Chitose
Is in the
Ramune
Bottle

6

Hiromu

Illustration by
raemz

c o n t e n t s

Atomu Uemura

On a Moonless Night

Chitose Is in the Ramune Bottle

6

Hiromu

Illustration by
raemz

YEN
ON
New York

Chit se Is in the Ramune Bottle 6

Hiromu

Translation by Evie Lund
Cover art by raemz

CHITOSE-KUN WA RAMUNEBIN NO NAKA Vol. 6
by Hiromu
© 2019 Hiromu
Illustration by raemz
All rights reserved.
Original Japanese edition published by SHOGAKUKAN.
English translation rights in the United States of America, Canada, the United Kingdom, Ireland, Australia, and New Zealand arranged with SHOGAKUKAN through Tuttle-Mori Agency, Inc.

English translation © 2024 by Yen Press, LLC

Yen On
150 West 30th Street, 19th Floor
New York, NY 10001

Visit us at yenpress.com
facebook.com/yenpress
twitter.com/yenpress
yenpress.tumblr.com
instagram.com/yenpress

First Yen On Edition: April 2024
Edited by Yen On Editorial: Anna Powers
Designed by Yen Press Design: Jane Sohn, Andy Swist

Yen On is an imprint of Yen Press, LLC.
The Yen On name and logo are trademarks of Yen Press, LLC.

Library of Congress Cataloging-in-Publication Data
Names: Hiromu, author. | raemz, illustrator. | Lund, Evie, translator.
Title: Chitose is in the ramune bottle / Hiromu ; illustration by raemz ; translation by Evie Lund.
Other titles: Chitose-kun wa ramune bin no naka. English
Description: First Yen On edition. | New York, NY : Yen On, 2022
Identifiers: LCCN 2021057712 | ISBN 9781975339050 (v. 1 ; trade paperback) |
    ISBN 9781975339067 (v. 2 ; trade paperback) | ISBN 9781975339074 (v. 3 ; trade paperback) |
    ISBN 9781975339081 (v. 4 ; trade paperback) | ISBN 9781975347956 (v. 5 ; trade paperback) |
    ISBN 9781975347970 (v. 6 ; trade paperback)
Subjects: CYAC: High schools—Fiction. | Schools—Fiction. | Friendship—Fiction. |
    LCGFT: Light novels.
Classification: LCC PZ7.1.H574 Ch 2022 | DDC [Fic]—dc23
LC record available at https://lccn.loc.gov/2021057712

ISBNs: 978-1-9753-4797-0 (paperback)
       978-1-9753-4798-7 (ebook)

10 9 8 7 6 5 4 3 2 1

LSC-C

Printed in the United States of America

Saku Chitose
One of the most popular guys
in the school.
Ex–baseball club.

Yuuko Hiiragi
A popular class princess.
Tennis club.

Yua Uchida
A self-made popular girl who tries
her best at everything. Music club.

Haru Aomi
A small and perky girl.
Basketball club.

Yuzuki Nanase
Every guy's favorite, along
with Yuuko.
Basketball club.

Asuka Nishino
A mysterious upperclassman,
difficult to read.
Likes books.

Kaito Asano
Popular jock.
Star player of the boys'
basketball club.

Kazuki Mizushino
A logical-minded, handsome guy.
A leading player in the soccer club.

Kenta Yamazaki
A former shut-in, otaku nerd.

Atomu Uemura
A contrarian boy with a tsundere
nature underneath. Has been playing
baseball since middle school.

Nazuna Ayase
A rough but cute girl. Often hangs
around with Atomu.

Kuranosuke Iwanami (Kura)
Homeroom teacher of Saku and his
group. Fairly hands-off and laid-back.

Chitose
Is in the
Ramune
Bottle

Hiromu

Illustration by
raemz

6

Hiromu

Born in Fukui, residing in Tokyo. Recently, I've been having more opportunities related to this series to meet or otherwise talk to people from Fukui. Even when I'm meeting a group for the first time, there's always at least one person I already know or who went to my old school, and it just makes me more fond of my hometown. "Yep, that's Fukui for you...," I'll think. The old-fashioned grapevine is the social media of the boonies—they say you can find anyone on there.

raemz

Born in California. Got a cat and has been eating lots of ramune candy lately.

PROLOGUE
My Normal

I've always lived a normal life.

I didn't really excel in many ways, but I also wasn't behind the pack in any particular aspects.

I didn't have any special friends, but I got along well with everyone, and a few kids from my class would even come to rely on me for some things.

I wasn't especially liked or disliked.

I passed the days quietly, modestly, eschewing both exciting entanglements and the sorrow that comes when they suddenly end.

It's okay to be average, I always told myself.

Being average leads to happiness, or so I seemed determined to prove.

So over time, I built up transparent walls around myself.

I wouldn't connect deeply with anyone, nor would I let anyone connect deeply with me.

Yes. I pretended that was what I wanted.

I cloaked the weeping little girl inside with an amiable smile.

But that day, in that classroom...

I met you.

I'd never even spoken to you before, but you marched right

into my most painful places with your heavy shoes on and rummaged through my locked drawers without even asking.

Even as I reminisce about it now, my first impression of you was that I hated you.

But that night, in a quiet moment...

You found me.

You took that word, *normal*, that I never really wanted to claim. You took my suffocating way of life that I'd been clinging to for years. You took the memories I actually really did want to cherish...

...and you lit them all up, there in the dark.

Now that I think about it, the emotion that quietly bound itself to my little finger was...

Well, anyway, that's why I made a wish to the moon I couldn't see.

It's okay if I'm not your special person. I don't have to be your girlfriend, or even your best friend.

But if you ever need someone...I want my name to be the one you say first.

I just want to be by your side, in that average way. That would be more than enough for me.

CHAPTER 5
A Kaleidoscope Colored with Scattered Tears

It would be nice, wouldn't it, to layer the night over a moonless sky and paint it with the color of sorrow?

Having cried all its tears, the weary sunset closed its eyes and dyed the evening with indigo.

The afterglow of the summer day still lingered in the shadows, but the darkness wasn't strong enough to cover the things I didn't want to see.

The familiar sight of the utility poles leading the way to the fateful classroom, the way the streetlights were strung between the stars. The soft light coming from houses awaiting the return of their inhabitants. And the shadows left far in the distance.

Far from blurring and blending in, the contours instead stood out vividly against the insipid darkness of the evening.

Splash. Sploosh. Splosh.

The water churned against the small sluice gate, like dammed-up tears threatening to spill over again.

I was still on the ground, and I'd only just uncovered my face. A wet stain was spreading like wings on my black uniform pants.

Why does it have to be like this? I thought, as the breeze gently stroked my hunched-over back.

I wanted to go deeper.

*   *   *

Take me away, to the very darkest depths of midnight, where even the sight of my outstretched fingertips would be swallowed into nothing.

Roll me away, to the very end of the darkest blue, too far away to fumble for pathetic excuses.

But even if I tried to lock myself away, in a safe place where the sunset could never reach…

—*Dan, du-la, da…*

That gentle sound enveloped me, as if reassuring me it wouldn't let me go.

*

I don't know how much time passed, but the music of the saxophone eventually ended.

I don't know if it was all one song, or if she'd played several songs continuously, without any gaps of silence.

The final note reminded me of a handkerchief being gently offered, and it lingered deep in my ears.

I wiped my eyes carefully with the cuffs of my blazer, then straightened my messy bangs with my fingers and took a quiet, deep breath.

Once I was finished pulling myself together, I carefully raised my gaze.

I hadn't been able to look at her before out of embarrassment, and guilt, and a sense of being utterly pathetic. Meanwhile, she was facing away from me, as dignified and graceful as ever.

The cool night breeze blew, sending the hem of her skirt fluttering just a little.

Beneath her wind-puffed school blouse, her back was solemn and still. I couldn't even be sure if she was breathing.

She was so beautiful that I bit my lip. *I need to say something now.*

A lame joke, an obvious show of bravery, or a carefully constructed laugh... Just something.

I had to get up, say thank you, and say good-bye. And I would leave this place without a single sigh remaining on the air.

I knew that, but then—

The strap of her saxophone dug into her shoulder, and I saw the nape of her neck, her sweaty hair stuck to it. And any words I might have said left me.

I'd made her bear my burdens. My selfish weakness, my naïveté, my cunning, my sadness, my regret, my mistakes...

She shouldn't be here.

Yua Uchida shouldn't be here, leaving Yuuko Hiiragi to cry alone.

But yet she stayed, watching—or watching over me.

"Saku."

A familiar voice called my name.

Yua turned around.

"Let's walk home together."

Then she broke into a bright smile.

...Why? Why was she being like this?

I had so many things I wanted to ask, but I didn't feel like I had the right to, just then. So instead, I found myself making vague *ah*s and *mm*s.

"We've got to buy groceries for dinner on the way back. We used up all the meat and stuff before the summer study camp." Yua kept on talking as she put her sax back in its case. "Any requests for tonight?"

She was acting as if it was business as usual, just another night with us two cooking dinner together.

"I mean..." Finally, I managed actual words. "I can't ask you to do that for me anymore."

I gathered the last little bit of my composure to express to her what I meant.

"Why not?" Yua asked. She gazed at me, and I could tell she was intentionally sidestepping the subject.

Why not?

I hung my head, clenching my fists.

There could only be one reason. There was really no need to spell it out.

I mean, look at what Yua was saying here.

The two of us, heading home side by side, having a cozy dinner together the way we always did? On the same night I'd hurt Yuuko so deeply?

"You know why not. Don't make me say it...," I mumbled without looking up.

But Yua wasn't playing along.

"Because you turned down Yuuko's confession, you mean?"

"..."

"That doesn't make much sense to me," Yua went on. "I mean, if you'd accepted her feelings, I could understand it. It wouldn't be appropriate to cook dinner with another girl if you had a girlfriend. But..."

Her voice was so level, almost indifferent.

"But you turned Yuuko down quite clearly, in front of me and everyone else. So there's no need for you to feel any type of way about what you do with anyone going forward, right?"

"Yua..."

She was technically correct.

If you picked up that high school over there, upended it and shook it around a bit, a dozen or more failed love attempts would spill out.

It happened yesterday, too. And today. And it would tomorrow, and the day after that... There's bound to be another boy, and another girl, and another confession, and another rejection, and another broken heart.

Unfortunately, the hands on the clock don't stop just because someone gets hurt. You might go home, take a shower, eat food that tastes like nothing, cry alone on your bed, toss and turn all night. But nothing about the world changes. It just keeps turning.

So all you can do is wash your face, brush your teeth, and start a whole new day.

"...I can't compartmentalize like that," I said, struggling to fully hide the tremble in my voice.

My mouth was dry; my lips stuck to my teeth.

This couldn't be right, could it?

How could it feel so bad to be the one rejecting someone else?

But though I tried to act strong and brush it all off, it felt like I had a gaping wound in my chest, and my bright-red heart was pumping itself out from the hole.

"*Unfortunately, dating just one girl goes against my personal principles.*"

If only I could have acted the player.

"*We can't date, but let's keep on being friends.*"

If only I could have given her a Band-Aid or sugarcoated it.

But the intensity in her eyes... Her words... Her heart...

*   *   *

—I knew that if I didn't give her a decent, straightforward response, I wouldn't be able to continue being the Saku Chitose that Yuuko had fallen for.

"Heh, just kidding." Yua laughed mischievously. "Whoops, I went kinda mean girl there. I guess I'm a little annoyed with you, Saku. And with Yuuko, too."
She tipped her head to one side, smiling slightly.
Give me some credit. It was obvious to me that what Yua just said wasn't what she really thought.
To rephrase, she meant more than what she was saying.
But trying to figure that out... Trying to guess why she came after me in the first place... Even us being together right now...
"Sorry, I'm really tired right now." I bowed my head. "Thank you, Yua. I really did appreciate the concert. But I'm okay now."
"—I won't let you say good-bye," Yua said with a somewhat reproachful tone. Then, softly and gently, she added, "I don't want you to have to be alone with those feelings."
Her smile was like a nodding yellow dandelion.
Those familiar words made my heart constrict in my chest.
For a moment, the image of a sunflower-like smile popped into my head, similar yet different. And I couldn't help imagining the state of that sunflower now—drooping sadly, pelted by torrential rain. I wished I could run to her.
But that wasn't an option anymore.
So at least, please let me be alone...
"You might think I'm the last person who has the right to say this, but I feel like this is unfair to Yuuko."
I wanted to be hurt as much as I'd hurt her.
Anyway, my summer calendar was already empty and blank.
When I was thinking about that...

*　　*　　*

"—Squeeze here, right?"

Yua took one step, two steps over to me, then pressed down on the nape of my neck with her slim fingers, as if she was depressing the keys of a saxophone.

"Listen, I'm not really in the mood for messing around right now…," I said, but Yua just chuckled.

"Saku…you don't know anything about Yuuko, do you?"

What do you mean? I was about to ask, when Yua continued.

"If you go home like this, will you take a proper bath? Will you eat? I'm guessing you won't sleep well, but will you at least get into bed and close your eyes like a good boy?"

She was poking me right where it hurts, and I unintentionally turned my face away.

Nope, I couldn't do any of that. Nor did I intend to.

"See?" Yua rolled her eyes. "You're planning to go home and curl up in the dark, right? Then when morning comes, you'll sit around with the curtains closed, not caring if you get sick. Nope, I bet you'll actually be hoping to get sick."

"…"

Wow, she read me like a book.

No matter how sad I was, it would be a tenth of what Yuuko was feeling.

So I deserved to suffer just a little, didn't I…? And if that mindset led to me getting sick like Yua said, what would that matter?

"Saku, do you really think Yuuko would want that to happen?"

When I slowly lifted my head to look up, I was met by her piercing gaze.

"You think anyone would be happy knowing that the person they love is devastated and in pain? Who'd be like, 'Yes, yes, suffer for me'?"

"Well... I..."

No one.

I was taken aback.

If Yuuko heard that I was a mess, she'd blame herself. Then she'd be in even more pain.

...Because that's the kind of girl she is.

I clenched my teeth. Ultimately...

Yeah, ultimately, did I just want to punish myself so I could get forgiven a little faster?

A shallow display of repentance won't undo the things I've said or the decisions I've made.

"See?" Yua said, the corners of her eyes softening gently.

"Right now, I'll be with you, Saku."

I took a deep breath and exhaled.

Loosening my clenched fists, I said, "I'm sorry. I promise you I won't do anything stupid."

"Yes, please promise me." Yua nodded slightly. "So let's go shopping, then go home." She lifted her saxophone case.

"No, I'm really okay now. I don't have the energy to cook for myself tonight, but I swear, I'll eat something."

But Yua shook her head, a hint of something in her smile. "Nope. This is an entirely different matter."

"What do you mean...?"

"I'll do what I want, too. If you really don't like it, you're going to have to force me out of the apartment and lock the door."

"...That's sneaky of you, Yua."

She knew I could never lock her out.

I still wasn't sure why, but it was undeniable that she was with me now. She'd come after me, instead of going to her friend Yuuko.

I would indulge in her kindness; then, as soon as I felt better, I'd dismiss her.

Normally, there wouldn't be two choices to make like this, so why today…?

Yua turned her back, as if she'd just read my mind.

"I just told you, didn't I? I'm a little bit annoyed right now."

She started walking off, leaving me no way of trying to decipher her meaning.

We still hadn't reached the railroad crossing yet, but I couldn't let her go alone on a dark street at night, so I quickly scooped up my bag.

Pausing, I glanced up at the sky. There were so many stars—and no moon.

I prayed.

Nanase, Haru, Kazuki, Kenta, or even Kaito.

Any of them would do.

Someone, please… Stay with Yuuko.

*

I cried and cried and cried and cried, and I couldn't make it stop. It hurt, and hurt, and hurt, and hurt, and it felt like my heart would burst.

"…Guh… Gck… *Sob… Choke…*"

I, Yuuko Hiiragi, continued from the school along the empty backstreets in the direction of my house.

I usually have my mother pick me up somewhere in the car, but even though my phone had been buzzing intermittently for a while now, I couldn't think straight.

If I stopped, something vital might snap inside me, and if that happened, I was afraid I'd cause a lot of trouble for people who are equally important. So I kept moving my legs, just to keep myself together.

My bag had slipped off my shoulder and was dangling from the crook of my arm, but I didn't have enough energy to put it back on.

The back of my hand was smeared with makeup from rubbing my eyes over and over.

"Ugh... Why...? Why...?"

How did this happen?
Why did I have to tell him?
I'd known the answer from the beginning.
He had his reasons. And I'd prepared myself.
But in the end... In the end...

"...Why?"

I was filled with regret. I just wanted a do-over.
I never thought it would be so hard to see something come to an end like this.
I never knew hurting someone you love could be so painful.

"See you, everyone. Next semester."

No, wait, Saku, don't say that.
Don't smile like that, like you're trying not to cry.
Don't leave me.
I don't want to hear "See you."
I want your usual, warm, crinkled...

...

*　　*　　*

Oh. Oh, right.

I can't see that smile, not anymore.

Can't hear him say "See you tomorrow" anymore.

Even when school starts again, we can't go home together.

We can't stop by the park and chat.

I can't call him on a lonely night just to hear his voice.

I can't force him to go on dates on weekends. Can't make him a bento lunch and watch him eat it. Can't invite him over to the house. Can't ever tell him how much I love him…

I can't do any of it anymore.

That's what it means to fail in love.

"There's another girl in my heart."

From now on…

I won't be the one laughing beside Saku, or the one making him laugh.

I won't be the one supporting him and comforting him when he's having a hard time.

It won't be me pushing him to be better.

It won't be me holding his hand.

It won't be me he looks at.

It won't be me who's the special one in his life.

—It won't be me. It'll be some other girl.

"Ugh… Ucchi…"

I uttered the name of my precious best friend; I couldn't take this anymore.

Hey. Could you come now?

I want you to listen to me talk, I want you to hug me tightly, I want you to smile gently like you always do, I want you to call me Yuuko.

But…but…

When Saku left the classroom, no one could speak or move.

I just stared absentmindedly at the door the person I loved had passed through alone.

About half a minute passed…

—*Tap.*

I heard someone taking a step.

I glanced over in confusion, just in time to see Ucchi grabbing her bag off her desk.

Through my tears, we made eye contact.

For just a moment, Ucchi's face distorted as if she was going to cry. Then she scrunched up her forehead, ran past me, and disappeared through the same door. She didn't even look back.

My knees trembled as I almost found myself running after her.

I couldn't go with her.

…Yes, Ucchi was the same.

She'd made a choice, as well.

No, I'm sure she'd already made up her mind a long time ago— that she would be by Saku's side.

All of a sudden, I found myself crouched on the ground.

Yuzuki, Haru, and Kaito came rushing over to me in concern.

Kenta hovered worriedly, and Kazuki just sat at his desk with an unreadable expression.

But I couldn't see anything, I couldn't hear anything, not a thing. Because…because…because…

"Waaaaahhhhh!!!"

Both my best friend, who I held dearest to my heart, and the person I loved had disappeared at the same time.

"…Guh."
The way I felt in that moment came back to me vividly, and a sense of pitch-black, muddy despair seemed to well up from the ground below me.
The happy days I'd spent with everyone—with Saku, with Ucchi, with the others… Our relationships, that I'd loved from the bottom of my heart… All the wonderful memories forged over those past four days…
I broke it all. I ruined everything.
The weight of it was enough to crush my mind.
After Saku was so sweet, too. He was saying thank you, how fun it was to spend time together. His smile was so innocent.
The toe of my loafer suddenly caught on the curb, and I almost fell to my knees.

"Yuuko!"

I heard someone call my name.
A rugged and powerful hand grabbed my shoulder from behind and supported me.
I slowly turned around, and…
"Kaito…"
I grasped his shirt tightly.

＊　　＊　　＊

After Saku and Ucchi had left the classroom, Yuzuki looked at me as I crouched there unable to stop crying. "I'll take you home," she said.

Beside her, Haru looked right into my eyes and nodded solemnly.

"*Sob... Sorry... I'm sorry...*"

If I stayed around others in this state, I'd only make everything worse. So instead I twisted away from Yuzuki's hand as she gently rubbed my back, and I dashed out of the classroom.

""""Yuuko!""""

The sound of them calling my name resonated inside so much it hurt, but I ran and ran and ran to the exit.

But even after I'd gotten a good ways away from the school, footsteps began to follow me from behind. They eventually caught up and came to a stop beside me.

"Um... Here."

He handed me a blue sports towel.

"It's one I haven't used, so..."

"...Kaito, I'm fine now. Please, leave me alone."

"No!"

He clenched his teeth and gazed at the ground, but the resolve was clear in his voice.

"I won't talk to you. I'll just walk along beside you. Can you let me do that much?"

"But—but... It's my fault you ended up..."

"Don't worry about things like that. I've been thinking for a while now that I'd kick his ass, if I ever got the opportunity. Besides, if I just leave you in this state, Yuuko, I can assure you it's Saku who'll be giving me a punch next time."

He forced a grin, and I slowly nodded.

...He's always been following along beside me, ready to support me when I stumble...

"...Why?!"

Before I knew it, I was pounding on Kaito's chest.

"Why?! Why did you punch him?!"

"Yuuko..."

I knew I shouldn't be saying this right then, but I couldn't stop the feelings spilling out of me.

"How could you do that...? That was a terrible thing to do, Kaito! After that, Saku won't feel like he can be around us anymore... He won't be able to come back to us... To any of us!"

The warmth through my little finger was so warm... I didn't know what to do with it.

"Ugh... Gah... Ngh!"

Kaito didn't step back or try to grab my hands. He just stood there.

"Why didn't you go after Saku right away?! You're supposed to be his friend! You didn't have to come after me! And also... And..."

I leaned against his strong chest with both hands, propping my weight against him.

My tears fell and disappeared into the dark ground.

Then I realized that Kaito's tightly clenched fists were trembling.

"I'm sorry. I'm sorry, Yuuko."

I lifted my head. "Why?!!!"

I kept repeating that same word again.

"Why are you apologizing, Kaito? You're not the bad guy here. You were just lashing out. This was all *my* fault. So why did you have to...?"

"Even if it's not my fault...I'm sorry," Kaito said with a gentle smile. "Because of me, you ended up getting hurt even more..."

Don't say that...

The boy in front of me was so earnest.

This was all because he was angry and worried on my behalf, and even now, he was deeply sad for me.

Even though I was saying irrational things, even though he should probably be losing his temper with me, even though he should probably be telling me to pull myself together...

Why, then, was he smiling to comfort me?

Oh, if only I could have fallen for this boy as my first love instead.

I'm sure I could have kept screaming "I love you" without a shred of anxiety, jealousy, or envy.

—But.

I still wish it was Saku with me now. I guess I really am just a bitch.

Here I was, thinking how nice it would be if it was Saku who'd run to comfort me. If I was hurt and crying for a different reason, if the reason I'd run off was something else. If only Saku could be the one hugging me from behind and saying kind words to me.

Is it wrong to desire that so much?

"I'm sorry, Kaito."

All I could really do was apologize.

"I'm sorry for saying such terrible things."

"Heh," he responded, a brief laugh.

"When you feel all torn up inside, it's best to get it all out, to scream, or punch a pillow or something. I'm glad I came after you, Yuuko, if that means I get to be your punching bag."

His voice was as bright as the clear sky. I was taken aback.

"I'm sorry for hitting your chest so many times. I'm sorry for acting like I'm the only one who's having a hard time. You were hurt, too, Kaito. It must have been terrible."

I should have realized sooner.

This guy has been Saku's best friend since first year.

Every day they goofed around together, arms around each other's shoulders, laughing.

"Don't be a dummy. I'm the basketball club's star player, I'll have you know. You can whack me all you want, Yuuko, 'cause your skinny arms…"

His empty words failed him midsentence.

"…don't hurt…"

I finished his sentence for him.

I was desperately suppressing my emotions, trying to speak it into reality.

"Kaito… Oh, Kaito…"

Burying my face in his warm chest and crying, I prayed.

—*Hey, Ucchi? Please…please…*

Please stay by Saku's side.

*

I'm the worst.

The worst of the worst of the worst.

I, Yuzuki Nanase, am…

After Kaito left the classroom chasing after Yuuko…

"We should go home, too. Not much fun with just us," Mizushino announced.

His voice was a little cold, as if he was saying we were all outsiders here. In reality, I suppose we were on the outside. Just bystanders.

We really didn't feel like going straight home, so Haru and I stopped by Higashi Park.

My teammate had changed into a T-shirt and shorts and was now single-mindedly practicing her basketball shots under the unreliable glow of the park's lights.

As I sat on the bench and stared blankly at the scene, I cursed myself over and over.

I really am just the worst.

The scene in the classroom replayed in my mind, again and again.

When I realized that Yuuko was going to confess her feelings to Chitose, I was attacked by a deep-blue terror that made me feel cold, like all the blood had drained from my body.

Ah yes. I suspected as much.

While I was trying to close the distance between us little by little in a casual way, *she* was…

She was jumping straight for the moon.

I thought, *Oh, maybe this is it.*

Maybe this is the moment my first love comes to its end.

If I'd had to witness Yuuko's wish come true…would I have to smile and congratulate her?

Hold on a minute. What, just like that?

That day, when Chitose came to my rescue… Although it's painful to remember it now, I felt like the heroine of a true love story.

It was fate, I thought.

My whole life had led me to meet this person.

I could dedicate my life to this.

I wouldn't need anything else.

So even though a rational part of me thought a day like this would come sooner or later…

In the future that I imagined each night, wrapped in my blanket, I was always the one who got chosen.

I'd fall in love with the same guy as my friends. Yes, we'd fight about it. We'd get angry, and cry, and make up, but in the end... I'd be with Chitose. It was a totally obvious happy ending.

Then together, we'd decide where to go to college.

Whether we went to the same college or not, we'd at least have to make sure we were in the same prefecture. After all, long distance is tough.

I'd like to go out of the prefecture, but if Chitose wanted, I'd be okay with Fukui University.

Realistically speaking, we could opt for Kanazawa or Kyoto— or maybe even push the boat out as far as Osaka or Nagoya?

I'd be a little worried about Nishino, out there in Tokyo, but despite his tendency to show off, Chitose is an old-fashioned guy at heart. A sleazy affair would go against his principles.

For the same reason, he'd probably refuse the idea of cohabiting at first.

We'd live separately for two years.

We'd go over to each other's places, having sleepovers on weekends and lonely nights, but we'd essentially both be living alone.

I'd need to get better at cooking so I didn't seem inferior to Ucchi.

When we turned twenty, we'd have a toast together at a bar that's a little weird, like we are.

Sometimes, we'd take a bath together and wash each other's backs while flirting.

I wanted to be smothered in so much love that I'd cry tears of joy in bed...

Then, in the spring of our third year, after meeting the parents, the two of us would finally start living together...

These might be ridiculous, childish delusions, but I couldn't help it.

No matter how much I try to act above it all, I still can't see the world without putting myself right in the center. I also don't like to spend my time imagining scenarios full of gloom and doom, so I keep my fantasies positive. So over time, I gradually fell into believing that my dreams would come true.

Maybe it's the totally baseless feeling of omnipotence that a lot of people tend to have when they're young.

Even so... I was so sure that I...Yuzuki Nanase...could shoot down the moon.

And that's why I felt this way.

I was left behind, as a play I'd never seen before unfolded on a stage I hadn't even set foot on yet. I was standing there helpless, feeling the frustration of watching from the audience.

I wanted to sink into the floor and disappear.

What was it all for, then? It makes me think of gum with all the taste chewed out of it, spat out onto the side of the road.

I should have stolen his lips instead of his cheek.

That stubborn boy who's always acting shallow—I could have been his first.

I wasted all this time side-eyeing Nishino and Haru.

I knew, even if I made it through the day, either one of them might overtake me at the slightest opportunity.

Out on the balcony, that day when Ucchi and Haru were over...I should have dashed back inside and just told him how I felt.

All that talk about giving it some serious thought.

I should have told Yuuko my feelings when she asked, and then we could have duked it out.

A truly kind friend would have hesitated before she made that leap.

...Wow, really?

I'm such a shallow person. I'm not worthy of him. He's willing to help anyone in need, and yet here I am.

I can't stand beside him with my head held high.

Even if I could go back in time, I'm sure I'd make the same choice.

No, that's a half-baked, self-serving excuse.

I was afraid to take the vital step.

There's a tomorrow where I can be loved by the one I love. But isn't there also a tomorrow where I fail to say what I'm feeling when it matters most?

If I weigh up both tomorrows on the balance board, it's going to slant toward the latter one.

Because I wasn't noble enough to just tell him my feelings.

I wanted to raise my chances of success, and then when the moment of truth arrived...I would make a beautiful shot, arcing through the air, dropping through the hoop without so much as a swish...

Umi said something like that to me before, right?

If I wait for the perfect conditions to make a shot like that, I'll be too slow to act when it really counts...

—Oh God, please give me just a little longer.

Give me more time.

Thank you, I'm sorry, good morning, good night. Chitose and Saku, I love you, I hate you, I adore you, I'm in love with you.

I have so many more words I want to say to him.

I don't want to regret this moment ten years from now.

I don't want that once-in-a-lifetime love to become just a bittersweet memory from a distant day.

The feelings in my heart aren't just summer fireworks.

Please, please, please...

*   *   *

"I'm sorry, Yuuko. I can't respond to your feelings in the way you want. There's another girl in my heart."

So...
When I heard those words...

My heart soared with hope.

My love will not end like this.

I looked at Chitose, smiling so earnestly.
I looked at Yuuko, gathering the last dregs of her courage to be strong, to laugh playfully.
And I envisioned a red thread linking my little finger to his...
A little red thread that was as yet unbroken.

Chitose said it very clearly.
He said he had another girl in his heart.
If it's not Yuuko, then maybe, maybe.

—Maybe it just might be...me.

I fell into a sweet dream.
The feelings of the two players in front of me were set aside.
My heart was pounding secretly.
However...

"...But no."

"If it's not you, Saku, I don't want anyone."

Yuuko's tears were so beautiful.

Facing up to her own self, telling the boy she loved how she felt about him. Then, when he didn't reciprocate, she smiled to make things okay for him... And the words that spilled from her lips were so heartfelt.

—What a jerk I am.

The moment I realized that, an indescribable sense of guilt surged over me.

This very moment, Yuuko was being swallowed up by the despair I'd just seen.

There was no way I could understand her sorrow and how it really felt.

And right now, there was no way the one I loved wasn't hurting, too.

I'm the worst.

The worst of the worst of the worst.

Yuzuki Nanase is...

In the end, I could only watch in a daze as Ucchi was the one to go running off after Chitose.

Rubbing Yuuko's back as she crumpled to the ground and broke down in tears, I kept repeating the words *I'm so sorry* over and over again in my mind.

★

What am I doing here? wondered Haru Aomi (that is, me) as I listened to the multitude of shots go bouncing off the rim.

I felt like I had to move my body or my heart would be torn apart. So on my way home, I snagged a ball from the clubroom.

But today, shot after shot after shot, I just can't get it through the hoop. With every failed basket, thoughts like *failure, miss,* and *pathetic* went through my mind.

I started playing basketball when I was in elementary school, and since then I've been part of a world that's all about winning or losing.

Of course, there are clear rules. Every game starts with a jump ball, and until the final buzzer sounds, we run around on the same court and compete for points.

As for how to win points… We all know which shots are worth one, two, or three. And we all know what constitutes a foul.

Every player in the game will fight to win while upholding those agreed-upon conventions.

Some things can affect the game—how everyone's feeling on the specific day, the team's momentum, whether they took advantage of the game's flow—but basically, the scoreboard reflects the difference in skill level between teams.

So it's generally pretty clear what you need to do to improve.

Maybe you need to get better at shooting. Maybe you lack physical strength, or you run out of stamina in the second half. Maybe your passing needs work. Or perhaps you have an issue with basic tactics.

There's always a chance of success if you put in the right amount of effort, and as long as you don't stop, you can always get closer to your goal, one step at a time.

And I…

—I thought love was the same.

It's just a matter of working hard toward a clear goal—dating the guy you like or even getting married one day.

If you work harder than anyone else, you'll be rewarded in the end.

All right, so I don't have a girly personality or appearance, and I'm pretty childish compared to those around me when it comes to beauty and fashion.

But that's like being short in basketball, right?

I'm used to competing with a handicap.

Many times, I've flipped things around to my advantage and won.

But despite that...

"Wait..."

At that moment, I almost cried out.

Wait. Just wait, please.

We haven't even lined up before the game and shaken hands yet.

The start whistle hasn't even been blown.

Come on. I was hoping to face off against you.

Of course Yuuko liked Chitose. We all knew that. She was always saying it.

That's why she would have needed to draw a clear line in the sand if she wanted to call him or chat him up over LINE or invite him to dinner as a potential boyfriend instead of a friend.

She and I have been in the same class for the past two years. She said I was cute. She helped me choose that dress, and that swimsuit for the beach. She taught me about fashion and beauty, two things I suck at. She broadened my horizons. Before I knew it, Yuuko had become one of my most irreplaceable friends. I knew I would have to tell her about my feelings: *I like Chitose, too, so let's fight fair and square.*

I thought that would be the starting line...

Hey, Yuuko.

It shouldn't be this way. This isn't fair.

You cheated. You cheated, Yuuko!

Yuuko has a lot of things that I lack, as a girl.

She has a cute face like an idol, long hair like in a shampoo commercial, a body that looks soft but well-rounded, big boobs, an innocent smile.

As for me? I'm still figuring out what love is.

It was so great, practicing for Chitose's big game.

It was an amazing excuse to be near him. Even though we're in different sports, I was still able to be of some help to him.

I secretly read books about baseball and memorized the rules.

After my own practice, I went alone to the park and tossed baseballs at the wall, just to train myself to be a good partner in our throwing and catching.

I also watched a lot of professional baseball games, even major-league games.

If Chitose decided to return to the team and aim for Koshien, I was going to be by his side, supporting him better than anyone else.

Whenever he was down, I would scold him. Whenever he was tired, I'd give him the push he needed.

But he gave a different answer.

I don't think he's ever going to give up baseball completely. Maybe he's even considering starting over from scratch in college.

I wasn't planning to question that decision.

But I was left hanging…

If our connection through the practice sessions ended, what possible pretext would there be now for me to be around him?

Will you give me your precious time?

How will you approach me?

Will you need me?

I had no answers to any of those questions.

Someone tell me. What does it mean to give it your all in love?

I had a vague inkling.

I'm not the kind of girl who can color Chitose's daily life.

The only thing I had to offer was a sports connection...and it was only for a short space of time that I was able to close the distance between us.

I'd told him how I felt. I'd even kissed him.

That was my one and only hand. What cards do I have left now?

My body? Who'd want that when Yuuko and Yuzuki are around?

Should I grow out my hair? Learn how to do makeup? Be more fashionable? Become more of a girly-girl? Focus on my words and attitude?

I could try to be graceful and modest, maybe do something about my lack of sex appeal.

If Chitose wanted me to, I could even learn to cook.

I could read a lot of books and study hard.

What should I offer to grab hold of your heart?

...It's not fair, Yuuko.

I gritted my teeth, that one thought repeating.

She had the luck to be in Chitose's class from first year. She'd spent much more time with him than I had, before I even had a chance.

That's why, when the chance to close the distance finally came around, and when I realized I was in love with him...of course, Yuuko was nearby.

Hey, what if I was more like you, Yuuko Hiiragi?

I can puff up my chest like you and bellow about how much I love him.

I can run up to him all innocent whenever I catch a glimpse of him. Chase after him when I spot him in a crowd. Call him on the phone, just because I want to hear his voice. Go to see him, just because I want to be with him. I can do all that.

*   *   *

Even without inventing some convenient reason, maybe I could still be a special kind of girl—one who could walk alongside a special kind of guy.

I'd never wanted to be like someone else this way.
Yuuko... Yuuko has been so far ahead of me since the beginning.

Now she was going to deny me the chance to go toe to toe with her?

Chitose. I called his name over and over again in my mind.
Are you going to say yes, just like that?
I told you at the beach.
I want you to take notice of me. I want you to see me as girl-friend material.
Someday, I'm going to sign up for a match for real.
And you said you'd be cool with that.
You liar. You liar, you liar, you liar...
Just then...
I noticed Yuuko's fingers, clenching her skirt tightly. They were trembling. Trembling, even as she waited for Chitose's response with a soft smile on her lips.
Oh. Oh, I see.

—Maybe I'm the one who wasn't being fair.

Actually, I figured this out a while back.
There are no set rules in love.
Here I am, whining about my own failures, how he and I hadn't met at the right time. I'm just like one of those weak players who doesn't try and attributes their opponents' skills to natural talent.

Yuuko has always worked hard on improving herself, looking better, being more feminine. So she was able to jump right in and get on with it as soon as she found a guy she liked.

Maybe, that night during summer camp…

"Okay, okay, so does anyone have a crush on someone NOW? Because I have a crush on Saku!"

That kind girl might have given me a chance.

If I'd made up my mind to confess to Chitose and then found the right moment to raise my hand and yell…

But no, I had to go and say…

"Right now, basketball is my only love!"

I was the one who turned away.

Meanwhile, I secretly carried on trying to get Chitose to notice me.

Even worse, I did tell him how I felt—but I was so casual about it that he wasn't able to give me a proper response.

The truth is…I was terrified.

My efforts were wasted in the wrong places.

It was an impromptu performance with no rehearsals. A tournament you can never join again once you lose.

A first-come, first-served game with no advance warning about your opponent's score, or the play style, or the start time, or the time limit…

I was terrified. Completely terrified.

I couldn't take that first step forward.

…You're amazing, Yuuko.

How could you be so straightforward with him in the midst of all this?

How could you announce your love for him in front of everyone, knowing it might all be over in a few seconds?

How could you bear knowing your crush might call another girl's name?

And if that girl likes Chitose, too...

"Sorry, Haru. Thing is, I like Nanase."

Just imagining it was like falling into hell.

Chitose and Yuzuki, shooting loaded glances back and forth in the classroom and waiting at the school gate after club activities to see each other back home. Him coming to watch our practice sessions—but only for my teammate. It wouldn't be me cheering him on at his big game. It would be Yuzuki.

But Yuuko knew the risks—and she stood up and took her chance.

She was amazing. And strong. And so cool.

Meanwhile...

—I'm just a coward.

Chitose's answer, Yuuko's smile and tears—none of it felt like it had to do with me.

It's like watching the finals of a tournament you failed out of a few rounds back.

I wasn't a player on the court, a member of the backup team, a coach, a manager, or even on the cheering squad at the venue.

I was just a random spectator, on the other side of the TV screen.

Even if I shouted out all my shoulda-woulda-couldas, no one would hear me.

So I just watched blankly as Chitose left, wearing a smile I didn't like at all. Then Ucchi ran off without looking back. And

I just stood there, like I was draped in a heavy cloth made of "if onlys."

I wondered if Chitose was back home in his apartment right now.

Maybe Ucchi was beside him, gently holding his hand.

Everyone has conflicted feelings. Yet we all make choices.

I really had no idea.

—I had no idea how painful love really is.

I was getting tired of chasing these balls around.

"Haru." Yuzuki picked up one off the ground. "Let's go eat."

The awful scene I'd pictured earlier crossed my mind, and I shook my head to dispel it.

Wiping my sweat away with my T-shirt, I smiled weakly. "Katsudon's the only cure for a time like this, huh?"

Yuzuki responded with an uncharacteristically loose smile. "Right."

I took the sports towel she offered and flopped down on the grass.

Yuzuki followed suit, and we looked at the sky side by side.

There was no sun or moon up there today.

We both reached for each other's hands and squeezed tight.

*

What should I have done?

I, Kenta Yamazaki, was walking home, ruminating on that one thought.

We all had such a fun four days, chatting about how summer vacation was still a long way from being over... So why did this have to happen?

I mean... I don't know the first thing about this stuff. How could I understand?

As far as I can tell, Asano likes Yuuko, but Yuuko likes King. That's probably why he's never let anyone know before now.

"If the person who could make them happiest is someone else, especially if it's a close friend, then I wouldn't want to get in the way of that."

I thought back to a casual conversation I once had.
Asano must have figured that if King and Yuuko ended up dating, then it was just one of those things.
He would have accepted that future and supported them both.
I felt a prickling in my chest.
I kinda understood that sentiment.
I can't really call it love, but it's an immature feeling—maybe something like admiration.
I mean… I can't lie and say I've never had similar thoughts.
But that feeling is so unrealistic; it's almost like stanning for the heroine of a light novel or an anime.
So…

—Somewhere in my heart, I thought it would be nice if she could be happy with the hero at the end of the story.

Any way you slice it, that's the happiest ending.
I think everyone can understand that. Everyone can celebrate a good old-fashioned True Ending.

"Why wouldn't you make Yuuko happy?"

I almost found myself nodding over what Asano had said.
Yes, it was perfectly natural for King and Yuuko to be together.
They made a perfect pair, shining bright.

But now it felt like that perfect relationship was crumbling right in front of my eyes.

King was always so full of confidence, and yet here he was hanging his head and in pain.

Yuuko was always so energetic with that big smile, and here she was openly sobbing.

Even just thinking about it now made my heart break. It felt so much worse than the incident that caused me to become a recluse.

My fingers dug into the front of my shirt, and…

"Why are you making that face, Kenta?"

Mizushino pulled me out of my thoughts as he walked beside me, pushing his cross bike.

After King left, and Uchida ran after him, Yuuko and Asano left, too.

Mizushino and I were the next to go, until the only ones in the classroom were Nanase and Aomi. They'd said they were going to stop by their clubroom.

While I was changing shoes by the entrance, Mizushino offered to walk home with me, which came as a surprise.

"Why…?" I paused for a while. "What you said, Mizushino… Was that how you really feel?"

I decided to just go for it, albeit timidly.

"What did I say?"

Whether he was deliberately dodging the issue or really didn't know what I meant, Mizushino was acting completely unaffected.

"'…I don't feel like covering for you, Saku. You saw this coming a mile away, didn't you?'"

"Ah, right." He chuckled, then continued on with his cool-guy expression. "Of course that's how I really feel, you know? He keeps playing the hero time after time. Of course girls are going to start thinking about wanting to lay a claim to Saku. Sooner or later, a day like today was inevitable."

I stayed silent.

"He's completely naive," he said dismissively.

"Yeah, but…!"

A wave of irritation washed over me, and my voice rose uncharacteristically.

I took a deep breath and looked entreatingly at Mizushino.

"But does that mean it's all King's fault?"

When I said it out loud, I finally realized.

I…I…

I can't believe King was cast out like some kind of lowlife.

I get how Asano feels. And I can appreciate what Mizushino's saying.

But for me—because of who I am and what I've been through—I think they're wrong.

Yeah, so King can be meddlesome.

He's pushy, he's bossy, he puts too much onto his own plate. Naive? Okay. I guess he is.

But…

—He also saved me.

If King wasn't such a hero, if he didn't have that savior complex, if he wasn't utterly incapable of turning his back on someone in trouble—I'd still be locked up in my room.

I wouldn't have even spoken to Yuuko, Uchida, Nanase, Aomi, Mizushino, Asano, or any of them for the rest of our lives, let alone become friends.

I would've spent this summer at home screaming about

how much I hated happy couples living their brainless lives. I wouldn't be trying to change or improve myself one iota. You're only young once, and I would have thrown that youth in the garbage without him.

And I'm not the only one he helped.

Now, I don't know all the specifics of the situation with Nanase, but...

Without King, she might have gone to pieces when she was terrorized by that Yan High guy and that creepy stalker.

Aomi might have lost her place in the basketball club.

And even Yuuko...

"I'd never blame Saku for showing kindness to me."

Ever since that day when she spoke to me through the door, she'd been clear about that.

I mean, if he was the totally self-serving type—like, say he only helped out cute girls—then maybe I'd get it.

Although, I don't think it's a bad thing that someone got help in the end, even if your motives are impure. Just from a moral standpoint.

But this was King we were talking about.

The first time I met him, I lashed out at him with selfish resentment and bitterness. But he stuck by me and helped someone who could do absolutely nothing for him in return.

He even offered me friendship.

No. I don't think this whole situation can be placed on King's shoulders.

No. I don't.

I don't think...I don't think anyone is in the wrong here.

*   *   *

I clenched my fist and opened my mouth again.

"Hey, Mizushino, listen here!"

But before I could say anything, he interrupted as if he'd been waiting for his cue. "You know, I think...I think you're right, Kenta."

"Huh...?" I was caught off guard.

"You wanna sit over there for a moment?"

Mizushino bought a can of black coffee from the vending machine right in front of him.

Then he took out another coin and turned to me. "Pick your poison, Kenta."

"Uh, no, I'll buy it myself."

"Aw, come on. My treat."

"Uh... Coke, then."

"You're the boss."

He tossed the can to me, and I caught it with a nod of thanks.

We sat down on the edge of the levee.

Mizushino pulled the tab on his coffee. "I guess saying 'Cheers' would be in poor taste."

So he took a swig without further preamble.

I realized I was thirstier than I'd thought, so I chugged my drink as well.

"Kenta..." Gazing vaguely at the flowing water, Mizushino spoke again. "Your impression is that Saku's not at fault here, right?"

"Right... But I'm not completely sure..."

"Hmm. You're another person he helped out, right? You've been hanging with him awhile, so I guess you've been able to get a pretty good read on him by now."

The corners of his mouth twitched, his expression somewhat melancholy.

I decided we needed to backtrack for a second. "You said something about not being willing to cover for him."

"I did. I said exactly that. But…," Mizushino continued, "Well, I also don't really feel like putting the blame on him, either."

Finally, I understood what Mizushino was saying.

Thinking about it, Mizushino's always the calmest one of the whole group.

He'd seen all of this coming, I bet. Heck, I was the last to join, and even I kinda did.

"In the hot spring…" Mizushino put down his can of coffee, stretched both arms, and looked up at the night sky. "Remember I said there's someone I have feelings for?"

I nodded, hoping he'd get to the end of this rabbit trail, whatever it was.

"Well, it's Yuzuki."

"Oh, right. I mean… Wait, *what*?! *What*?!"

So much for the pensive atmosphere.

Nanase? And Mizushino?

Hmm. But in terms of their stats… They're both way OP. So it kinda makes sense.

But I'd always had this weird impression that Mizushino wouldn't ever fall for any of the girls in our group.

"Are you that surprised?" Mizushino's shoulders shook, like he was laughing.

"Uh… But…but why haven't you told King or Asano about it?"

"Hmm, I think Saku guessed already. Not sure about Kaito. I wonder why I haven't said it openly, though…"

He took another gulp of coffee before speaking again.

"It's weird and random, but I guess I was just seized by the desire to share this pointless emotion with someone."

"I didn't know you had feelings like that, Mizushino."

To be honest, Mizushino strikes me as someone who's just hard to read.

Even when he's goofing around with King and Asano, he's

always so cool. Or maybe detached is a better word—viewing things from a step or so away.

So it was really a shock for him to suddenly confess something this personal.

Mizushino was lying down beside me now as he continued.

"Do you remember when I told you about what sparked the whole thing for me?"

"—*I fell for her when I saw her fall for another guy.*"

I silently nodded and waited for him to continue.

"Well, it was when Saku and Yuzuki were duking it out with that Yanashita guy from Yan High."

I wasn't there, but I heard the details later.

As I recall, Mizushino was tasked with filming the encounter, so we'd have proof that Yanashita dealt the first blow.

"You know, I always thought that Yuzuki was more like me. Refined, sophisticated, moving skillfully through the world and getting what we wanted from people. There's something inside us both that'll always be cold."

Truthfully, even now, I still have pretty much that exact impression of both Mizushino and Nanase.

Of course, I don't mean it in a bad way; it's just that the two of them seem more mature than the rest of us.

"To be honest, I think that was a fair assessment until then."

Mizushino's voice sounded somewhat nostalgic and a little sad.

"But then she stamped her foot, gnashed her teeth, stared right at this terrifying guy, a kid intimidating enough to scare a grown man… And she yelled: '*I'm Chitose's girlfriend! I won't let you hurt a single hair on his head!*'"

He chuckled, shaking his head.

*   *   *

"She was so noble in that moment. Like a queen. It was incredible. I'd never seen anything so beautiful."

Mizushino's speech accelerated, as if he couldn't keep his pent-up emotions inside anymore.

"Well, I was heartbroken in that moment. I became a blushing schoolgirl in love. And of course, it wasn't *me* who brought out the true beauty inside Yuzuki."

"Yeah..."

"After seeing what I saw... I thought, if only Saku hadn't been the one who reached out to help her. Not that I could ever say as much."

So that's what he meant when he said he didn't want to blame King.

Mizushino twisted to look up at me.

"Well, the rest is history. Any way you slice it...I have no chance of winning. So I stuck a knife in my feelings overnight. Functionally, I'm Team Sakuzuki. And I guess...yeah. I can be cool with that."

"But...," I muttered doubtfully. "I know how this sounds, and I'm not saying it should be this way, but...but if the two of them don't work out, then...you'd have a chance with Nanase yourself, wouldn't you...?"

Mizushino looked at me sadly.

"Like a certain someone we know, I have my own code for myself. I don't wanna be the kind of guy who secretly hopes for that."

Then he smiled. There was something pure and refreshing about it.

Ah. Right.

Asano and I were of the opinion that King and Yuuko would make a happy couple, but life's full of wishes. Doesn't mean they're all gonna come true.

"So," Mizushino continued, "I get why Saku's conflicted, and I understand Yuuko's feelings, and I also get why Kaito's mad. I don't think any of them are wrong, really."

I suddenly remembered what King had said in my room.

"But if it's someone you actually like and value as a friend who catches feelings and asks you out... Well, it sucks to have to wreck a friendship."

"No matter how handsome you might be, or how good at sports you are, or how high your grades are, or whatever, it doesn't automatically mean the girl you like is gonna like you back."

At the time, I just took it like, *Oh, maybe he's experienced unrequited love before.*

Or maybe, he knew that this day would eventually come.

What a sad ending, then.

I wonder how it could have been done better, though?

There's no way I could understand something that even King himself didn't.

I let out a big sigh and opened my mouth again.

"But you know..."

There was one thing I still wanted to ask.

"Why'd you speak up right then? It sounded like you had an actual grudge... That doesn't jibe with what you just told me at all. Or was that just my imagination?"

Mizushino's eyes widened in astonishment, and then he scratched his head.

"...It was because Yuzuki looked sad," he muttered softly, looking embarrassed.

"…Pfft-ha!"

I burst out laughing. That was so not him.

"Hey now, Kenta, that's not nice."

"I'm sorry, but… Hearing you say something like that… Geh-heh-heh!"

"Okay, so there's this wrestling move—do you know the soccer kick?" Mizushino lifted himself up and put his arm around my shoulder.

"What?! That's a headlock!"

After we wrestled for a minute, I spoke again. "I wonder how the others are getting along."

Mizushino answered without hesitation, in his usual tone. "Beats me. But knowing them, they'll probably be all right."

His short response brought to mind various scenarios. I nodded.

I wished I could do something to give back.

Mulling it over, I drank the rest of my rapidly warming cola.

*

Tap, tap, tap, went the knife on the cutting board.

The water was boiling.

Clatter, clank, went the dancing pot lid.

The familiar and soothing rhythms of cooking were so everyday, so humdrum, that they almost offended the senses.

I, Saku Chitose, turned on my Tivoli Audio and set it to randomly play music from my phone, which was connected via Bluetooth.

From the speakers, the sound of SUPER BUTTER DOG's "Sayonara COLOR" began to flow.

In the end, I wasn't able to get rid of Yua, so I ended up going to the supermarket with her and then bringing her back to my place.

This everyday ritual, this routine for the last year, was now accompanied by an indescribable sense of guilt that tightened like a vise in my chest.

While I'm over here doing this, Yuuko has to be...

I wondered if she even got home safe.

I wondered if Kotone came to pick her up.

What if she was wandering the city alone, at night?

I just wanted to know if she was safe.

No matter how selfish and cruel it might have been of me, I just wanted to call her and ask her, "Hey, you okay?"

But I couldn't do that.

Even so..., I thought.

Is it okay for me to be sitting around, casually waiting for a hot meal while she's out there?

Shouldn't I kick Yua out and wallow?

And I should keep wallowing, day after day, until summer vacation is over.

...Wow, look at me. Self-pity city. Yua's right. I would have done exactly as she predicted, if she wasn't here.

I sighed.

I just couldn't make sense of today.

How was I supposed to handle a girl when I'd made her cry?

If I just went back to ordinary life without spending some time punishing myself first, it would be like the time Yuuko and I spent together, the choice I'd made, meant almost nothing.

As I sat on the sofa ruminating...

"Saku." Yua turned around and called from the kitchen. "I've filled the bath with hot water, so why don't you go and take a soak?"

Her expression was as calm as ever.

Why? I wondered.

Over the past year or so, Yuuko and Yua have always been together.

Not only at school, but also on days without club activities, and on Saturdays and Sundays. I always get texts with shots of them having fun together.

Each time, I'd laugh and think, *Wow. They're really like sisters.*

This didn't make sense.

Yuuko had broken down in tears in front of her friend. Those tears must have affected Yua deeply.

And yet here she was.

"Saku?" Yua said again.

"Ah, right. Okay, I guess I'll go get in the bath."

Maybe it was all my fault.

Nanase, Haru, Kazuki, Kaito, and Kenta all stuck around with Yuuko.

Yua put aside her feelings for her best friend, left the cleanup to the other guys, and chased after me when I ran off alone.

Her chest must have been swirling with conflict and regret.

But she was acting like her usual self, so as not to make it too obvious.

I'm…I'm so pathetic.

The least I could do right now is try to avoid causing any further worry for others.

I grabbed a towel and a change of clothes and headed for the bathroom.

"If the day ever came when I had to make a choice…I decided a long time ago that I would choose the one I liked the most."

For now, I wanted to keep the meaning of those words locked away in the night.

⋆

I closed the bathroom door and turned the shower handle, and cool water began to rain down from the high hook where the showerhead was attached.

I put my hand on the wall and dunked my head under the spray.

"...Guh."

At least I kept from sobbing in front of Yua.

I had a feeling this day would be coming, in the not too distant future, and I thought I was ready for it.

I'd have to confront someone's feelings, and my own. And I'd have to provide a response.

But the world this spoiled brat imagined was much kinder than the one we live in.

Let's all share the pain, little by little.

But in the end, we should smile and head toward a new tomorrow.

I never imagined I'd ever even cross a point of no return, much less so suddenly, without any time to prepare. Like a sudden crease had appeared in the fabric of reality.

My cheek stung where Kaito struck me.

It's certainly not the first time I've been rejected by a girl I used to be good friends with. It's not my first time being hated by people who were my friends the day before.

As I told Asuka, I'm tired of cycles of idealization and delusion. And especially when it comes to girls, I've tried to build a wall around me made of shallow behavior and arrogance.

I always knew the end was coming.

Meeting Yuuko shouldn't have changed any of that.

So then why couldn't I stop crying?

Why did this hurt so bad? I felt like I was being crushed from the inside out.

It would have been so nice, so easy, if I could say that I liked Yuuko that way, too.

I wished I could take it all back and have that be the reality.

I could start tomorrow as her boyfriend and walk the usual path home with more nervous fidgeting than usual. We could awkwardly hold hands at the park we always stopped at on the way.

If only I could have chosen that future...maybe it would be so much happier.

This happened because it got too comfortable for me, being with you. No...it's because it was so comfortable that I forgot something important.

That sooner or later, it would end up like this.

When you were someone I couldn't stand to lose.

"Was Yuuko really nothing to you? Was she worth being discarded in ten measly seconds?"

"...Of course not."

With a thud, I hit my fist against the bathroom wall.

Yuuko, Yua, Nanase, Haru, Kazuki, Kaito, Kenta.

The days we spent together were so much fun. That was precious to me.

I knew I was coasting on a lot of goodwill, but I kept procrastinating... Just a little longer... Just a little longer...

If I could have... I wanted to keep that lukewarm happiness going forever.

In fact, I kept wishing for it in my heart.

—But.

I had no choice but to deal with the fact that Yuuko had confessed to me—and that I had told her no... And I would be dealing with that when tomorrow arrived.

I needed to move forward, even just one step at a time.

It'd be disrespectful to Yuuko for me to remain so hesitant.

If I was going to regret it so much, why did I turn her down?

Why didn't I make it a beginning instead of an ending?

I'm sure that, for me, that's one way of drawing a clear line in the sand.

—Even at this stage, I haven't come to terms with my own feelings.

I brushed back my hair, lifted my head high, and relaxed in the water.
Like I could wash off these past four days.
And I was not to recall the scent of the ocean, in the middle of the night.

*

After soaking in the bath for longer than I usually did, I got up and smelled the sweet-savory scent of ketchup on the air.
Looks like I kept her waiting.
I quickly blasted my hair with the dryer, then changed into a T-shirt and shorts.
I pulled back the curtain of the changing room area.
"Did you have a nice bath?" Yua, seated at the dining table, smiled brightly.
Ignoring the pang in my heart, I nodded a little. "I mean, I've been in some pretty amazing hot springs the past four days." Now I was bringing it up of my own volition, and I felt the wounds rip open a little more.
"Right, but isn't it kinda reassuring to take a bath in your own tub after a trip?"
"Hmm. I think I see what you're getting at."
She giggled.
"It's like being reminded that you're really home or something. It's fun while the trip's happening, but it's also kind of draining. Then when it's over, it feels kinda sad. But then you get that rush of relief over being home and finally relaxing all the way."
"Sorry. I know you should be at home in your own space right now, Yua."

"It's okay," Yua said. "This place is like another home."

"...Uh-huh." I went over to the fridge. "Is barley tea okay?"

"Sure!"

I filled two cups with ice and then poured from the big plastic bottle of barley tea we got at the supermarket.

When I brought it to the table, I found two plates of beautiful yellow omelets over rice there, one on either side.

I believe Asuka asked me about omurice once... But I think my preference is for rice with heavy ketchup, wrapped in a thin omelet in the old-fashioned style.

"Huh. It's been a long time since you made this, hasn't it?" I said.

Yua lowered her eyes a little. "It's kind of a special dish for me."

I was wondering if I should ask her to tell me more, when she tilted her head, looking slightly embarrassed.

"It's my mom's recipe."

"...I see."

"Mind if I elaborate?"

"Of course not, if you want to."

At that, Yua began to talk, her voice tinged with warm nostalgia.

"In elementary school, when I got a bad score on a test, or when I had a fight with my friends at school, or when I couldn't play well at a piano recital...my mom always made this. And she'd draw a little message on it in ketchup."

"That sounds like a nice memory."

Yua giggled, smiling softly. "So even now, when I'm having a hard time, when I'm sad or angry, I have a habit of making omurice to cheer myself up."

"I see. So this is for me."

To cheer me *up*, I was about to say, but Yua shook her head slightly.

Then with a faint smile...

* * *

"This is for us both. See? It's the moon tonight."

Ah yes.
It's shaped like a waxing moon, I thought.

For some reason, I was relieved that I could catch a glimpse of Yua's innermost thoughts just from that short exchange.
She really is putting on a brave face, I realized.
I forced myself to make a joke, hoping to lighten the burden for her a little.
"But where's the ketchup message? Isn't that the most important part?"
The top of the omelet was still bare and clean, while the ketchup sat right next to it.
Yua's eyes widened in surprise, and then her expression relaxed slowly. "You want me to write something?"
"Depends what you write."
"Hmm… How about REPENT?"
"…That joke's in poor taste, isn't it?"
Then we both burst out laughing.
My heart felt a little lighter, but at the same time, I was sad that I could still smile on a day like this.
"You know, Yua…"
I took a breath, trying yet again to distract myself from my guilt, but…
"…Never mind." I changed my mind immediately.
Because "Why haven't you questioned me about any of this?" makes it sound like I want to be questioned about it. I can't keep heaping my burdens on her.
Yua placed her hands together and chose not to pry. "Shall we eat?"
I followed her lead. "We shall. Thanks."

"Here," Yua indicated, leaning forward, ketchup bottle in hand.

She added a splort of ketchup just to the left of the center of the omelet.

It spread out on the white plate, making the whole thing look like one of those picture-perfect wax food replicas from a retro coffee shop.

After taking a sip of barley tea, I picked up the matte-blue soup cup with a handle.

This was a hearty consommé soup with finely chopped cabbage, carrots, onions, daikon, celery, and bacon. A sprig of dried parsley floated on top.

"Thanks," I murmured again, scooping it up with a spoon.

After soaking in the bath, I'd cooled myself down again in the shower before I came out, and the soothing consommé flavor and the sweetness of the vegetables gradually warmed me up again.

"…It's good," I commented absently, and Yua beamed.

"Really? I noticed you didn't eat any vegetables at all at the buffet or the BBQ. And I figured you'd be able to handle some soup, even if you didn't have much of an appetite."

"Yeah, it's delicious. Can I put some pepper on it?"

"Seriously, that again?"

I scooped up some of the ketchup on the plate with a spoon and then cut into the edge of the omurice.

When I put it in my mouth, I got a hit of butter, a fairly comforting flavor.

The inside was simple, just chopped chicken and onion.

Maybe it was because of what Yua said earlier.

But for some reason, the sweet-savory taste of the ketchup reminded me of days gone by.

But not when I was a kid.

It was here, in this apartment…

Ah, come to think of it…

The soup cup. The plate.

Originally, I had a mishmash of dollar-store plates, but Yuuko complained that they weren't cute, and that was how we went to choose new tableware together.

For my birthday last year, she gave me some loungewear from Gelato Pique. I was a little embarrassed by how nice it was, and I didn't want to ruin it. I've been keeping it neatly in the closet ever since.

The coffee cup that I use every day...the multiple sets of chopsticks, even though I live alone...the luncheon mat that I barely use because it's a hassle...even my hair dryer.

This room is filled with things that Yuuko likes.

And yet here I am, surrounded by her things, eating comfort food...

"...It's delicious, isn't it?"

The tears spilled out before I could manage to choke them back.

Ha-ha. Ridiculous.
What, you're not so devastated that the food has no taste?
You're able to eat omurice?
Wow.
Once those thoughts started, they didn't stop.

A thin, transparent film started to form on top of the ketchup.

Drops of water dripping down my cheeks slipped into the edges of my lips, and I tasted salt on the tip of my tongue.

But despite that, I...

I kept my head down and shoveled the food into my mouth.

The spoon hit the side of the plate with an unsophisticated clang.

I was going too fast, and I began to choke.

"Guh... Gack..."

It was delicious. So good. But very, very salty.

Without saying anything, Yua stood and turned up the volume of the music a little.

*

"Thank you for the meal. Really, it was delicious."

As soon as I finished eating the omurice and consommé soup, I rushed into the dressing room, washed my face over and over again in the sink, then finally returned to the living room.

"I've made better, but thank you."

Before I knew it, Yua had finished eating, too. Now she was about to carry two dishes to the sink to wash them.

"Oh, I'll do that."

"Sure."

Yua withdrew, since we both had our usual jobs.

I was grateful that she didn't try to comfort me and just left me alone.

I squeezed some detergent onto a brand-new sponge, then washed the drinking glasses, soup cups, spoons, plates, and so on, starting with the cleanest items first.

Yua once told me that this was the most efficient method.

Rinsing is done at the end, and if something's very dirty, wipe it off with a paper towel first.

I think it had become a habit before I even knew it.

While you're at it, clean the sink thoroughly with the old sponge you haven't thrown away yet.

As I went about my work, my feelings gradually calmed down.

I looked at the clock and realized with a jolt that it was already ten PM.

"Yua."

"Saku?"

                              *   *   *

Suddenly, we spoke at the same time.

I held out a hand, signaling her to go first.

Yua nodded and said, "Can I take a bath here?"

"...Huh?"

"Didn't you hear me? I want you to lend me your bath."

"No, I heard you very well, and then I wanted to hear it again."

It was way too late for a young woman to be in a guy's apartment.

"I'll take you home. You can have a nice hot bath there."

Yua tilted her head. "Uh, but I'm sleeping here tonight, though?"

"Oh, I see, then that's... WHAAAT?!!!"

I was so taken aback that I yelped like a puppy.

"Wait, didn't I mention that?"

"Hold on... It's not about whether you mentioned it..."

"It's okay; I have a spare change of clothes."

"You thought that far ahead?!"

"While you were taking a bath, I explained things to my dad on the phone."

"I'm begging you, please don't tell me something that crazy..."

Yua blinked at me, like I was being ridiculous... And she showed no hint of embarrassment. Almost like she was being intentionally frivolous about this.

I sighed deeply, then...

"There's no possible explanation that could be given for a girl to stay at a guy's house. A guy who isn't even her boyfriend." I had to state the obvious.

Yua laughed a little. "Aw, Saku. You treat me like a real girl."

"How else should I treat you?"

"As your mom? Someone who cooks you dinner?"

"Listen here..." I slumped my shoulders. "Please. I'm not in the mood to talk about girls like that."

However, Yua pretended not to know what I was saying. "You let Yuzuki stay over, though."

"Well, there were extenuating circumstances..."

That's right; I remembered the scribbles Yuzuki drew on my neck, as a prank...

"You know," Yua said, scratching her cheek.

"Since this isn't the first time, don't you think it's a bit too late to be making a fuss about it?"

"..."

I didn't know what to say to that.

Yua peered at me. "If you don't want me here, wanna try kicking me out?"

She didn't wait for my reaction before she continued. "I'd turn you down either way, but just to check, you don't feel guilty, do you?"

"That's not what I'm worried about."

I'm not some kind of lowlife who'd abandon all rationality just because a girl was staying over. Especially not on a day like today.

But sleeping in the same apartment seemed like a serious betrayal.

Even though I'd already committed the ultimate betrayal.

"Saku, you probably won't be able to sleep tonight anyway. Sure, I'll be staying over, but we'll just be here chatting like it's any other visit."

It was like she'd been reading my mind.

"But why...why go to all this trouble...?"

"I told you, didn't I?" Yua said, gazing straight at me.

"Just like you did for me that day. This time...I'm going to be the one who's with you, Saku."

*　　*　　*

She smiled, and I thought I saw pity in it.

I couldn't say anything more.

"Well, then," said Yua, picking up her own bag. "I'll borrow your bath."

"…I'll take a walk until you're done."

"All right. I'll be about an hour."

I nodded, stuck my smartphone in my pocket, and left the apartment.

*

Outside, it was still slightly humid and warm.

Up until a few hours ago, I'd been smelling the sea breeze. Now the familiar scent of the riverbank tickled my nostrils.

Crick crick, chirp chirp. The sound of the insects created a very specific atmosphere.

The night had grown awfully thick.

I had an inkling as to why Yua was being so stubborn.

That was why I wanted to keep my distance. But in the end, I caved.

What am I doing?

It sucked—really sucked—and I knew I shouldn't be doing it, but I wasn't able to stop myself from crying in front of Yua.

No matter how desperately I tried to act cheery, I kept seeing Yuuko's smile, her tears, hearing her words in my mind. And I lost the ability to judge what's right and what's wrong.

I realized my phone was buzzing, and that it had been for a while now.

Nanase had sent me one LINE message, and Haru had sent a whole bunch.

But I wasn't brave enough to open those messages now.

I could imagine what they said well enough.

It would be nice if they sent things like, "It's okay," or "Don't worry about it." But thinking of Yuuko again…I realized I didn't want to see that.

While I was thinking…

—Brrrrr.

Now my phone was buzzing continuously, letting me know I was getting an incoming call.

I was just thinking about how I was going to opt out of answering (sorry) if it was Nanase, Haru, or even Kenta, but then I blinked and looked at the display again.

Asuka Nishino, it said.

"Asuka?" I muttered to myself.

After that trip to Tokyo, we'd started communicating over LINE, but this was the first time I'd received a sudden phone call.

I wondered if something was up.

Nanase and the others knew the current situation, so they'd understand if I didn't answer.

But if I left Asuka hanging…

And what if…what if it was an emergency?

I couldn't ignore it. I hesitantly tapped the display…

"Evening. It's a beautiful moon tonight."

…but her voice was completely calm.

"Uh… Yeah." I managed an answer of sorts.

"Huh?! I'm sorry; were you busy?"

"Uh, I was just taking a walk. What's wrong?"

After a short silence, Asuka spoke.

"…Nothing's wrong. I was just wondering what's up."

It was an unusual and uninformative response.

While I was contemplating how to answer…

"Do I need a reason to call you?" Asuka sounded somewhat uneasy.

I tried to be as bright as possible. "I just got home, took a bath, and ate dinner."

I guess I performed well. Asuka's voice was peppy when she spoke again.

"I see! Well, what did you have?"

"The kind of old-fashioned omurice a certain person favors."

"Nice. So you cooked for yourself, right after coming back from summer camp?"

"Uh, yeah, I guess I did."

I'm sorry I'm being so evasive.

"Okay then, once I've learned how to cook meat-and-potato stew, the next on the list is omurice."

"...It's surprisingly difficult."

"Hey, you've been acting like I'm useless lately, you know?!"

"Nope, you're still the same older girl I look up to."

"........."

Suddenly, the conversation ground to a halt.

"What happened?" Asuka said.

"What? Nothing happened."

"Liar!"

Ah, it was going so well, I thought, giving in to the inevitable.

"I'm just a little tired. You're being weird, Asuka."

"Hey, it's a new moon tonight, you know."

One of the first things Asuka said to me came back to me then.

"If everything was all normal with you, then you'd be like, 'Would that we could meet, but alas' or something, wouldn't you?"

"Sorry. I was just surprised by your call, so I was being glib. Anyway, I really did want to look at the night sky tonight."

"All right, well enough of the usual sarcasm and snark. It's obvious to me that something happened. So come on, spill it to me. Didn't I tell you I wanted to talk about as much as I can with you in the time we have left?"

"But…" I fumbled for words.

"Hey, you're not mincing words on my behalf here, are you? Like, you don't want me to get involved, or you're worried that telling me might wreck my mood? You know…" Asuka's voice was a little sad. *"Being left on the outside of the mosquito net really sucks. I mean, we have a one-year age gap. I don't know anything about your life at school. It might be selfish of me, but I'm always worried something big's going to change right out of my reach, and by the time I find out about it, it'll be too late. There are times when the wounds you don't know about go deeper than the ones you do know."*

"Asuka…"

"I don't want that to happen again!"

I heard a sharp intake of breath, and her voice softened again.

"I don't want to see you playing baseball again when nobody told me anything."

Oh, I see.

That day…on the baseball field… That's how Asuka felt.

…

I'm really sick of my selfishness.

Of course, I was planning to tell Asuka about the baseball club.

But I wanted to be fully prepared when I told her, "Hey, I'm going to play in a game, so make sure you come watch."

Because when we met again in high school, all she saw was me sulking.

I wanted to show her that I was facing the game I loved again.

…But thinking about it from Asuka's perspective…

Despite all our talks, it would have looked like I'd just decided to go off and play baseball again on a whim, leaving her out of it completely and goofing around with my classmates.

Yeah, I could see how she took it like that.

Hey, I did it again. Without even realizing it, I've hurt someone I…

"All right. I don't know if I'll be able to explain it that eloquently…"

"I don't need it explained eloquently. Just tell me what happened in whatever words you want."

I took a breath, mentally going back over those days spent with Yuuko.

After I finished telling her everything…

"I'm sorry." Asuka's response was brief.

"I'm sorry, too. About the baseball."

"It's okay. I know you had your own reasons. You weren't in the wrong. We just misunderstood each other…"

After a short silence, I heard the sound of swallowing, the clink of ice in a glass.

In the background, I could hear Bump of Chicken's "Embrace" playing low, so as not to drown out the call.

"I wish I had some good words to give you right now." Asuka forced a laugh. *"It's no good, though. Whatever I say is going to sound trite."*

She was putting herself down, but I…

For some reason, I felt like I'd been saved.

No doubt, she'd imagined the whole story unfolding almost as if it was all happening to her. And this girl, who valued the importance of words more than anyone else I knew, was now at a complete loss.

I was helpless in a maze with no exit in sight, and I felt like I had a little bit of affirmation that things really were as dire as they felt.

"It's tough, isn't it?"

"Yeah. It is."

I let my weakness show after fighting so hard to hide it from Yua.

When that song was over, we said good night to each other.

★

After ending the call, I stood there motionless for a long time. Maybe even a few minutes.

I, Asuka Nishino, was snapped back to reality by the sound of my phone dropping onto the bed.

I was the one who'd pushed him to talk, but I still hadn't wrapped my head around what exactly he'd said yet.

I noticed it right away, the desolation in his voice. I'd wondered if it was my imagination when he started goofing around as usual, but the more we talked, the more certain I was that something was off.

You're always like that. You stick your neck out for others with no regard for who or when.

I'd assumed he'd been up to more of his usual schtick.

So I figured, *Hey, I'll be Big Sis Asuka and make myself useful.*

I...I...

I've been so naive.

The time we spent together during summer camp was so amazing...and even though it was only for a brief time, it felt like we were actual classmates. When we got home, I was on edge, though.

I wanted to hear his voice even more. I wanted to talk even more.

I want to go back over each and every moment to make sure that these four days weren't some kind of summer mirage.

So there I was, floating up off the ground...

Meanwhile, this whole other thing was unfolding.

It was over and done before I even knew it was happening.

Hiiragi's determination, the confusion of the others, Asano's anger, the tears I know you cried. It all happened without my involvement.

Hey.

Why did I have to be born before you?

Why aren't you my classmate?

That's the only thing I would have needed, and I could have been a main cast character.

I could have jumped in and confessed my feelings to you first, before you got a chance to respond to Hiiragi's. I could have been there to stick up for you with Asano. I could have been the one to run right after you when you split from the classroom.

—But I wasn't even given the chance to make those choices.

I'm so jealous of Uchida and Nanase and Aomi. It feels like my soul is filling up with dank mud.

I could easily hate Hiiragi.

You girls are so lucky to be his classmates.

Even if you confess your feelings all in a rush and get a disappointing response, the new term will start again once summer break is over.

You're going to have to see him every day. After all, you're classmates. You're friends.

Any bitterness will soon disappear, and you'll be hanging out like normal all over again before long.

And as you continue to spend time together, you might get another chance one day.

Maybe even far into the future, during a class reunion or something.

But I'm a year ahead.

If I try and fail, even once, it's over for good.

It's not like we have close friends in common. We don't always have a specific place or opportunity to meet, and we don't have an inseparable bond.

The moment I try for your heart and miss…

…That's it.

The moment I realized that, I was terrified.
This wasn't some hypothetical scenario.
One single misstep.
What if you'd accepted Hiiragi's feelings?

Then that call just now would have been a good-bye call.

"Yuuko and I have started dating. I can't meet up with you one-on-one anymore, Asuka. But let's chat every now and again at school, okay?"

I hate that.
I can't stand the thought of it.
I hate it, I hate it, I hate it!
When I decided to go to Tokyo for university, I'd thought I was prepared for not being able to see him anymore.
I'd come to terms with not being his wife someday, or so I'd thought.
But in a corner of my mind, I let my imagination run away with me…
We'd message back and forth every day over LINE, talking about my new life… Maybe call each other once a week or so… And when I came back to Fukui in the summer, we'd go on a long-anticipated date.

Maybe you'd even come to Tokyo.

This time, I'd play the part of the older sister and show you around, have you stay at my place and feed you the meat-and-potato stew I'd specifically learned how to make.

It was lost time that could never really exist in the first place.

Yeah. This is the truth about me.

—Even though I was prepared to live apart, I wasn't prepared to leave you, at all.

I know, it's not Hiiragi's fault.

She just summoned up her courage.

We traveled together, slept in the same bed in the same hotel.

What am I doing, blaming Hiiragi for stealing the lead? I stole the lead ages ago.

If we're not classmates, and we have no opportunity or reason to meet—if there's no thread tying us together—then I'd just have to build my own thread.

I need the single golden ticket that gives me the right to be with you: the girlfriend ticket.

But...even so...

Thinking back on it now... Back when I was that shy little girl, you came to visit me in the summer and took me to all kinds of places.

Thinking back on it now... After we met again in high school, you'd seek me out and sit down right beside me.

Thinking back on it... You've been leading me by the hand all this time.

I don't have the slightest idea of how I can take the initiative. How can I take hold of you and turn you my way, when it seems like you're on the verge of leaving?

Don't go, don't leave me, don't leave me out.
I don't want to feel sad every time summer comes.
Not after a miracle brought us together again.
Let's go on adventures together, again and again.
Take me to the festival again, like you did that day.
"Saku…" I hugged my pillow tight.
Everyone's out there standing under the spotlight, yelling, *"Here I am! I'm here!"*
They're living out their respective stories and holding their happy endings in their hearts.
Even right now, I wish I could have asked him one thing.

Hey. Who was the one who made you omurice while you sat crying…?

*

After the phone call with Asuka, I, Saku Chitose, took a walk to kill some time, and after an hour or so, I returned home.

I'd thought that moving my body would distract me a little, but it just made the ruminating worse.

I should have taken my baseball bat if it was going to end up like this. I could have broken a decent sweat and then just taken another bath.

If I'd concentrated on my swing, I wouldn't have been in my thoughts so much.

I pressed the doorbell. *Ding-dong.*

Immediately, there was a clattering inside, and the door swung open.

Yua had changed into blue satin pajamas covered in little white stars.

"Why'd you ring?"

I frowned at her.

Her hair, which she usually wears in a side ponytail, was loose.
"I guess you wouldn't be freaked out either way, but I figured just in case."

If by any chance I caught her in the middle of changing clothes in the living room, I'd be sleeping on the balcony tonight.

"Hee-hee. Well, thanks for your concern."

She held the door open for me, and as I passed by her, I suddenly caught a whiff of a scent that struck me as significant in two ways.

That was the shampoo I always use. And it was the shampoo Yua insisted I buy.

When I took off my shoes and entered the apartment, trying to shake off the mood that seemed stuck to me, the smell of strong coffee reached my nose.

"Would you prefer it hot or iced?" said Yua, squatting down to straighten my Stan Smiths. "We didn't get a chance for after-dinner coffee earlier, see."

She said it so casually that I felt my shoulders relax a little.

"But it's already almost midnight," I said.

The clock read just before eleven thirty.

"Sorry. I figured you wouldn't be sleeping much even without coffee…"

"No, it's okay… Can I have mine hot?"

"Black, right? No milk?"

"…Yeah."

She read my mind again.

I tuned my Tivoli to a frequency I liked and sat down on the sofa.

Yua placed two mugs on the coffee table and sat down beside me.

We both took our coffee black.

"You don't have to stay up with me," I said. "Why don't you have some hot milk or something?"

She gave me a devilish little grin. "I have to stay up and keep an eye on you, at least until you go to bed properly."

"You don't trust me at all, do you? You don't need to worry. I won't be able to sleep right away after drinking this, but I'll lie down and close my eyes at some point tonight. That's what I promised you, after all."

"Then I guess we'll have to move the sofa again." Yua turned to me. "Let's keep chatting until one of us falls asleep." She smiled, the corners of her eyes crinkling a little.

"Like I keep saying, you don't need to stay up with me."

"No, I won't be able to sleep right away anyway. Besides, I was very relieved at the time."

"I see. Well, you can use the bed."

"Even if I say no, I guess you'll keep insisting. So I'll take it gladly."

The air filled with slurping sounds as we sipped our coffee together.

"I think I feel a little better," I muttered to myself. "I wonder how she's doing right now."

Obviously, Yua knew who I was referring to. "Probably still crying," she said without hesitation.

"Don't sound so callous…"

But whose fault is it anyway? …I mean, I guess that's true, but I was curious about her indifference.

"No point ignoring the obvious facts. Yuuko's crying, you're suffering, and I'm here. We all made our own choices."

"…I guess so."

Yua's been like this ever since our talk by the riverbed.

"The other day, I met Kotone," she said.

"Yeah, I heard. Yuuko acted like she was annoyed, but I think she was actually pretty happy about it."

Just picturing that made my chest hurt again.

"When Yuuko went to the bathroom, Kotone told me a little bit about her childhood. When I saw the two of them, they seemed to get along really well. To me, they looked so close, like friends, or sisters. It was so wholesome. I thought it was nice she had a family like that."

When I glanced over at Yua, I saw that her expression had shifted to one of total calm.

"Yeah. I've been over for dinner several times. I had the same impression."

"At the time," I said, taking a sip of coffee, "Kotone told me that she was relieved to know that Yuuko had me in her life. And I told her I'd always be around. As her friend."

"...I see."

"So that's another promise I've broken."

Yua shook her head. "Yuuko was the one who tried to change your current relationship. You did your best to stay her friend. Anyway, Kotone said the same thing to me. She said she wanted me to help dress Yuuko for her coming-of-age ceremony. She said she hoped that Yuuko and I would always stay friends."

She trailed off for a moment.

"But...the way I feel about Yuuko right now..."

For the first time, Yua's voice trembled slightly.

Oh, right. I kinda guessed.

I stood up and turned up the volume of the Tivoli, just like Yua had done earlier.

Then, for a while, we listened to an unknown piano sonata on the radio.

Still, Yua didn't let me see any tears.

*

"Mom... Oh, Mom..."

I, Yuuko Hiiragi, sat on the sofa in the living room. Only the overhead light was on. I was clinging to my mother, who sat clutching a glass of wine in one hand.

In the end, Kaito ended up silently walking me home.

I didn't even have the energy to take the keys out of my bag. When he rang the doorbell, Mom came out and saw me with Kaito. I think she knew immediately that something was up.

"Thank you for bringing Yuuko home. Um, I'm afraid I don't know your name…"

"I'm just a classmate. Well, see you around."

And Kaito turned and walked off.

I really should have thanked him, but I was so relieved seeing my mom, and the tears welled up all over again.

She didn't say anything, just took me to the bathroom and brought me a change of clothes and a bath towel.

I was standing there like such a zombie that Mom almost started undressing me herself. So I snapped out of it and told her, "It's okay. I can do it myself."

After that, I took a shower, then soaked in the bathtub and thought about all kinds of things. Eventually I started to boil, so I got out of the bath and did my usual skin care routine, even though it seemed pointless now. Finally, I carefully dried my hair.

When I returned to the living room, Mom was waiting on the sofa.

Dad should have been home by now. Maybe Mom asked him to go upstairs to spare me the awkwardness.

Mom patted the sofa beside her, and I sat down.

She put her glass on the coffee table, then poured some Welch's grape juice into a second glass for me.

"Take your time, Yuuko."

"…"

And then I told her, all in a rush, about the events of the past four days. About my confession to Saku and his response. About my true feelings, the ones I hadn't been able to tell anyone. I told her everything as my voice broke.

"Mom… It's all over."

She patted my head a couple times. "I see. You did everything you could, Yuuko."

Then she stroked my hair gently.

"Did I…do the wrong thing? Did I just run off a cliff like a giant idiot?"

Mom took a sip of wine. "Well, as far as a romance tactic goes, yeah, you messed it up."

Her blunt reply made my vision go white for a second.

"Mom! That's horrible! You didn't have to say that…"

"But you know it yourself, Yuuko, don't you? You knew that if you confessed now… Well, it was never going to go well. You knew it was still too early."

"…Yeah. I knew. But there are so many other girls around that probably like Saku, too. And some of them are my best friends! I just didn't know what to do…"

"If it was me…I would never have done what you did, Yuuko."

Mom was giving it to me straight.

"I guess… I guess you're right…" My voice faded to a whisper. "But you know…"

Mom looked at me, with infinite kindness in her expression.

"I'm proud of you. You've grown up to be an earnest girl. You really cherish the people important to you."

Mom paused for a moment. Then…

"I'm so glad you're the way you are, Yuuko. Thank you for being my daughter."

*　　*　　*

Mom grinned.

I...I just...

"Really? You don't think I'm the worst? I hurt the people I love—my best friends."

And Mom said...

"—I'm sure the people in your heart will tell you."

I drew my knees up on the sofa and hugged them, and my tears spilled down my cheeks again.

*

After drinking coffee and brushing my teeth, I, Saku Chitose, joined forces with Yua to drag the sofa into the bedroom.

We just needed to be close enough to chat, so I positioned it a little away from the bed.

I set the shut-off timer on the Tivoli in the living room, turned down the volume, and clicked off the air conditioner.

Yua called to me from the bed.

"It's okay. I have a blanket."

I run pretty hot, so I always have the air conditioner running at a low temperature.

On the other hand, Yua, who tends to run cold, sometimes pulls out a hoodie from my closet and puts it on when she's over.

"No, I'll point the fan at myself. Besides..." I opened the window that led to the balcony. "It feels more comfortable like this."

The curtains filled with air, and a quiet midnight breeze stole into the room.

It had gotten much cooler outside.

Lying down on the sofa and closing my eyes, I smelled the summer grass.

But I was still wide awake. No escaping into dreams just yet.

I could hear Yua tossing and turning.

Glancing over at the bed, I saw her lying on her side, her cheek resting on the pillow.

"Let's talk about something." Yua clutched the edge of the blanket with both hands as she spoke.

"You're seriously going to stay awake with me?"

"I told you. I don't think I can sleep, either."

"I see." I turned on my side, too. "But having a cozy bedtime chat alone with you feels..."

"Unfair to Yuuko?"

"Yeah."

Yua giggled, shaking the bed. Her hair, unbound by its usual scrunchie, spilled over. "It's weird. You know, Saku, you're the one who taught me what to do in a situation like this."

"Huh...?"

With a tender expression, Yua said...

"—Let's talk about Yuuko."

She smiled softly.

"That way, it doesn't seem like we're discounting the time we spent together. It doesn't sound like we're turning our backs and saying we never should have met. It's almost like it's the three of us here, having a fun sleepover together."

I blinked.

Right... Yua was talking about that time when...

"Okay. Then tonight, the three of us will sleep lined up next to each other."

I finally gave a real smile.

*   *   *

"She hides it well, but Yuuko's the type to get lonely easily, huh?"

I propped up my cheek with my elbow on the pillow.

"Oh, totally!" Yua laughed and continued. "Yuuko often comes to your place, but when I do the same thing, she's always like, 'Hey, Ucchi, no fair!'"

"Well, the reverse is true. She's often like, 'Why is it that Saku's the only one who gets to eat Ucchi's special homemade omurice, huh?'"

"She's so pretty, and friends with everyone, but sometimes she gets insecure. Like if I'm not talking much, she'll be all, 'Ucchi, are you mad at me?'"

"And when I went shopping with her, we went to Hachiban's after, and I had just a regular spicy ramen. And she was all, 'Saku, are you tired? I'm so sorry for making you hang out so long. I mean, usually I have a double helping of ramen.'"

"Hee-hee. Yuuko's so innocent. She lives in tune with whatever she's feeling. One time, I didn't have any side dishes in the fridge, so my lunch bento was just rice with *furikake*, pickled plums, and one omelet. I was super embarrassed, so I tried to hide what I was eating. And Yuuko was like, 'Open wide, Ucchi' and shoved some of her food in my mouth. I just know she noticed."

"I know what you mean. Normally, Yuuko acts pretty selfish, right? She's not the type to agonize over things. She just tells it like it is, and her charm makes up for the rest."

"Yeah, totally. Like, 'Hey, there's a new shop in front of the station, so let's go there right now.'"

"Yeah. Or 'I bought so many clothes today! I'm gonna hold a fashion show at your place right after this, Saku.'"

"Oh, that's so Yuuko. What else?"

"Around this time last year…you weren't hanging with us on

the daily yet back then, Yua, but this was when I was down-and-out after quitting baseball."

"I know. I think I mentioned before how I saw you practicing for games over the summer at the sports field."

"Right, you mentioned that when we went to Kenta's house... Wait, during summer vacation, I..."

"Now, now, that's not the part to focus on here."

"Right, well anyway, I couldn't talk to Yuuko, Kazuki, or Kaito about what really happened. But around then, Yuuko stopped being so selfish. It was summer vacation, so usually she'd be all over me about hanging out, but there was none of that. Instead, she sent me perky messages over LINE every day, with pics and stuff. Like a sunflower she'd seen on her walk home, or a pretty sunset, or the moon when it was really big in the sky. Stuff like that."

"Sounds like she was aware that you were going through something."

"I think so. When I came through the worst of it, she dragged me all over the place. It was way more than before."

"Yeah, and by that time, I'd started hanging with you, too."

"Yeah, that's right..."

Would we...

Would Yuuko...
Would my best friend, Yuuko...

...ever be...
...ever be...

...with me, Saku...
...with me, Yua...

...ever again?
...ever again?

*　　*　　*

We spent the next little while with memories of Yuuko.

We didn't think about anything else.

Like looking for pretty seashells on the beach, like counting the stars one by one, like chasing a contrail at dusk, like running away from a tomorrow that has already arrived.

We were afraid—that if we fell asleep, we'd be locked out of the world of yesterday, never able to put things right again.

I think we were both quietly hoping that if we kept talking like this, all night, then Yuuko would suddenly appear, and summer vacation would continue as if nothing had even happened.

I think we were both trying to prepare for what came next.

—But the future would arrive no matter what.

"Hey, Yua?"

"Hmm?"

"Do you think I can make it up to Yuuko and Kaito?"

"I don't know. I don't think it will ever be the same again."

"I guess that's true."

"Hey, Saku?"

"What?"

"Do you think Yuuko and I can still be friends?"

"I don't know. Not without changing something, at least."

"I guess that's true."

So for now, for just a little longer.

Let's pick up beautiful candy balls, rolling around at the bottom of a box of midnight.

Let's let the color of our sorrow run its deep-blue course.

So that, someday, we can walk through the twilight again together.

CHAPTER 6
Us Two Together with No Moon in Sight

—In the spring, at sixteen years old, I, Yua Uchida, entered Fuji High School.

To be honest, I was surprised when I got the top score in the entrance exam and was tasked with delivering the commencement address as the new student representative, but I was on board with the idea.

In junior high, I got the top test scores.

That said, I'm no genius.

It's not like I can understand all the concepts just by skimming through the textbook, and I can't rattle off a bunch of correct answers to complex problems I've never seen before.

Like most kids, I didn't like studying when I was little.

I had much more fun playing the piano and flute, which my mother encouraged me to do, and my report cards were generally only just above average.

But sometime in the fourth grade, I made up my mind that I'd work hard and help my family stop worrying. I started studying and working hard to prep for my classes until late at night, every night.

Meaning the practice of studying for entrance exams has always been part of my daily routine. I've just spent more hours than most doing it.

Things might be different when it comes time for college entrance exams. But so far, at least, I've managed to get high scores on every test just by studying hard and memorizing well.

Just by working your way steadily through books of practice problems, you can pick up the important vocabulary, figure out the standard procedures for answering questions, and learn the patterns.

I spent more time doing that than most people, so as a result, I got better grades than most people.

I've never thought of myself as smart.

What I do is make sure that when I take a test, many of the questions are at least familiar. In the end, it's not much different from having the answers in advance.

But occasionally, when I'm up against a problem that requires flexible thinking and responsiveness, I make careless mistakes, even when I try to think through things methodically.

So am I what people call a hard worker?

I wouldn't exactly say that, either.

In terms of pure process, sure, I'm diligent.

But I lack motivation and drive. I didn't study because I wanted to be good at school.

My motivation was always about not giving my family any reason to worry about me.

Also, I just didn't have friends, so the time that might have gone to socializing was saved for studying instead.

In fact, I studied because I had nothing better to do, so I feel guilty trying to pass it off as some sort of decisive effort on my part.

Way back, I did have some friends in school, and in music class.

We weren't close enough to be called good friends, but when we ran into one another, we would chat and eat lunch together.

At least, I don't remember being alone.

But when I entered fourth year, I made up my mind to study hard.

One by one, my friends disappeared.

We didn't argue or fall out, and I wasn't bullied.

It was just that everyone else found other friends they vibed with better, and they prioritized spending time with people who weren't me.

I don't think anyone really knew what to do with me.

For a long time, I've been aware of the fact that I'm considered "plain."

I'm not that good at talking, and I'm not perky and outgoing, so I spent a lot of time with the quiet kids in class.

I wasn't savvy to trends or fashion, and that was around the time I started wearing glasses, too. In fact, I actively tried to distance myself from fashion and so on.

When I had nothing better to do, like during breaks at school, I just studied.

Before I knew it, I was cast in the role of "quiet honor student."

I'm a little hesitant to say it myself, but everyone in my class put me on a pedestal a bit as one of the smart kids.

I would let other kids sneak a peek at my homework when they came to class having forgotten to do theirs. And before tests, the popular kids would come to me to borrow my notes or ask me to explain problems they didn't understand.

I wasn't the type to tell people, "You've got to do it yourself," so I tried to help them as much as I could.

Tutoring others helped me understand, too, so I never felt like I was being taken advantage of.

And so it continued for a long time.

Before I knew it, a transparent wall had formed around me.

People would crowd around me and call my name, but it was

like they were talking to a walking puppet who'd been designated the perfect, subdued honor student.

No one wanted to get to know Yua Uchida. No one wanted to get inside Yua Uchida's heart. No one wanted to be friends with Yua Uchida.

It was very comfortable for me.

I was able to study more than ever, but now I had to shoulder the burden of the role.

—Because I wanted to be a normal girl, more than anyone else in the world did.

I wanted to be someone who doesn't stand out too much. Someone who doesn't need to have a ton of friends, or any really close friends. Just someone who doesn't look lonely and pitiful. Effortless, riding the breeze of school life. That's what I wanted.

I liked having clear boundaries around me, though.

Eventually, when I entered junior high school, my title of "quiet honor student" faded. And once I started getting treated like "a good girl who helps everyone else study," I felt like I'd gotten what I wanted.

You might be like, what does a kid know? But really, just living a normal life was enough for me.

I didn't get any great fortune, but at least I escaped the fate of being shoved to the bottom.

Sure, I wasn't showered with adoration from everyone around me. But I could avoid causing any pain to those I cherished.

It's fine like this. This is what I want.

Please let it continue like this, in high school…

*

Within a few days of admission, much sooner than I expected, I was once again treated as a quiet honor student by my classmates.

Unlike in junior high school, where students were automatically sorted by school district and many of them graduated from the same elementary school, high school students come from all over the prefecture.

What's more, this is Fuji High we're talking about.

I didn't really want to be the honor student. Honestly, I was fine with being thought of as sort of mousy and plain. But as the first-year class representative with the highest entrance scores, I'd ended up overshooting the mark a little. And I got cast in a role that I quickly grew comfortable in.

My new life at a college prep high school was actually much more comfortable than I'd imagined it being.

And there weren't any high-octane, ruckus-causing students at Fuji.

The girl sitting next to me said, "You're smart, aren't you?" But after we'd talked for a while, she seemed to figure me out pretty quickly. She ended the conversation smoothly, in a way that would avoid any future connection.

As soon as the class started, even the people who'd been standing in the middle of class laughing and chatting were suddenly all quiet and listening to the teacher.

Lots of students here studied during their breaks, too, so it was a relief to find that my natural habits made me normal in this environment.

But one day, in homeroom, there was an incident in which I was actually involved.

Mr. Iwanami, who's the opposite of what you'd imagine for a prep school teacher, suddenly announced that we were going to choose the class president.

I was like, *Uh-oh.*

I put my face down so as not to make eye contact with anyone.

There's a type for the president, you know? In novels, movies, TV dramas, there's always a good-girl character who wears glasses and acts fussy about rules and so on.

Except for that last characteristic, those all applied to me. So whenever it came time, I was always put forward as a recommendation almost as a matter of course.

Usually someone in the middle of the class would say something like, "How about Uchida? She's smart!" and everyone would agree.

For example, in this class...

"Yes!"

The very person I'd been expecting to volunteer flung her hand into the air.

—Yuuko Hiiragi.

I know this sounds terrible, but when I first saw her, I was surprised that someone like her got into Fuji High.

She's as pretty as an idol who just stepped out of the TV screen, and even though she wore the same plain uniform as everyone else, she made it look so stylish. She had everyone's attention.

But somehow it didn't seem to have gone to her head at all. She always smiled cheerfully and talked to everyone in a friendly way.

She was the complete opposite of me, in other words.

I'd only known her as my classmate for a few days, but watching her, I started feeling embarrassed for wishing I could be normal.

After all, I'm the definition of normal. Next to someone like Hiiragi, I'd blend right into the background and disappear, no matter how much I tried to fight it.

...So I had a glimmer of hope in my heart.

Maybe she was going to volunteer for the position herself.

If so, I would gladly give her my vote.

However, after a short exchange with Mr. Iwanami, what she ended up saying was...

*　　*　　*

"How about Uchida? If she's up for it, of course?"

Ah, those familiar words.
There were casual mutterings of agreement and scattered claps of approval around the classroom.
Yeah. Called it.
I look like the type who loves enforcing the rules, right?
No… That makes it sound more obnoxious than it is.
I'm sure Hiiragi was just saying that I looked on top of it.

"Er, uh…"

I hesitated, but I'd mostly resigned myself to it already.
If you asked me if I wanted to be class president… Well, not particularly.
I mean, I'm not one of those people who relishes taking the lead and demonstrating leadership. And if there was some kind of issue in class that needed hashing out, I'd have to mediate… The very thought made my stomach hurt.
Seeing me hesitate, Hiiragi continued.

"Ah, sorry to just spring it on you. But you were the representative for the new students at the entrance exam, and so I thought you'd be the best option for us all. But if you don't want to, you can simply say no, okay?"

Her empty equivocation drove me into a corner.
I know she meant it.
But it wasn't fair for someone like Hiiragi to say it.
Looking at the reactions of the people around me, I saw that the class was already welcoming the idea, and if I turned it down now, people would be left feeling negatively to some extent or another.

And that would affect the normal student life I was after…

I slumped my shoulders and let out a sigh.

So just like I've done all my life, I chose the path that was easiest to deal with, the one that wouldn't make big waves.

"No, it's okay. If that's okay with you…"

Hiiragi looked relieved.

Plus, you know, this is Fuji High. I couldn't see any student squabbles arising. Even if I was the class president, all I'd really be doing was leading homeroom and assisting the teacher.

It'll be fine. Okay.

Yes. This is all right. It's cool this way.

I was trying to convince myself, when…

"—Nah, I'm not into it."

Someone's voice sounded, quietly but clearly…

""Huh…?""

Hiiragi and I both spoke in surprise at the same moment.

Looking in the direction of the speaker, I realized it was the boy who'd been sort of catching everyone's attention these past few days. He'd scraped his chair back and was now standing.

As I recalled, his name was Saku Chitose.

Right after we entered this school, he and two other boys had become pals, and the three of them really stood out in class with how much noise they made. So he'd left an impression on me.

And I'd noticed how the girls had giggled and reacted to him, too.

To be honest…my first impression was that he was someone I really didn't want to get involved with.

In elementary school and junior high, there always were people like this, the center of attention in class.

For boys, they're usually star players in some sports club or other, like baseball or soccer. Or they're just really good-looking. Sometimes both.

Some of them were arrogant, but some were kind to everyone. You can't really lump them all together and dismiss them as jerks.

But the common denominator is that, for better or for worse, they have way too much of an influence on those around them.

When they laugh, when they get mad, when they get a crush on someone, when someone gets a crush on them, when they say literally anything, it affects everyone else, and some people get either really overexcited or completely despondent over them.

—So…why?

If he'd left it alone, I would have become the class president and everything would have been settled.

Why was he interrupting right now?

Especially because Chitose and Hiiragi seemed to get along really well.

I mean, just before class, I saw them standing together chatting animatedly about something or other.

I guess this was a continuation of their banter or something?

But why was he going to the trouble of speaking out against this…?

As I sat there in confusion…

"You know, Hiiragi…"

Chitose continued.

*   *   *

—And then…

I sat and watched the exchange between the two of them as it heated up, and it seemed like the atmosphere was about to darken.

To my surprise, every single word that Chitose spoke seemed to reflect feelings that had been buried deep in my heart.

I was surprised by this, by *him*…which probably just proves that I had my own unconscious biases.

Like, how could a guy like him understand how it feels to be swept along and cornered?

Then I realized…

"Sorry! I said something selfish!"

Hiiragi was suddenly gripping my hand.

"Oh, it's okay, I…"

As I spoke, my hand stiffened up, and I flicked my gaze around the classroom.

I'd been prepared to just accept it, but maybe a part of me was secretly relieved.

All of a sudden, a restlessness washed over me.

I squared my shoulders, my breaths coming quicker.

Right. I was pretending not to see it, but the truth is, I've felt this way all along—and much more deeply than I myself even knew.

"You too, Uchida."

Seeing me sitting there frozen and mute, Chitose spoke again.

*   *   *

"You kinda got dragged into it this time, but next time, at least make a face when you don't want to do something. Then maybe someone'll notice, and you won't get into a bad habit of having to fake a smile all the time."

…Huh?

I was just planning to thank him after this.
I have no idea why, but this person stuck out their neck for me.
Thanks for that, I was going to say.
Then I would introduce myself properly, and even though we'd never really be friends, we could get along as classmates going forward, too.
But…

"—I don't think you have any right to say such a thing."

Before I knew it, I was glaring at Chitose.
The rest of the class was watching as I squirmed with discomfort.
I was biting the hand that was trying to help me up.
Why am I doing this? I wanted to ask myself.
I shouldn't be making a scene and arguing with him. That was the last thing I'd ever want to do.
Especially not with someone who'd been trying to help me. If I wanted to live a quiet, normal high school life, I should really try to stay on good terms with him, of all people.
But while I was thinking all that, he shrugged, as if my words didn't bother him at all. And he said…

"Maybe not. My bad."

And then Chitose grinned.

I stared at his childish expression.

Oh, phew, it didn't turn into a big deal. I'll just have to make sure I apologize later.

But before I could start thinking anything else rational...

I felt anger boiling up inside me.

—*Oh. I'm mad. I'm pissed!*

Usually, I never even thought anything like this.

Who the hell is this guy? He's never even spoken to me. He's never even glanced my way until today.

And here he is, pretending like he knows everything. Look at him! His whole life has been a walk in the park, huh?!

Yeah, he's good-looking—not like I'm remotely interested—and sure, he can play sports.

He's always surrounded by friends. Has this guy ever faced a single moment of inconvenience in his life?

No. That's how come he can stand up in front of everyone and speak his mind without worrying about backlash.

Biting down on my lip, I scowled at Chitose, who'd moved on from the likes of me and was now putting himself forward for the position of class president.

In my usual rational state of mind, I'd have seen that as a gallant act.

He'd glossed over my emotional outburst and made me inconspicuous again.

But...but...

Even that was pissing me off now.

With just a few words, he'd trespassed into a tender place inside me.

Like the way I'd lived my life until now meant nothing.

And his words showed me...

*　　*　　*

...that someone had noticed me. That thought kept rattling around in my head.

It made me realize that...I really didn't like myself all that much.

...What did he know about the reasons I had for my fake smiles?

I was so mad.

I hate people like you.

My heart was pounding with burning hot emotion toward another person. And I thought I'd left all that behind a long time ago.

*

I didn't sleep well that night, so the next morning, I left the house early, rubbing my eyes.

The moment I entered the classroom, those words came back to me, and I was irritated all over again.

After about half an hour, the classroom began to fill up. Everyone was calling good morning over my head or behind me.

No one seemed to remember me from yesterday, thank goodness...

"Uchida!"

A voice rang out with my name, a voice that reached every corner of the classroom.

When I looked toward the door, I saw Hiiragi skipping toward me. She seemed to be worrying about something—I wasn't sure why, but I gave her a greeting in response.

"Good morning, Hiiragi."

"Yeah! Morning, Uchida." Hiiragi squatted down by my desk and grabbed my hand. "And I'm really sorry about yesterday, okay?" She gazed up at me, concern in her eyes. "It was all a bit of a mess, so I planned to give you a real apology after homeroom, but you left so quickly."

Oh well…

That was something unavoidable.

I was so agitated and flustered, I ended up dashing out of the classroom when that homeroom finally ended.

It was a surprise, though, to see that Hiiragi was still hung up on yesterday, too.

I gave her my brightest smile.

"Thanks. But it's really okay. I was a little taken aback, but you nominated me with pure intentions. I know that."

"But I never stopped to consider *your* feelings. I'm sorry. I'm so sorry. Really!"

As I saw the regret in her face, I suddenly had a thought.

For Hiiragi, this was no doubt an insignificant event, something that wouldn't really stick with her, but she'd taken my hand in the classroom, after the entrance ceremony…

"Hey, Uchida! Your speech was super good! These kind of things tend to get sooo boring, but what you said actually got to me!"

And complimented me.

For some stupid reason, I felt my eyes growing hot and prickly.

It might have been unavoidable, but standing up in front of the whole class and delivering the address was awful. I wished I'd been able to say no.

But I was the one chosen. So rather than putting together a speech full of trite clichés, I wanted to talk instead about how happy I was to enter Fuji High. About how much I looked forward to high school life, how I hoped that what I had to say might help all the other new students to feel more positive about the upcoming years, too.

Up until the night before the speech, I was tying myself in knots. Maybe no one would even listen to me, maybe my hopes for a normal, pleasant high school life wouldn't touch anyone.

So it felt like Hiiragi had given my speech the seal of approval. *She really must be an earnest and kind girl*, I thought.

I squeezed Hiiragi's hand back as she crouched there gazing at me with worry in her eyes.

"Well, let's have a good year together, okay?"

It was clumsy and lacking decorum. Hiiragi was a gorgeous girl, and everyone seemed to love her. No way was she ever going to be a special friend of mine.

But it would be nice if we could chat like this, as classmates, every now and then.

Hiiragi gave me a big smile and said, "Sure! Well then, can I call you Ucchi?"

She sounded so happy.

I smiled awkwardly and scratched my cheek.

I wasn't used to getting close to people, especially not like this, so honestly, I wasn't sure how to respond.

"Uh… Um… Well, that might be a little embarrassing."

"Oh, come on! It sounds so cute. Or would you prefer it if I called you Yua?"

"Wh-whatever's easier for you, Hiiragi…"

"Ucchi it is, then! Oh, and you can call me whatever you like!"

"For now, Hiiragi's fine…"

"Aw, that's so boring!"

"Well… I mean…"

Hiiragi beamed—her expression changed moment by moment.

Hmm, I thought, narrowing my eyes.

How long has it been since I had an interaction like this?

When I was in junior high school, everyone called me Uchida, like it was a foregone conclusion, and I only ever called people by their surnames, too.

That was when my thoughts were interrupted.

"Ah!" Hiiragi stood up and looked to the front of the classroom. "Saku! Good morning!"

The name made me stiffen in my seat.

Since getting home the day before, I had thought about this over and over. There was no world where I didn't owe Chitose my thanks after that. Still, just thinking about it made me feel all weird inside.

It was the first time I'd felt this strongly toward someone who wasn't even family.

Hey, didn't Hiiragi call him by his last name yesterday...?

"Hiiragi and Uchida. Good morning."

I couldn't just ignore him now. I lifted my head.

Chitose, one hand raised in greeting, walked over with a big yawn.

I sighed internally.

Look at him, acting all casual. Well, why wouldn't he be? He didn't have a thing in the world to worry about.

Still, after preaching to Hiiragi about keeping in mind the influence she had...I thought he ought to be more aware about how his words affected others, too.

If he'd lectured her while fully aware of his own shortcomings...that would make him a huge jerk.

...No, stop it!

Why was I being so combative, even in my own mind?

I had to thank him properly today.

While I was sitting there arguing with myself, Hiiragi spoke. "Hey, Saku! Don't call me Hiiragi! You make it sound like we're strangers! Call me Yuuko!"

She spoke as casually as if she'd been discussing the homework.

I mean... She was the complete opposite of me.

I found her request really ballsy... But maybe I was just too old-fashioned?

Chitose laughed, rolling his eyes. "You got super mad at me the other day when I called you, '*Hey, you.*' Now you want to make it more casual?"

Right, I thought.

Those two were going at it in front of everyone yesterday, even without my involvement.

Actually, I didn't have time to think about this yesterday, but how come Hiiragi ended up as the vice president?

Meanwhile, Hiiragi was charging ahead. "Okay, starting today you can call me 'Hey, you' if you want! Let's keep it chill, okay?"

"Agh, look..." Chitose looked somewhat confused. He scratched his head, then said, "All righty, Yuuko."

It was like he was admitting defeat of some kind.

"Okay! Let's swap LINE contacts later! Oh, and you too, Ucchi!"

"Ah... Okay."

Startled by the sound of my name, I just nodded and went along with it.

When I looked at Hiiragi, I felt like a fool for spending last night being mad.

I should just say thanks and put this whole matter behind me.

It was thanks to Chitose, 100 percent, that the weirdness with Hiiragi was resolved.

If just one thing had gone differently, I might not have remembered those sweet words she had for me after the entrance ceremony—or the happiness I felt when she said them to me.

Just then, I met Chitose's eyes. "Morning to you, too, Uchida."

I felt bad he had to repeat himself after I'd neglected to respond to him.

I took a deep breath, and...

"Um, good morning. I hope you're having a good day."

I returned the greeting with a little hesitation.

Chitose stared at me for a moment, then...

"'I hope you're having a good day'? What is this, customer service?"

And he burst out laughing.

Suddenly embarrassed, I lowered my eyes. After a whole night of being confused and extremely aware that I shouldn't get too close, I was being way too formal.

I wanted to melt out of my uniform and into the floor.

I decided to push through. "I mean, I don't know you very well yet."

Just get through this, and we would probably never exchange another word the rest of high school.

"Then..."

When I looked up, Chitose was still shaking with laughter, hand over his mouth.

"Once you let your guard down a bit, at least call me by my name. Saku's fine, or you can stick with Chitose."

"..."

There he goes again.

Every single thing about him seemed to be pretentious.

Dammit, I was supposed to be thanking him.

If I just smiled and said, "Thank you for yesterday," that would be the end of the story.

But...but the thought freaked me out.

Next to him, Hiiragi was looking at me curiously.

This boy and girl were so different from me.

They didn't have to think over and over about the things that had happened. They laughed and had fun when they wanted to. And even when they butted heads with their peers, they'd just make up.

There's no way either of them would know how it felt trying to be normal.

It's okay. It's fine.

My emotions bubbled up again.
A secret little mantra that has sustained me since I was little.
It's been that way for a long time.
If no one tries to get to know me—if I prevent anyone from getting to know me—sure, I won't be very happy. But I won't have to suffer through the pain of having everything fall apart in front of my eyes.
I can get by with a friendly smile, just like I've always done.
So before I realized it...

"—I don't think I like you very much."
Those words made it through the transparent wall.
Huh...?
What am I doing?
I had no idea why I just said that.
I'm not being formal. It's just that we barely know each other, so I wasn't sure how to address you. Also...I'm sorry about yesterday.
Those are the sort of things I should have said.
I've never spoken this way to anyone before in my life.
"Er... Uh..."
Seeing me rushing to fix things...

"Yeah, I kinda got that impression."

...Chitose smiled, a little bashfully.

...Grr!

*　　*　　*

His attitude pissed me off!

What was he smirking about?

I wish I could have been annoyed. I wish I had some kind of brilliant comeback.

Why was I the only one off-balance?

...Don't you worry about being disliked?

Is it just because I'm a mousy girl with glasses? Is that why you don't care?

But then, he acted like this with Hiiragi, too, yesterday.

I don't understand this person. And it's so frustrating.

I've never had anyone treat me like this before. Like they're peeling away that label that reads "quiet honor student" and taking a peek at the person inside.

As I sat there, fists clenched, Hiiragi burst out laughing. "Ah, I get it! I totally get it!"

Her reaction was off-script, too, and now I really didn't know what to do.

"Saku's sooo annoying, isn't he? It's like, hey, who do you think you are?"

"Erm..."

"If you have something to say, I think you should say it, just like I did yesterday. It might do you good!"

I sat there, nonplussed, and then...

"You know, Uchida..."

The boy I disliked was speaking again.

"Why don't you relax your shoulders a bit? You're too beautiful to ruin it with a frown."

Oh, and now a little negging? Come on...

＊   ＊   ＊

"I don't care what others think of me."

…I HATE you!!!

＊

Starting the following day, after Hiiragi and I exchanged LINE details, my life at school became a little more colorful.

Take this one day, for example.

"Hey, hey, Ucchi, where do you usually go shopping?"

"Uh… Maybe at the supermarket. Or Genky."

"Huh?"

"What? You mean, like, groceries and stuff, right…?"

"No! Definitely not! I mean things like clothes and makeup!"

"Oh, sorry. I don't know much about those things."

"Oh, really? Well, let's go shopping together sometime!"

"Um… I'm not really sure…"

I was happy but also a little worried, if I'm honest.

I had a lot of things to do at home after school and on weekends, and I didn't want to do anything too far outside my comfort zone.

Take this one day, for example.

"I told my mom about you, Ucchi! And she says she wants to meet you!"

"…Um, thanks. Well, I appreciate the sentiment."

"Oh, sorry. Of course. It's a bit sudden. But I hope I can introduce you someday!"

"Yeah. Sure. Someday."

I was certain that day would never come.

I had no idea why Hiiragi was so chatty with me. But when I paid closer attention, I realized she was chatty with everyone in class.

I'd be comfortable if we could just be classmates who chatted casually now and then.

It was clear to me that Hiiragi was a really nice girl, but I didn't feel like deepening our relationship any further.

Take this one day, for example.

"Ucchi! Let's go eat together."

"But, Hiiragi…you always eat with Mizushino and Asano…"

"Yeah, so let's all go together!"

"…No, really, it's fine. Please, don't worry about me."

I mean… *He* would be there, too.

I was certain, at the time, that I'd gotten rid of him for good.

But he kept on talking to me, and he seemed a little confused.

Take this one day, for example.

"Uchida, why are you always so frosty when I talk to you?"

"You're imagining it."

"You always smile when you talk to the others. And with Yuuko, you're a little less stiff. Aren't you?"

"I just don't really think we vibe."

"Hmm. Well, I prefer this to that weird fake smile of yours. It's like you're wearing a mask."

"…You… You're just so…"

We weren't even friends. He was so rude!

And more irritating than anything else, he hit me where it hurts.

Take this one day, for example.

"Uchida, would you mind explaining this problem to me?"

"Actually, I would mind."

"Ah! Now you've added irritation to your repertoire."

"Yes. Thanks to you."

"Now, now, don't flatter me."

"You realize I don't like you, right?"

"Well, that doesn't bother me. I don't take these things personally, y'know?"

"...You don't even know the first thing about me."

"It doesn't bother me," he said, and it sounded like he meant it, too.

But the truth is, I...

Take this one day, for example.

"Uchida...do you make your own bento lunches?"

"...Is there a problem with that?"

"No, not at all. Man, I sure wish you'd teach me to cook sometime."

"Yet again, you're making inappropriate suggestions."

"Actually, I was serious..."

"Ask your mother to teach you to cook."

"Well, I can't really..."

"Oh, too cool to hang with your mother? Must be nice to be rebellious."

"You know, sometimes, you're pretty cute."

"I hate you more and more with every passing second."

I was aware I wasn't exactly doing my usual light and breezy thing. In fact, I was starting to sound kind of harsh.

But I'm stubborn, too.

Although... If only..., I caught myself thinking.

I wondered how he would react if I told him everything.

For some reason, I wanted to know.

*

One day, after school.

My relationship with Hiiragi remained the same, not growing or receding, and as we entered July, we continued to interact.

The first semester was almost up.

For the most part, I was able to lead the kind of school life I'd wanted.

In class, cliques had already formed, and I wasn't included in any of them. Fortunately for me, though, I wasn't viewed as some sad outsider. Maybe because I was spotted chatting with those two every now and then.

Actually, sometimes people asked me stuff like, "How come you're so friendly with Chitose?" or "Does Chitose have a girlfriend?" and it was tough to keep the "freaking out" reflex buried.

As I was walking down the hallway deep in thought...

"Ah, if it isn't Uchida."

Someone said my name from behind.

"Yes?" I said, turning around, and there was Mr. Iwanami.

"Have you seen Chitose?"

"...No, I haven't."

"Bet he's still yakking in the classroom. Sorry, but would you mind doing me a favor?"

"Of course..." I nodded.

"I have a bunch of handouts on my desk in the staff room, and I want him to bring them to the classroom. It would be helpful if you could pass along the message. I asked him to come after school, but I forgot to specify a time. I have a meeting after this."

My response caught in my throat.

I didn't really want to go out of my way to talk to Chitose, but that wasn't a good enough excuse for saying no.

"Of course," I said reluctantly.

Mr. Iwanami just raised one hand, said "Thanks a lot," and walked off.

I let out a small sigh.

Then the slapping of wooden sandals against the floor paused.

"Speaking of which, Uchida." Mr. Iwanami turned. "If you have the chance, you should talk a little more openly with Chitose. You and he have some things in common."

"What do you mean...?"

"That's for you to discover."

Then Mr. Iwanami walked off at a brisk pace, leaving me to puzzle over his cryptic comments.

Me and him?

No. No. No way, never.

He's got everything. He's always brimming with confidence, surrounded by friends, living life free as a bird.

Compared to that, I'm just...

Well. Maybe Mr. Iwanami has some kind of problem with his vision.

I let out a big sigh.

Agh. Help. I don't want to talk to Chitose. He always says such weird things.

Should I just go and get the printouts myself?

I turned around and headed to the staff room.

"Excuse me," I said, stepping inside.

I'd been there to ask teachers things lots of times before, so I was able to quickly locate the seating chart posted by the door.

As I could have predicted, Mr. Iwanami's desk was piled up with textbooks and materials in no particular order.

In the center, a massive tower of papers sat precariously balanced.

This was way more than I'd been expecting.

"I don't know if I can carry all that...," I mumbled.

I pulled the stack of papers toward me bit by bit, and when half of it was hanging off the desk, I put my other hand on the bottom and lifted the whole thing.

"Gah."

It weighed more than I could have predicted, and I felt my spine curve forward.

Hmm. I think I can just about make it.

During club, I sometimes help carry heavier instruments, so it's okay.

I'd come this far anyway. I'd hate to have to put all this back on the desk and seek out Chitose after all.

With a little effort, I straightened my back and held the stack of papers against my body.

Okay, I'm managing.

It might have been bad manners, but with no one around to help, I was forced to use my foot to open and close the staff room door.

Regret soon followed.

With every step I took, the edges of the rough paper cut into my fingers, and my arms trembled with the strain.

I should have just gone to get Chitose, after all.

He could lift this weight and look cool while doing it.

Eventually, when I reached the stairs, my arms were getting numb.

I couldn't climb step by step like I usually do, so I had to raise my right foot one step, then lift my left foot onto the same step, and go up a little at a time.

I must look pretty dumb right now.

Oh no, why is this happening?

Suddenly I felt hopelessly miserable.

The inner corners of my eyes grew hot.

The tears weren't because of the stupid handouts, but because of everything that had happened since I'd entered high school.

This wasn't how I'd wanted it to go.

I felt so frustrated, all the time, even though I was actually doing all right. I should have been satisfied with how things were going.

It was all his fault.

Every time we speak, he annoys the heck out of me. He's constantly pointing out things I'm trying not to acknowledge. *I'm really like you? Am I?*

"Uchida!"

Just then, I heard a voice I'd grown accustomed to.

Light footfalls came tripping up the steps.

"I just saw Kura. There weren't any printouts in the staff room, so I figured…"

He stopped right behind me.

"You could have just come to get me. Sorry you ended up doing my job. Here, let me take those."

I scowled at his carefree smile. "I'm fine, actually!"

My voice was hard as steel. He seemed dazed. Well, I could hardly blame him.

I was lashing out my own internal frustrations without any rhyme or reason.

"Why are you being like this? I just said I'd take them."

The way he spoke irritated me again.

"I was asked to do this job."

"No, all you were asked to do was pass the message to me."

"Whatever. Please go away."

I twisted my body to escape from his hand as he reached out toward the paper.

—I felt a snag.

The heel of my left foot got caught on the raised, nonslip rubber strip at the edge of the step.

"Eek!"

Yikes, I thought, and I started to tip backward.

The heavy stack loomed over me, as if trying to assist gravity in taking me over.

My heart shrank with a sensation of weightlessness, and it was like my knees had been kicked out from under me.

No. Don't cause a fuss!

But just as I thought that...

"—You idiot!!!"

...a pair of rugged arms wrapped around me.

The handouts fluttered in the air like falling petals in slow motion.

My glasses flew off, and with a crack, I could hear them break.

But the sensation of landing was much softer against my back than I'd been anticipating. It was like falling on something small and firm, like one of the old gym mats.

"...Yikes."

Hearing his voice over my shoulder, I thought, *This feels warm.* Not the kind of thought I should have been having, but my mind was all over the place.

The heat coming from the arms wrapped around my stomach, the body pressed against my back... His temperature seemed to run higher than mine.

It felt like when I was little, and my mom read picture books to me.

But...
I inhaled.
It smelled like sweat and dirt. Like a boy.

Huh? Wait... What am I doing?

"Chitose?!"

I finally snapped out of it, and with an ungainly wriggle, I got away from him.

Looking over my shoulder, I found my frosty mask again as the reality of the situation sank in.

There lay Chitose, head at the foot of the stairs, still grasping the handrail with one hand.

He cushioned my fall? Like a gym mat...?

"Um... I..."

Chitose smiled a little and said...

"You finally called me by my name!"

He grinned.

"..."

I stood up and tried to act as if nothing had happened.

"Tch. I may act like a handsome playboy, but I really do have those lightning-fast baseball player reflexes, huh? If ol' Chitose hadn't been there, you might've cracked your head."

"Uh... I mean..."

"Heh. But seriously, Uchida, you're lucky I was there to cushion your fall, huh?"

His casual words made my chest tighten.

"Sorry. That must have been scary. Are you all right?"

"I'm...fine. Thanks."

"Sorry for how things have been. I understand that you don't like me, but for some reason, I just can't seem to leave you alone."

"...Um."

"I'm sorry to bother you. But just let me say one last thing."

Chitose continued in a gentle voice.

"I get frustrated seeing you, Uchida. I can tell you've got stuff going on... And I know I have no right to say this, as an almost perfect stranger, but..."

Then he suddenly paused, before saying...

"—Your life *is* yours, isn't it?"

Then he grinned, a rakish, slightly embarrassed grin.

Badump.
My heart thumped.
Badump, badump, badump.
There you go again, acting all bigheaded. I suppose I have to say thank you properly this time. Wow, I really do hate you. Maybe we should both go to the nurse's room. Could you do me a big favor and never speak to me again after this?
The pounding of my heart was so loud that those other thoughts got drowned out.
Badump, badump, badump.
The shock of falling was nothing compared to this.
Maybe it was frustration over being indebted to a guy like this.

Maybe it was embarrassment, being caught and held by a guy I don't like.

Thump. Thump. Thump.

But this pounding was nothing like I felt back in the classroom.

…It was sweet. Almost soft…

As I stood there frozen, Chitose deftly gathered up the spilled printouts.

Wait. Hold on.

I haven't caught up yet, emotionally or verbally.

Chitose picked up my glasses and handed them to me after first arranging the stack of papers.

"Here you go, then."

Yes. Here you go. We're done here.

Just like that? After you had your hands all over me?

Chitose lightly waved his hand, jogging up the stairs holding the stack of papers.

He didn't even look back.

Like he forgot I existed.

My gaze fell to my hand. Oh.

The lenses of my glasses were cracked.

I clutched them, and…

"Um, Chitose!"

I called your name.

I don't know why I did that.

My mind was blank, and I didn't even know what to say.

But strangely…

Thump thump thump thump thump

Thump.

*　　*　　*

If I don't do this now, then I feel like, many years from now, I'm going to regret this day so much that I'll want to cry.

Chitose looked down at me, puzzled.

Oh, help. I have to say something.

Um. Er… The thing is…

"—My glasses!"

Before I knew what I was even saying, the most asinine thing I'd ever said came out of my mouth. It was…

"I mean, Chitose, what do you think about me without glasses?"

It was like my lips were moving on their own. I couldn't stop them.

The moment the words left my mouth, I was so embarrassed, I wished I could just vanish into a puff of smoke.

What was I saying?!

Now he was going to think I was some kind of freak.

This, after I'd been so standoffish with him? After acting like I didn't care what anyone thinks of me?

Even though I hadn't been conscious of how I look in others' eyes for many, many years…

…Why was I saying this now?

After blinking at me, Chitose grinned mischievously.

"It works for you, Yua."

On the way home, I stopped and had my glasses repaired, and I also ordered some contacts.

The next day, Hiiragi kept squealing about how cute I apparently was, right from first period.

Meanwhile, Chitose said, "How about now you do something about those frown lines?"

I really do hate him.

...It's just that I was nervous right then. That's all.

*

The first half of August.

Surprisingly, I had a somewhat unsatisfactory summer vacation.

This was completely self-inflicted and actually something I'd hoped for a little bit. But I guess, over time, I got slightly used to having Chitose tease me and chat with me all the time, while I'd fire back with some frosty response.

I'd started to call him Chitose without worrying about it, and he would sometimes call me Yua in this jokey kind of way.

Maybe the wall I'd put up around me had cracked a little, the same as my glasses.

Strangely, the feelings of anger, irritability, and frustration had started to fade away. In their place, I was now experiencing annoyance, exasperation, and impatience.

What's the difference? Hell if I know.

Little by little, Hiiragi taught me how to do makeup and take care of my skin.

I was too embarrassed to put it into practice right away, but I was thinking it'd be nice to give it a try during this summer vacation.

I seemed to have accepted the new changes in my school life. I was actually counting the days until August 31. Maybe I really was excited for the new semester.

There was just one little glass shard, stuck in my heart.

Before summer vacation, Chitose's smile had faded away. The genuine one, to be precise.

To preserve my normal life without rocking the boat, I often keep a close eye on other people's facial expressions. So I immediately notice subtle changes in the people I talk to almost every day.

He'd completely stopped teasing me, too.

I'd been acting like I hated it all this time, but when it stopped, I felt a surge of anxiety.

Did I say something offensive? Did I accidentally cross a line?

But thinking rationally, I hadn't really changed anything about how I reacted. And it was obvious that Chitose didn't care at all about me or how I reacted or whatever.

But somehow, I almost missed it.

"Uchida."

I realized someone had just tapped me on the shoulder.

I was in the music room, on the fourth floor of Fuji High. I'd been spacing out, right in the middle of club.

"Sorry, I drifted off there."

My band partner giggled. "That's unusual for you. We're all talking about going to the convenience store for lunch—what about you?"

"Oh, thanks. I brought a bento lunch, so I'm good."

"Okay. Well, we'll be back in a bit."

I watched them leave, until it was just me.

—*Clink.*

Suddenly, a high-pitched metallic sound reverberated through the quiet music room.

Finding myself drawn to the window, I opened it.

The steamy summer air rushed in.

I could hear boys' voices yelling "Come on!" and "Over here!" loud enough to drown out the din of the cicadas chirping away.

I pulled up a chair and sat down, putting my arms on the windowsill and resting my chin on it.

Apparently, baseball club was having a practice game.

I wondered if Chitose was out there, too.

We'd lost the summer tournament, apparently, but I'd heard he was a great player.

Even though he was just a first-year, he was already playing an active role as the main driving force of the team.

Come to think of it, I'm always up here when Chitose practices on the field, but I've never really watched.

For some reason, I couldn't see a guy like him playing baseball.

What would I do if he looked up and spotted me?

Heh. That's a stupid thing to worry about. My eyes followed the players running around below.

Everyone was wearing hats and helmets, but it was still possible to tell who was Chitose and who wasn't.

My contacts had felt weird at first, but I was used to them now.

After about five minutes of scrutinizing every player on the field, I realized...

Chitose's not here...?

I'd looked carefully. I couldn't possibly have missed him.

Maybe he was off, with an illness or injury.

I hope he's all right, I thought, and just then...

—*Clack.*

The ball hit by the opposing team rolled outside the white line drawn on the left side.

Wow, baseballs are so fast!

"Foul!"

Someone yelled as the ball went behind the batter.
It hit the high net that separates the tennis and handball courts from the sports ground and came to a stop.
A member of the baseball team who was just running there picked it up, and…

"Hirano!"

Even from an amateur's point of view, the guy threw a great ball back.
I knew that voice…
"Oh…!"
I knew right away that it was Chitose.
I hadn't spotted him because I was just watching people on the field and around the benches, but he was there all along.
And he wasn't wearing the same uniform as the others. Just worn-out practice clothes.
Why…?
The game resumed as if nothing had happened.
After watching for a second, Chitose started running laps. He was at the edge, just silently going back and forth.
He didn't look injured or anything to me.
Beneath the deep-blue sky and the heavy thunderheads in the distance…he just kept running back and forth. Like he was afraid that if he stopped, even for a moment, something would catch up with him.
No one was watching him back there. Why not cut corners? Nobody would even care, probably.
Why was this happening?

The only thing I knew for sure was that this was not a good thing for Chitose.

Maybe this was some kind of penalty for making a mistake. Or maybe he was injured, but in a way that running wouldn't hurt?

Being unable to participate in the game and running around the corner of the field... It must be frustrating, embarrassing, awful for a dedicated member of the baseball team.

But Chitose—the guy who was always trying to act so cool—was struggling away by himself, not even caring who was watching.

For whatever reason...he was just pounding away, never looking down, totally focused on his task.

—Somehow, the sight of it made me wince. My heart ached.

Had I ever faced up against myself like that?

Have I ever fought head-on, without looking away?

Unable to bear it any longer, I suddenly stood up from my chair and clenched my fists.

I took a deep breath.

Go for it. Go for it. Go for it...

"Go for it, Chitose!!!"

I yelled at the top of my lungs, with all my air, like I was blowing on my sax.

Shoulders heaving, I suddenly felt a wave of embarrassment wash over me, and I quickly crouched down.

Maybe it was the hot summer breeze that flowed into the air-conditioned room.

For whatever reason, my chest was suddenly burning hot.

*

Somewhere in my heart, I was waiting impatiently for the second semester.

Chitose had taken to staring blankly out of the window every day, and even when he was around Hiiragi and the others, he didn't look very happy.

He was like a different person. Almost mute, and that mischievous smile of his had gone.

I'd heard from Hiiragi that he'd quit the baseball club. Even she seemed at a loss as to how to handle Chitose, so she ended up chatting with me more and more.

It can't be! I wanted to yell.

Even after that practice game, when I spied him through the music room's window, I kept seeing Chitose at practice. Always working hard, and always alone.

If he was still at it, they must be putting him through the wringer. But he was gritting his teeth and refusing to crack.

Just how bad was it?

I desperately wanted to hear it straight from him.

Maybe there was something I could do to help.

…Who do I think I am anyway?

If Chitose can't even confide in Hiiragi, why would he tell me? How could I help where Hiiragi can't?

Anyway…

Ever since that day when he rescued me on the stairs, I felt like the distance between us had shrunk a little. But in reality, I was just one of his many classmates.

All that was different was how we referred to each other. There was no logical reason for me to feel like he and I were more familiar now.

I hadn't even spoken to him once during the long summer vacation. I mean, I didn't even have his contact info.

All this…is just a waste of my mental energy.

*   *   *

What on earth am I thinking anyway?

Wasn't this where I wanted to be?
I was keeping to myself. No one was intruding on me.
I was just drifting on the breeze, day by day.
This has to be good, right?
No matter how much I tried to convince myself, I couldn't keep lying. I wasn't okay with staying this far removed from everything.

—Several weeks went by.
In the end, Chitose gradually got his energy back, and I still didn't know what had happened.
I had more opportunities to talk to him like before, and I got to hear his silly jokes again.
One day, on the way home...
I saw him talking to a short-haired girl by the riverbed.
Even though I could only see her from the side, I could tell she was very beautiful.
Chitose's face was relaxed in a way I hadn't seen before. Like he was drawing strength and comfort from this girl.
What if I was the one beside him like that? I thought, and then I laughed at myself over how ridiculous that concept was.

*

Then, one day after school at the end of September...
All club activities were canceled for some academic reason or other.
After finishing classes and homeroom, I was about to go home early.
"Ucchi, wait a minute!" Hiiragi stopped me.

"What's up?"

I was used to her suddenly calling out to me, but she didn't often stop me like this on my way home.

"You don't have club today, either, right, Ucchi?"

"Uh, right, but why…?"

Hiiragi's face brightened, and she grabbed my hand. "I was just chatting with Saku and the others, and we're planning to hit up Hachiban Ramen on the way home. Why don't you come, too, Ucchi?"

"Er, but…"

Hiiragi had suggested hanging out a few times before.

And even over summer vacation, she sent me a few messages on LINE.

It was always awkward, so I tried to be evasive. I was sure she was just trying to be nice.

This was the first time I'd received such a specific invitation.

To be honest, I no longer even wanted to be as stubborn as I was when I first entered high school.

I'd still have plenty of time to cook for my family after I got back home. And yes, I was interested in hanging out after school like a real high schooler at least once.

But I'd barely ever spoken to Mizushino or Asano.

And what about *him*? What would he think of me tagging along?

While I was hesitating, filled with various worries…

"You should come." Chitose, watching from a distance, called out to me point-blank. "It's just ramen. What are you worried about?"

His blunt words gave me the push I needed.

"All right, then I suppose I could tag along, if nobody minds…?"

"Of course we don't mind!" Hiiragi jumped up and down.

Giggling a little, I actually did a little hop myself.

*   *   *

When I passed through the door of Hachiban Ramen, I was hit with a nostalgic aroma.

When I was little, my whole family used to come here on weekends.

How many years has it been? I wondered, smiling a little.

Going there alone would feel weird, and eventually my family stopped suggesting eating at Hachiban's. So I hadn't been there in a while.

We took our seats at the table and ordered.

I wasn't sure what to get at first, but I decided to opt for veggie ramen with miso butter topping.

Way back when, Mom always ordered this. She never got sick of it.

At first, I tried to copy her and order the same thing, but eventually I became more of a salt ramen person. Today, though, I wanted to eat the ramen from my childhood.

While we were waiting for the ramen to arrive…

"You know, Ucchi!" Asano, who was sitting across from me, leaned in.

"Y-yes?"

His enthusiasm made me shy.

"Ah, sorry. Yuuko always calls you Ucchi. Is it okay if I call you that?"

Asano scratched his head calmly, and I relaxed a little. "Yes, it's fine."

"Oh, cool. So hey, Ucchi. Why is it that Saku's the only one you're all buddy-buddy with?"

"Huh? We're not buddy-buddy," I immediately replied.

Mizushino spluttered with laughter from his adjacent seat. "Sorry, Kaito's an idiot. Can I call you Ucchi, too?"

I nodded. "Yeah, that's perfectly fine, but…"

"Anyway, you talk to Yuuko and Saku a lot in class, Ucchi. Kaito gets why you chat with Yuuko, but he's always whining about how Saku is the only one of us guys you seem to want to talk to."

Asano piped up before I could respond. "Well, can you blame me? A graceful, beautiful girl ranked number one in her grade in the entrance exam. She's always smiling, but she doesn't have any specific friends. She's a total enigma!"

"Er… Who are you talking about?"

"Well, duh! You, Ucchi!"

"Huh?!" I yelped in surprise.

Beautiful girl?

Enigma?

Where? Who?

I'm just the glasses-wearing plain Jane, you know?

"Aw, come on." Mizushino grinned, hand on his chin. "Kaito only started saying stuff like that after you got contacts, Ucchi."

"Hey! You jerk! Don't go telling her that!"

What were these people talking about? Did they have no shame?

Mizushino, Asano, Hiiragi, and—yeah, Chitose, too.

All so different, but they're the clique of hot guys and girls that everyone in school envies.

And those people were saying this stuff about someone like me.

If it wasn't for Hiiragi's genuine smile as she watched us, I would have mistaken it for a new and inventive type of bullying.

I mean, I was still a little skeptical.

It's a mean thing to think about Hiiragi and Chitose, who always chatted to me in such a friendly way, but part of me wondered if the whole thing wasn't just a big joke to them.

Ignoring my frozen reaction, Hiiragi piped up from her seat beside me.

"Kaito, you have no eye for cute girls. *I* saw how adorable Ucchi is right from the entrance ceremony!"

"H-Hiiragi?!"

"You know, Yuuko," Mizushino said. "Why did you want to get to know Ucchi?"

Want to get to know me?

The things they were saying so casually embarrassed the heck out of me.

It's not like that anyway.

Hiiragi gets along with everyone. She doesn't discriminate. I'm just another classmate to her.

So hearing this kind of thing is really annoying.

Actually, I'm starting to get really uncomfortable here!

But Hiiragi continued like it was no big deal.

"Well, at first I just went to apologize, but gradually I realized that talking to Ucchi had a soothing effect on me. And I wondered why."

That's...how she felt?

Hiiragi looked at me and smiled. "Then I realized! For whatever reason, she always carefully weighs up each situation and environment. She never says anything that would hurt someone's feelings, make them sad, or cause them to be depressed. That's why I'm so comfortable around her, I think."

You're wrong, I muttered to myself, although I couldn't vocalize it. *It's nothing nearly that laudable. I'm just keeping my head low to preserve the normal, quiet life that I want. It's not some big noble thing.*

Hiiragi continued. "Oh, but not with Saku, though. It's weird."

"Really?!" Asano yelped. "You know, I had the impression Saku's sweet talk had her under his spell."

"Absolutely not." I was quick to deny this.

Mizushino looked at Chitose and grinned. "Uh-oh. It sounds like she doesn't like you at all."

I heard a haughty sniff.

"I'm the only one she's mean to, huh… I understand. There's a thin line between love and hate, right, Yua?" Chitose grinned, and I retorted right away.

"Uh, no."

"Really? Not even just a little bit?"

"Yeah, really. Not in the slightest."

"…Aw, man."

Everyone cracked up.

"Aw, Saku struck out," said Asano.

Mizushino was next. "That's our Saku."

Hiiragi grabbed my arm and clung on. "Hey, Ucchi is *my* friend here, you know?!"

Chitose shrugged, still grinning. And I grinned back.

⋆

How long had it been since I'd chatted with classmates for hours like this?

Both Asano and Mizushino were lively and funny, and they were both really nice to me, even though we'd never really interacted before.

Of course, Hiiragi and Chitose seemed much more relaxed than I'd ever seen them, and I was a little envious of this group's carefree relationships.

What if I could spend every day with everyone like this? Maybe that's getting ahead of myself.

The sun went down outside the window before I even realized it.

I seemed to come out of some sort of trance.

Hmm? What time is it?

I checked my phone for the first time since walking into Hachiban's. It was already almost eight PM.

Oh no, I thought, my heart sinking.

Even on a normal day, this would be the time I needed to go home and cook dinner after club.

I wasn't expecting to be this late, so I hadn't even texted home.

When I checked my notifications, I found more than ten unread LINE messages and six missed calls.

The only people from school who had my LINE info were the girls from the music club and Hiiragi. So all these messages were probably from home.

I thought it was overkill, a little. But although I'd mentioned that there wasn't any club practice today, this was my first time being this late without checking in since I'd started having a phone. So I'd caused an undue amount of concern.

I knew it. I really had been getting ahead of myself.

I'll make my excuses to the others and leave the ramen restaurant first, then I can call as soon as I make it outside.

Well, that was my plan, but…

—*Brr. Brr. Brr.*

The phone in my hand vibrated.

The name on the display was my younger brother's, who was right in the middle of studying for the entrance exams.

I guess he planned to tell me something like, "I'm hungry. Hurry up."

He's a growing boy, and lately he's like a bottomless pit.

"Ucchi, you should answer that."

Beside me, Hiiragi seemed to have noticed my phone.

"I'm sorry. It's my brother. I'll just call him back…"

Then I answered the call.

"Hello? Sorry I'm late. Yes, I'm coming now."

"Sis. Just stay calm and listen, okay?"

*   *   *

The voice in my ear was strained, desperate.

"They took Dad to the hospital."

He was speaking slowly, deliberately.

Clatter.

My phone slipped from my hand, hit the table, and bounced onto the floor.
"Huh...?"
My mind was blank.
With my empty hand near my ear...
"Why?"
I mumbled to no one.

"...?"
"..."
"...!"
"..."

Hiiragi, Asano, Mizushino, and Chitose were all talking to me with some alarm.
But I couldn't understand what anyone was saying.
Dad's in the hospital?
But he was fine yesterday.
Even this morning, he told me to have a nice day.
No. No, this can't be happening.
I jumped to my feet, and before I knew it, I was running toward the exit.
I bumped into the waiter who was carrying the ramen, and bowls clattered together with a sharp sound.
I'm sorry, I'm sorry, I'm sorry.

                        *   *   *

"Uchida!"
"Ucchi?!"

Chitose and Hiiragi were calling my name.
I didn't have a second to stop and explain.
I jumped up and ran off without knowing what I was doing.
I have to run, run, run...
I don't know where to go or what to do.
But even so...
I felt like if I stayed still, Dad would disappear, and I would never see him again. So even though this made no sense, I knew I had to keep moving. Keep moving and try not to throw up.
BEEEEEEEEP
A car horn blared.
I'm sorry, I'm sorry, I'm sorry.

Where's my phone?
Gone.
Where's my bag?
Gone.
Where am I?
I don't know, I don't know, I don't know.

No. I have to calm down.
Go back to the restaurant, apologize to everyone, ask my brother where the hospital is, and then...
  ...
I couldn't force myself to calm down. Bad thoughts swirled like a dirty river, filling my mind with thick mud.
These are the times when I have to be strongest.
It's okay.

It's okay, it's okay, it's okay.
It's okay, it's okay, it's okay, it's okay, it's okay.
Help me, someone help me.
Mom…

"Uchida!"

Just then, someone grabbed my arm from behind.
Why? Why are you talking to me when I'm freaking out?
I knew whose voice it was immediately.
Why? When I'd done everything in my power to avoid him?
Why, then, did I still want to fall into his arms and have him take care of everything?

"…Chitose…"

The one who was chasing me was the boy I should have hated.
"Wow, you music club girls sure do run fast. Your skirt was flapping so much I almost saw your panties."
Idiot! Even at a time like this…you're such an idiot!
"Why'd you suddenly run off to the riverbed? Can you just try to calm down?"
But I couldn't hold myself back anymore.

"What do I do?! It's all my fault!!!"

I clung to Chitose's chest, clutching his shirt tightly in both hands.

"It's because I didn't come home at the usual time. I didn't keep my promise. I told myself I'd be normal and quiet so this wouldn't happen again. I wasn't going to cause any more worry to anyone. Dad's all I've got left, but now…"

                    *   *   *

"Yua!"

Chitose grabbed me and hugged me tight.
Just like he did on that day when I almost fell down the stairs.

"It's okay. Maybe it's not as bad as you're imagining."

I could hear his heart pounding, pounding in his strong, warm chest.
"It's okay. It's all right." Chitose kept repeating, over and over.
Those words made me think of Mom again.
"But they took him to the hospital…"
Chitose patted my back reassuringly as he spoke. "The call was still live, so I asked your brother what happened. Basically, it sounds like just a simple wrist sprain."
"…Sprain?"
"He was working overtime and ended up leaving later than usual, so he was hurrying down the stairs at his office and slipped. A colleague called an ambulance just in case, since it sounds like it was a pretty dramatic fall, but apparently he's fine besides the sprain. I guess clumsiness runs in your family, huh?"
"You pig!" I lifted my chin.
Right in front of me, Chitose was smiling softly. "Have you calmed down now?"
His eyes, so magnetic, suddenly colored with embarrassment over how close our faces were.
Chitose loosened his arms and took two brisk steps back.
"Your brother said to tell you sorry. He knows you worry, so he was trying to explain things to you slowly and calmly, but instead he ended up making it sound much more dire than it actually was."

Recalling the conversation we just had, I went limp.

"Yes. He did say to stay calm and listen."

Chitose continued. "Your brother was at the hospital—sounds like he ran over there himself. So I was able to talk to your dad on the phone. He told me to tell you, 'Don't worry about anything. Just have fun with your friends.' Oh, and he asked me to take care of his daughter, too."

When I calmed down a little, I was flooded with embarrassment for my distraught reaction, and I felt horribly guilty for running out on everyone so rudely.

"Um, I, uh—I'm really sorry. Oh, at the restaurant…"

I suddenly remembered how I'd knocked over those bowls on my dash to the door.

"Yuuko said, '*Leave this to us, and you go after Ucchi.*' She said she'd call later."

"Oh gosh… I'm such a mess!"

"Hey, listen, Yua…" Chitose paused.

I'd figured him using my first name earlier was just to get my attention while I was having a full-on panic, but the fact that he was still using it now made me feel a little squirmy inside.

"If you don't mind, can we talk a little?"

"Um, but…"

"I can't just walk off and leave you here now that I've found you. Also…I don't think you should be alone right now."

"…All right, then."

"I'll buy you a cold drink from the vending machine. What would you like?"

"I'll pay."

Chitose snorted with laughter. "You don't have your wallet, do you?"

"Oh…"

Right.

I left everything behind when I split.

Great. I was totally pathetic; I couldn't do anything right.

Chitose glanced at his phone. "Yuuko's got your bag and stuff. Let's go get it from her later. I did manage to grab this on my way out, though."

He handed me my phone.

"Do you want to call your family?"

"No, it's all right. Thanks."

When I took it from him, I found that the screen was cracked.

I frowned and let out a sigh. "When I'm around you, Chitose, something always breaks."

"Just so you know, the glasses weren't my fault, either, you know?"

Chitose gave me a goofy grin, then dashed off along the embankment.

"I wasn't talking about the glasses," I muttered, staring at his back.

*

As I sat down on the riverbed and listened to the sound of the water, Chitose came back.

"I tried to pick something a girl might like," he said, offering a choice of two drinks. I took the *houjicha* latte.

"Thank you."

"Don't worry about it," Chitose said, sitting next to me and prying the pull tab on his café latte.

After taking a sip…

"What did you mean, 'It's your fault'?" he muttered.

"Huh…?"

"Not sure if you meant to say it, but that's what you said."

Honestly, I could only sort of half remember saying that.

A half remembrance was enough, though.

As I sat there wondering how to answer, Chitose continued.

"Ah, if you don't want to talk about it, then don't worry about it. Let's talk about something else. Which restaurant has your favorite sauce for katsudon? Do you prefer grated soba noodles with lots of toppings or dipping sauce? Or we could talk about the season? Flowers, cats, constellations..."

He kept talking, almost as if he was poking fun at me and trying to comfort me at the same time.

"You don't have to talk to me about it anyway. You could talk to Yuuko, or your mom, or someone else. I recently learned that just talking to someone can really kind of save your soul. So I thought it could help you out, too, Yua."

Suddenly, I thought of that beautiful girl with the short hair.

Was he trying to be there for me, in the same way she'd been there for him?

All right. But just this once.

Maybe I can show someone what's inside my heart...just a little bit.

"Would you mind..." My voice was weak and faint. "...if I talked about my mom?"

Chitose's eyes widened a little, and then he nodded at me to go ahead.

*

—Mom was a kind person.

I don't remember her ever yelling. She just smiled all the time.

When I was little, she often played the piano or the flute for me instead of lullabies.

The music was like a whisper, like a hug.

I was more of a mama's girl, and I loved to listen to her play. I'd fight to stay awake, not wanting to miss a note. But I always ended up dreaming before I knew it.

I can still recall how excited I was when Mom said, "Would you like to learn to play, too, Yua?"

When I went to elementary school, I started going to music classes on Mom's recommendation.

When you start practicing the piano and the flute in earnest, it's not all fun.

The set pieces for the recital were difficult, and when the teacher scolded me for not being able to play them well, there were times when I wanted to just give it all up.

Kids who started learning later than me kept passing me, and I often cried and sulked and threatened to quit.

But whenever that happened, Mom would always say…

"It's okay."

She'd stroke my hair softly and hug me tight.

"You don't have to compare yourself to others or compete with them. It's enough for me if you just enjoy music normally. Love it for its own sake."

Normal. Mom was always using that word.

Even when my test scores sucked.

"It's okay. If you just do your best and get a normal score, it's fine."

Even when I fought with my friends.

"It's okay. You can just make up. That's normal."

Even when I was asked about my dreams for my future at school and couldn't answer.

"It's okay. Just living a normal life is all you need to be happy."

*   *   *

When I entered elementary school and then in junior high school, too, I began to realize that there was nothing about me that made me stand out.

Many kids were better at sports, studying, and music than I was.

But each time, Mom repeated, "It's okay, it's okay," like a soothing mantra.

Mom always told me it was okay to be normal.

That that was where happiness truly lay.

Her piano and flute playing were beautiful—but honestly, in many respects, Mom really was just a completely normal, average mother.

She was a stay-at-home mom, waking up early in the morning to make a packed lunch for Dad. She did cleaning and laundry in the morning, then shopping in the afternoon.

Every night, she would prepare all kinds of meals.

I loved watching my mom cook, and I would always grab on to her leg and ask what she was making or what she was using.

When she had time, I asked her to teach me certain dishes while I did my best to help out.

When I first got a child's kitchen knife, I was so happy to cut cabbage and cucumbers.

So that was who Mom was. But one day, Dad told me a secret.

"Your mom used to be somebody amazing, you know."

"Amazing how?"

"I don't know all the details, but when she was at the university in Kansai, she won a prize in a big piano competition."

"Really? But then why didn't she go pro?"

"…Well, that was my fault. She could have lived in a more glamorous world, but she followed me when I went back to Fukui to find a job. She always said she'd be happiest just building a warm, loving family. I tried to convince her to consider becoming a music teacher at least, but she said that if you only hold on to your dreams halfway, you'll always be left with regrets."

"I see... Then I guess she must be the happiest ever right now!"

"Hee-hee, well, I certainly hope so."

In this way, our family lived a peaceful life.

We'd wake up in the morning and go to school or work, while Mom did the housework, and at night we'd all relax together.

On weekdays, we'd go through the same routine, and on weekends, the four of us would often go to Lpa or Hachiban's together. Sometimes we'd go to the cinema together and sing karaoke. When it was someone's birthday, we'd go to revolving sushi at Kaisen Atom. That was always a big treat in my eyes.

A slight change came when my younger brother entered elementary school.

Mom had more free time, and when I came home from school, I'd often find her playing the piano by herself.

Not the gentle songs of my childhood lullabies. She'd be pounding the keys—the sound was like screaming or crying.

When I started taking lessons myself, I finally came to understand how amazing Mom was.

Probably much better than a classroom music teacher.

Whenever Mom noticed me, she'd laugh like I'd caught her doing something silly and stop playing. So I took to listening secretly, outside the door.

She would just play without stopping until it got dark and it was time to start getting dinner ready.

One night, while I was listening to Mom playing the piano, I asked a question.

"Mom, won't you ever do a recital or anything?"

Mom looked surprised for a second.

"Hee-hee. Well, I'm playing in front of a little audience of one right now, aren't I?" Mom answered softly.

"Not like this. Like in a real concert hall or something."

"I'm happy just playing normally at home like this."

"My music teacher said she has some adult students. We could do recitals together!"

When I said that…

—*Ding!*

Mom's nimble fingers made a rare mistake.

That sharp tone was like an angry shout, and I recoiled in shock.

Did I say something wrong?

I thought it would be fun to play a duet together in a large hall; that's all…

"Whoops, I messed up."

As I sat there, thoughts whirling, Mom stuck out her tongue and looked at me.

"Maybe I should have your teacher teach me, too."

Her smile seemed fake. I wished I hadn't said anything.

Then one day, when I was in the fourth year of elementary school…

After school, a classmate actually invited me over, and we played together until it was late.

When it got dark, and I finally realized it was past curfew, I rushed home and found my father sitting alone at the table in the living room. He was despondent.

There were empty beer cans all over the table, along with a piece of paper that looked like an official form, in green ink.

"Sorry I'm late. Where's Mom?"

Dad stared at me emptily. "She left."

"Like shopping?"

I looked around the living room and saw my younger brother holding his knees on the sofa, crying and sniffling.

A terrible feeling washed over me.

It was like my entire world had been overwritten. I was standing in an entirely different today from what yesterday had been.

Dad shook his head slightly and said, "She's far away. She won't be coming back." His voice was unsteady.

Huh?

What did he say...?

I threw down my school bag, ran over to Dad, and shook his limp shoulders.

"Hey! Dad?!"

Choking back tears, I started to yell.

If I started crying, it would be like acknowledging that any of this was happening.

"What do you mean? She's on a trip? She's at Grandma's house?"

Gently, Dad took my hand and shook his head again. "No, Yua. We've decided to part ways. From now on, it's just the three of us."

"I don't believe you!" I snatched my hand away and banged on the table. "Mom would never leave us! She always said she was happy! She said she was glad she met you and that we were born. She said she'd teach me piano and flute until I grew even better at it than her. She said when I grew up, we'd wear fancy dresses and do recitals together. So what you're saying...doesn't make any sense!"

Finally, a tear fell from Dad's eye.

"Maybe she got sick of a normal life."

—Ding!

*   *   *

I heard it again. Mom's wrong note on the piano.

It's not true, it's not true, it's not true!
Mom always said the same thing, like a mantra.
Normal is fine; normal is best.
What's wrong with normal? Eating meals with the family every day and watching TV together—isn't that enough?
Just yesterday, Mom went with me to practice. She said I played well.
We took a bath together and slept on the same futon.
This was horrible.
She didn't even say anything!
I didn't get a chance to process it!
Was I never going to see Mom again?
Did she get sick of us?
Was she angry because I broke curfew?
If I did something wrong, I'll fix it.
I'll do my best even if I'm not good at studying; I'll never break a promise again…
So please… Please…

Drip.

Finally, the tears fell from my eyes.

"No!!!!!!"

My brother leaped up and hugged me. "Sis… Sis…"
Dad leaned across the table and held on to us, and the three of us sat huddled there together.

*

It was the first time I'd said this to anyone outside of my family.

Even within my family, we haven't properly discussed it since then.

Dad doesn't usually talk much, so he didn't tell us what was said when they broke up. He didn't explain why he hadn't tried to talk her out of it. He didn't even tell us whether he'd filed the divorce papers.

Maybe he thought it was too heavy for his nine-year-old daughter and seven-year-old son, or maybe he just didn't want to put it into words.

Chitose sat next to me and just listened in silence.

All of a sudden, I recalled that time in my life.

As soon as my elementary school friends learned on the country grapevine that my mom was gone, they avoided me like the plague.

I guess I don't blame them.

It's natural for a young child to have trouble reacting to the fact that a classmate's mother is gone. Especially when she left just because she wanted to.

What was I doing, telling Chitose?

Sure I was upset, but that's not the only reason.

I'm not sure I would have said this to anyone else.

Maybe I figured he'd laugh it off with another of his crude jokes.

Maybe his second hug had me seeking further affection. Pathetic.

Once I finished telling my story, I was still puzzling over my choices when…

"So that's why you reacted like that?" Chitose said softly.

I knew he was referring to my panicked reaction from before.

I nodded and cleared my throat. "It may sound dumb, but I had a flashback to that day. I got all excited, being invited out with friends for once, and I lost track of time… And while I was distracted…"

"Yeah. I get it," Chitose said. "What happened after your mom was gone, Yua?"

"What do you mean…?"

"What did you feel? What were you thinking? How did it change you? Of course, you don't have to tell me. But if you want to talk, I'll stay until you're done."

…Honestly, I didn't mean to even tell him this much.

Talking won't solve anything. And it's far too personal.

But Chitose…

He didn't seem deeply sympathetic, overly concerned, or unsure how to respond.

At least on the surface, he was the same as ever, just continuing the conversation normally.

Well, I thought.

Now that we've discussed all this, we can't go back to the casual relationship we had when we were eating ramen.

I wish I could have spent a little more time like that. But if he was willing, then I should tell him the whole story.

My mind made up, I cleared my throat again.

"…At first, I remember feeling sad. Like maybe it was my fault, and raising us was too much of a burden. If I'd been a better kid, if I'd been better at piano and flute, maybe she would have taken me with her."

Chitose remained silent, looking off into the distance.

"Once that finally subsided, the next thing I felt was uncontrollable anger. I mean, who could blame me? Mom *was* selfish. She didn't explain anything to me or my brother. She didn't even say good-bye. Even thinking about it now that I'm older…I think what she did was completely unforgivable."

As I spoke, the feelings I had back then came rushing back.

"She told Dad she'd be happy just to get married and build a warm family. She gave birth to my brother and me. And then she just… I don't know how Mom felt when she left. Maybe she really did want to pursue music again. Maybe she found someone better than Dad. But even if she did…!"

I gritted my teeth.

"It's like saying that all the good times were a lie. You know what Mom always said? She said, 'It's fine to be normal.' Was she just trying to convince herself of that? 'It's fine to be average. It's okay.' Was there a part of her that was whispering that it was a lie the whole time?"

Drip, drip. Tears rolled down my cheeks.

"If that's the case, then what about me? I lived my life by those words. Was I just being jerked around by my mother's selfish excuses? 'It's okay, you don't have to be special. You can be happy even if you live a normal life. It's fine to be the way you are.' It's like…"

My tone was harsh, and I gave a pathetic laugh.

"It's like, how am I supposed to handle my father now, after my mother basically told him, 'Life with you is average and boring'?"

* * *

Hesitatingly, I continued.

"Ever since then, my father's been an empty shell. He's never once blamed Mom. He's just quietly raised my brother and me."

So... So...

"—So I made a promise that I'd be normal, like she taught me to be! I'd be the very 'normal' she herself turned her back on. I'd stick with my father and brother and bring back our happy family life. I would take Mom's place. And that's what I decided."

I had kept these feelings in my heart for a long time, but once they overflowed, I couldn't stop them.

"I did my best, Chitose. Even as a nine-year-old child, I thought hard about what I should do to keep Dad and my brother from ever feeling sad again. I wanted them not to have to worry. I began to study seriously, so there wouldn't be any concerns about how I was turning out. I maintained moderate relationships with my classmates so they wouldn't worry about me quarreling with others or getting bullied. I didn't want any uncomfortable entanglements, so I kept away from the kind of kids who followed the latest fashions and trends. If I screwed up, I knew the school would call Dad. I kept smiling, even when I was upset, or in pain, or when I had to deal with someone I didn't like. I kept the peace…so I wouldn't cause any trouble to anyone.

"—I did everything I could to live a normal life!!!"

                    *   *   *

Gack, ack. I coughed—I basically never shouted like that.

"Ugh… Guh…"

I gazed at the sky, as if I could find more air that way, but I couldn't see the moon at all.

"…But I want to be like you guys, too. I want to make close friends, have fun every day, joke around, fight sometimes, make up again. I want to get all excited when a good friend of mine has a crush on a guy. And maybe confide in them, if I ever get a crush on someone myself."

I first started having those feelings when I encountered the boy I was speaking with now.
I don't want this kind of life.
I'm just trapped in the past.
What I really want is to be like you. To live life openly.
I wanted to know what it felt like to laugh so hard I couldn't breathe.

"Before I knew it, I was looking forward to chances to talk with you and Hiiragi. When you invited me out for ramen, my heart was racing, but I was so happy. I wanted it to continue…"

I clenched my tear-spattered fists.

"But I can't! I have to prove that I can be happy even if I'm normal. I don't want to do a single thing to hurt my father or my brother. I don't want to be like my mother who abandoned us!!"

My chest heaved.

*   *   *

"And more than that…if I ever get close to someone…if someone ever becomes important to me…then maybe one day, I'll lose everything again. I've been so afraid to be hurt like that again. I don't want to get used to holding someone's hand and have to let go. It scares me… It scares me so bad."

As I spoke, I kept desperately wiping away tears that wouldn't stop flowing.

"…So please, don't get involved with me anymore."

Because…you shine too bright.
The closer I get, the more my contradictions become apparent.
Because you try to see what's on the inside.
Because I could see myself relying on you too much.

"Thank you for listening to all that."

That, in itself, was more than enough.
Under a strange set of circumstances, I'd been able to reveal a secret I'd been holding on to all alone for years, even from my family.
For the first time since Mom left, I was able to cry in front of someone.
With this memory alone to sustain me, I think I can do my best again.
So thank you, thank you, thank you.
I'm grateful to you, the boy I thought I hated.

"…Yua… No, wait, maybe I should call you Uchida."

Chitose looked confused.

Yeah, that's fine, that's fine.
Starting tomorrow, I can just be Uchida to you again.
It's okay.

Chitose took a deep breath, and…

"What the hell?! What are you, stupid?!!!"

He really yelled it, too.

…Huh?

"Agh, man. I mean, what a load of crap."

Why…why was he mad at me right now?

"I knew you were living a boring life, but your reasoning is completely twisted! I mean, you're supposed to be smart, Uchida. But I only get about half of what you've been saying, here."

In my shock, my tears stopped flowing.

"I can understand not wanting to worry your family, or trying to live a normal life and be happy when you've been through something intense. Like, when you have a really painful experience in elementary school… I can see how a kid would come to that conclusion."

Chitose looked me straight in the eye as if almost glaring at me.

"But how long do you plan to be nine years old? You're Yua Uchida, aren't you?"

*   *   *

"Now, wait a second…!"

He's always been like this.
He's always getting the wrong idea.
Intruding on others' private feelings.
Talking like he has any idea.
Hitting me where it hurts, every time.
Yeah, now that I think about it again… I really, really…
HATE YOU!!!

"You have *no* right to say something like that to me!"

I bellowed at the top of my lungs.

"You don't know a damn thing about me! *You* grew up in a happy family with nothing to worry about. *You've* got friends all around you and all the good things in life. What, you want me to grow up into a rebellious teenager and fight my mom? How?! There's no one to fight! Even if I want to, I *can't*!"

Then…

"—Yes, you can, if you get creative."

Chitose smiled and grabbed my hand.

"Come with me."

He got up and started walking off.
Without knowing why, I let him tug me along.
Please, let me go.
I could have said that. I could have shaken him off.

He really does face things openly.

The strength in his eyes…

I wanted to hold on to the warmth that came from his hand in mine…just a little bit longer.

*

After I apologized and thanked the store staff at Hachiban Ramen and collected my bag and bicycle, Chitose brought me straight to a four-story apartment building.

It wasn't exactly a very nice building, but the babbling of the river nearby was pleasant to listen to.

"Here…?"

I called up to Chitose, who'd climbed the stairs to the top floor and stopped in front of a door.

"Yeah. It's my place," he replied.

"Oh, right, you live here… Wait, what?"

He spoke so naturally that I almost just nodded along, but how could this be Chitose's place?

"Wait a minute. I just cried a ton; I must look terrible. And I don't have a gift or anything for your parents."

Why did he bring me here anyway? What does this have to do with what we just discussed?

Chitose shrugged off my concerns and smiled. "It's okay. There's no one else here."

He was already unlocking the door as he spoke.

No one here? Maybe his family was all away? So it was just going to be the two of us?

And we would do…what, exactly?

Of course, I didn't expect that Chitose, who was always surrounded by beautiful girls like Hiiragi, would want to do anything to me anyway.

But it was getting late, and if his family wasn't home…

"Um, I think I…"

"Just come in, Yua. I want to show you something." Chitose opened the door and softly pushed me in the back.

When I stepped inside, the place was pitch-black and silent.

Coming in behind me, Chitose switched on the lights with a snap.

The soft light of an incandescent bulb illuminated the room.

We'd walked right into an open living room, and I could see some random furniture like a dining table, a sofa, and bookshelves.

There was a faint sense of incongruity. Something was missing.

Chitose quickly took off his sneakers and put on his slippers, then fumbled around inside the shoebox.

He pulled out a cheap-looking pair of slippers, probably from the hundred-yen store.

Not to be snooty, but they were a bit thin, and they were still connected with a little plastic thread.

Blowing any stray dust off them, he bit the plastic thread with his teeth, pulled the slippers apart, and placed them on the floor in front of me.

"Come on in."

There was no way I could back down at this point, so I timidly slipped out of my loafers and arranged them neatly with Chitose's sneakers, which he'd randomly kicked off.

Seeing the two pairs of shoes lined up tidily by the door was satisfying.

"Excuse me…"

I walked in, and…you couldn't exactly call the place tidy.

I always cook for my family, so I couldn't help but look at the kitchen.

There was a cup of instant ramen sitting out with broth left in it, but there were no plates, chopsticks, or other tableware to be found anywhere.

On the dining table were plastic bottles, half-drunk cups of coffee, and empty convenience store food containers.

The sofa was occupied by T-shirts and shorts heaped in a laundry pile, and it was impossible to tell if they were dirty or clean.

A baseball bat and a glove sat in a discreet corner.

"You know," Chitose said to me as I looked around, "maybe it's a little too soon for you to see inside this room…"

As he spoke, he opened the sliding door in the living room.

"Um… Excuse me…"

Somewhat nervously, I went and stood beside him to look.

It was a small room of about six tatami mats in size, adjacent to the living room.

And all that was in there was…a single bed.

"Huh…?"

I live in a stand-alone house.

I don't really know much about the floor plans of apartment buildings, but…

But this…

"It's a 1LDK. One bedroom, with a living/dining/kitchen room," Chitose explained.

For some reason, even though this was just his home, I got chills down my spine.

Thinking back on it, there were clues.

A strangely clean entryway, brand-new slippers waiting to be used, a cluttered room with only boy things in it, an unused sink that suggested no one ever cooked there.

Only one bed in the bedroom.

And above all…there was no atmosphere of cozy, mixed clutter, like in places where several people lived together.

No signs of Mom in the kitchen, none of Dad's bottles of whiskey or hobby tools, no scratch marks left by naughty younger brothers…

The room reflected only the occupancy of the boy named Chitose.

"Figured it out?"

Embarrassed, Chitose scratched his head.

"I don't have my parents, either. Neither of them. And it hurts."

I should have been prepared, but I couldn't help but gasp.

"…Uh… I…I mean…"

The things I'd said to Chitose came back to me in a rush.

"Ask your mother to teach you to cook."
"Oh, too cool to hang with your mother? Must be nice to be rebellious."
"You grew up in a happy family with nothing to worry about."

…What was wrong with me?

Why did I think I was the only one?

I was just stewing in my own thoughts. Anyone who laughed in such a carefree way must have grown up in a happy environment. People with sadness in their past would let it show on their faces.

I was too wrapped up in myself. I was just lashing out without any idea of what was really going on.

Chitose continued, as if it was all no big deal.

"My parents got divorced when I was in junior high. We actually all discussed it together, and the writing had been on the wall for some time. It was my choice to live alone, and I can call them whenever I feel like it."

*   *   *

He looked me in the eye.

"Still, I think we're in kinda similar situations. So I guess I have the right to intrude a little, huh?"

He smiled bashfully.

God. This guy is really...

"Pfft..."

"Uh, Yua?"

"...Ah-ha-ha-ha!"

Before I knew what I was doing, I was belly-laughing.

"Is that the right response to be having, really?"

Chitose sounded confused.

"I mean...that's such a forced comparison! You react totally different to trauma in elementary school than you do in junior high. And you knew it was coming... You weren't blindsided. It's so *weird* that you'd think we're in the same situation!"

"Well, all right, I'm sure it was tougher for you, Yua. But come on, it's kinda the same thing, right?"

No, it's not!
It's really, really not!
You may think I suffered more. But I'm not so sure.

They'd shared even more years and memories together—separating after that must have been even harder.

A nine-year-old has nothing else to do but to cry, but he was old enough to understand better, and that probably meant more conflicts and frustrations, too.

The relationship between his parents slowly breaking down before his eyes, the helplessness of having to stand by and watch, the loneliness of being able to call them, but maybe not wanting to, of living alone instead of choosing one or the other. He must have been really sad.

And it's okay to let yourself be immersed in that sadness.

Who could blame him for crying or complaining?

But…he was being so casual about it?

Offering up his past pain as a way to get through to me?

I mean, seriously.

What a warm, kind, strong person he must be.

You might look at him and think it's a normal reaction to divorce.

Maybe he's just coldhearted. Maybe he's just gotten over it already. Maybe he just doesn't really care.

But I know how it really feels. Boy, do I.

When someone's been there since the day you were born, the most natural thing in the world, you start believing they'll always be there. In fact, it's not about believing or not. You just never imagine anything different. Your parents will always be there. Of course they will. And then to part from them is incredibly painful.

It's like having half of yourself, half of your life as you know it, ripped away from you.

And honestly, you wouldn't want anyone else to know about it.

The moment someone finds out, you see the pity in their eyes. And you feel so alone, like you've been cast out of the world of normalcy.

It's like you're just walking down the road, and someone points at you and yells, "Hey, everyone, don't you feel sorry for them?!"

Even if the day comes when you find someone to open up to, it's normal to sugarcoat and give disclaimers and carefully select your words.

But if there's a reason why Chitose has been able to be so blasé about this...

Then it's for the sake of the person he decided to tell about his parents... Or perhaps she found out quite by happenstance.

In that moment, that person is me. Yua Uchida.

And his casualness was to stop me from having to feel the weight of his sad past in addition to my own pain and confusion.

He was protecting me from the regret of my own careless words. This was to preserve our future conversations, too.

No, he and I aren't alike at all.

He's so much more mature than...

"Do you want to keep talking?"

Chitose asked.

"...Yes!"

I answered without hesitation, then looked around the room before saying...

"But before that, can I clean up a bit?"

He scratched his cheek pensively.

*   *   *

"Wow, now I feel embarrassed."

As Chitose stared at the floor like a scolded child, I burst out laughing.

*

I threw away empty food and drinks, washed the cups and gave the sink a wipe, folded the clothes on the sofa (turns out the pile was clean laundry), and disposed of the expired food in the refrigerator. Then finally, after making coffee, I settled down on the sofa.

During that time, Chitose was sitting on his knees and fidgeting uncomfortably.

Several times he asked me, "Is there anything I can do?" and a few times he said, "Oh, you can just leave that!" until I told him to "Sit there and be good!" Which he meekly did.

I took a sip of coffee. "All right, thank you for waiting."

"...Uh, thank *you*."

"Hee-hee, you can sit normally now."

Chitose, beside me on the sofa, unfolded his legs with some embarrassment and got up as if he'd just thought of something. He went over and switched on his little radio.

Maybe even a guy like him gets nervous being alone in private with a girl.

From the radio, a nostalgic piano sonata was playing at a low volume.

"It's 'Für Elise.'"

When I was in elementary school, I couldn't play it properly on the keyboard, and I remember practicing with my mother many times.

Chitose came back and sat down heavily beside me, as if to dispel the slight tension in the atmosphere.

He turned to me. "Hey, you know…"

I shook my head. "I know what you want to say."

Chitose narrowed his eyes, which I took as a gesture to continue. "You think it's messed up, don't you? My way of life. My philosophy."

"Hmm, well."

"A little while ago, you asked me how long I plan to stay nine years old."

"That was a little harsh."

I shook my head, looking down. "I've been pretending not to notice it myself, but it's true. I'm still bound by a set of self-contradictory rules dreamed up by a pathetic nine-year-old girl."

"Specifically when it comes your mother. And how the word *normal* features in your memories of her."

"There you go again, poking where it hurts…"

I realized that, at some point, I'd stopped keeping him at arm's length in the way I talked to him.

Chitose stretched out his legs. "But what's a normal way of living anyway? You enter Fuji High as the highest exam scorer, and you think you can just be normal? You'll get a protractor triangle between the shoulder blades sooner or later if you try that."

"Well, I guess… I guess I wasn't expecting to score the highest. It just happened accidentally because I study every day…"

"I could stab you with an ear pick right now if you'd prefer?" he said. "Thing is…avoiding making friends, not dressing nicely, just putting up with it when you don't like something… That's not 'being normal.' It's being a loner. It's being drab. It's being a pushover."

"Wow, don't hold back on my account!"

Honestly, he ought to have a license to use that tongue.

I sighed, then composed myself again and cleared my throat.

"I guess you're right, Chitose. But to me, a normal life meant not creating any trouble for my family. It all got confused. But ultimately all that matters is not causing a fuss."

"Incidentally, what about hanging out with fashionable kids is 'causing a fuss'…?"

"…I mean, like, hanging out on the streets and getting mixed up with delinquents…"

"High school girls are delinquents? What is this, the fifties?" Chitose exclaimed.

Now that he pointed it out…I wanted to dig a hole in the ground and disappear into it.

After laughing for a while, Chitose gave me a teasing look.

"You've lost sight of what normal people are like, Yua."

"What do you…?"

But he interrupted me as I was responding.

"You should take a step back and try to view things more normally, first off. Go to school every day normally, make normal friends, hang out like kids do. Fight sometimes, make up, don't study or work in your club *too*, too hard. Enjoy dressing nicely, catch feelings for someone, and fall in love. All normal. Isn't that the kind of happiness your mother wanted for you, Yua? Think about it rationally. Normally. Isn't that what being normal is? …I think I'm saying the word *normal* too much. Normal. Nor-mal. Ugh, it's lost all meaning."

Yes… Yes, he was right.
All those things were ridiculously commonplace.
However…

—In the farthest recesses of my heart, that was exactly the world I always wanted to live in.

* * *

Crack. I could hear it splintering.

Again.

Because of him, something was about to break again.

The words were so simple.

What Chitose was saying here wasn't exactly complex philosophy.

If you ask the average person what "normal happiness" is, maybe nine out of ten would give you the exact same answer.

But, I thought.

No one had ever told this sad, misguided nine-year-old that her way of living was wrong.

Of course, that was all my fault.

I didn't want to confide in others. I didn't want to rely on them. I didn't want anyone to know me.

But him…

It was like he'd been able to see my secret suffering right from the start.

That's why he rubbed me the wrong way so much. Why I tried to push him away. Why I couldn't stop thinking about him.

"Besides," Chitose said, crossing his arms behind his head.

"Yua, you say you don't want to worry your family, but they've gotta feel like you're shutting them out. They're sad that you don't lean on them. Right?"

"Huh…?"

Pointing at my chest with his finger, he said…

"I mean, when your mom left, didn't you wonder why she didn't talk to you if she was in so much turmoil? Why did she suffer alone? Why didn't she confide in her family?"

157

*　　*　　*

Ask yourself, it was like he was saying.

"…"

This time, it hit me like a fist to the side of the head.
Right.
After Mom disappeared…I've had that thought almost daily.
If it had gotten too hard to care for us, why couldn't she let us know?
I could learn to clean and do the laundry. I could get really good at cooking and take over.
If Mom wanted to play the piano again, why didn't she just say so?
I never rebelled. I always tried to be a good kid.
Even if she had a new boyfriend or something, I could have helped her remember what's so great about Dad. I could have changed her mind.
Right, I…

"…I've become just like her."

That path only leads to a dead end, until you have to throw everything away, and still…
Chitose half smiled.

"Most parents live however they want, so why should we be the only ones to suffer the consequences? That's the case with your household, too. Of course, your mom was wrong for leaving. But your dad was selfish, too. He kept it from his kids and just let her leave, too.

"Still," he said, continuing.

*   *   *

"Isn't that the way it goes? Not just with family, but with friends, and boyfriends or girlfriends, too. I think everyone lives as they please, inconveniencing others or being sneaky for our own benefit. I mean, you're more than just your parents' kid. You're more than just your younger brother's big sister. You're more than just a quiet honor student. You're more than just some normal girl."

Chitose patted me on the shoulder.

"You're Yua Uchida, right?"

Then he laughed out loud.

Crash. Patter, patter.

In my head, I heard the sound of breaking glass.
How...how?
How do you know me better than I know myself?
I've been wanting someone to tell me this for a long time.
For someone to notice.
For someone to discover me.
To say, *You don't have to live like this. You can lift your head and face the future.*
I want good friends. I want to laugh with others every day. I want to dress up and wear makeup because, dang it, I'm a girl. When I don't like something, I wanna be able to say it. When I fall for someone, I wanna be able to tell them.

"...*Your life is yours, isn't it?*"

The jagged shard that had been stuck deep in my chest finally melted away.

Finally, I understood.

Chitose has lived his life this way.

He doesn't blame things on the past. He doesn't use others as an excuse. He stands on his own two feet.

But...

"Can I, though? I've been so docile for such a long time... I built a wall for myself and shut myself in, so if I suddenly throw all of it away..."

I was still afraid to take that next step. My mouth made a pathetic whine.

Chitose suddenly flicked my forehead.

"Ow, hey...?!"

The pain spread slowly, and it was somehow...reassuring.

"Don't be ridiculous. You think Yuuko and I chat with you as part of some nerd outreach program? Don't ask me to explain why, 'cause it's embarrassing, but we've both taken an interest in you. We both want to be friends with you."

Chitose softly placed his hand on the spot between my neck and shoulder.

"I don't know much about the value of living, though. After all, you can kill a person with a good squeeze here. No one knows what will happen tomorrow. You might get into an accident or get sick. Your family might suddenly disappear, someone you thought was your friend might turn their back on you, you might lose sight of your dreams. I mean, you and I know that better than most, right? So..."

*   *   *

He moved his fingertips from my neck to my cheek.

"I can't replace your mother or make it so the past didn't happen. But together, we can create new memories for the future. Here, today, right now. We'll never get the chance to do this time over again. And it just so happens that we come from a similar set of circumstances. If you don't mind being friends with me... then we can have fun, and laugh, and cry, and fight, and annoy each other...just like another kind of family."

He stopped talking, smiling with his eyes.

"—Let's become the kind of friends who can make up for each other's shortcomings."

At that moment, I burst into tears.
Heavy drops left my cheek and your fingers wet.
The warmth of your touch was gentle, reassuring, reliable.
Honestly... He really is just so...

"Honestly, Saku, you really..."

I grabbed his proffered hand and held it tight.

"...All right, then!"

And I laughed, my face all screwed up with emotion.

*

After that, I went out on the balcony and called Dad.
I suppose it would have been better to look him in the eye and tell him directly, but it took a lot of courage to reveal the feelings

I'd kept hidden in my heart for all these years. I felt more confident telling him here.

When I told Saku that I might be a while, he smiled with those gentle eyes and said, "It's cool. I'll be taking a bath, so take as long as you need."

The day Mom left, I had made several decisions. I set doctrines for myself. But now I planned to do things differently.

I told Dad everything, with no pretenses, as gently as I could.

Halfway through, I could hear Dad's voice trembling. "I'm so sorry. I didn't notice. I let you worry... I let you suffer in silence..."

He kept apologizing like that, over and over.

At the end, I even had a little talk with my brother.

My long, long fight against no one was finally over.

Then I ended the call and reentered the room, to find...

"—Hng?!"

...Saku, shirtless, with a towel around his neck, sipping a soda, cool as you please.

"Can I ask what you think you're doing?"

By reflex, my stiff way of speaking returned.

"Say what now?"

"Clothes! Please! Put on some clothes!"

"Oh, right."

Saku randomly pulled out a T-shirt from the laundry I'd just folded and yanked it on, as if under duress.

"You're used to living in a house full of men, aren't you?"

True, my brother lounges around like that after a bath, and sometimes he even gets changed when I'm in the room.

"That's not the point here! Do you dress like that when other girls come around?!"

"What other girls?"

"Uh, like, Hiiragi…?"

"You're the first, Yua," Saku said casually.

"Huh?"

"You're the first girl who's been to my place. That's what I'm saying."

"Oh… Really…?"

My heart skipped a beat.

"The heck? You think I have a revolving door of girls coming in and out of here or something?"

"…Uh, yeah, a little bit."

"I'm not going to dignify that suggestion with a response."

After a short silence, we both snorted with laughter.

All of a sudden, everything just seemed hilarious to me.

I'm the first, am I?

Me?

Thump, thump, badump.

No, this isn't what it looks like, I thought, trying to deny my own joyful heartbeat, but then I realized…I don't have to do that anymore.

I settled back against the sofa, mulling through emotions I'm not used to fully feeling yet, and…

"How'd it go with your dad?" Saku asked, beside me.

"He apologized a lot for how things have been. He said he's leaned on me too much. From now on, he's going to help with the housework and cooking so I can go out and have fun more. He said that's what he always wanted anyway."

"Right. I see."

"It was kinda…anticlimactic. I should have said something earlier. It was so simple, but it took so long to be able to say it… I told my brother I was sorry for not making dinner tonight, and he must have been starving…and he just laughed."

"Heh. What did he say?"

"He said I smother him. He's already in junior high and can

feed himself. He can just grab instant ramen or something from the convenience store."

"Well, yeah."

"Ha-ha." I laughed, showing my teeth.

I was a little bit fascinated by how he looked from the side— and how his hair was shining, still slightly wet.

Then suddenly, Saku looked at his phone.

"Yikes, it's kinda late."

I grabbed my own phone. It was already eleven PM.

"I'll take you home, Yua."

But as Saku was getting up, I shook my head. "Er, I was think-ing I'd sleep over?"

"Oh, right, I… Wait, *what*?!"

Now it was his turn to be all freaked out.

I got the reaction I wanted and had to fight a grin.

"Hey you, are you nuts?"

Now I kinda understood how Hiiragi felt when she said he could call her, "Hey, you," if the urge took him.

This kind of informality isn't bad at all.

"But I already got Dad's permission, you know?"

"Don't give me a heart attack, here."

"Well, I left out the part where you're a guy. I said I was at a sympathetic friend's house and planned to sleep over. Dad actu-ally sounded happy. I've never asked to stay over at anyone's place before."

"You left out the biggest part of this setup, and you barely even batted an eye, huh?"

I giggled. "Would it be an imposition?"

"An imposition? I mean, yeah?!"

"But, Saku, you said we have to live as we see fit, sometimes incon-veniencing others, sometimes being sneaky for our own benefit."

"Yeah, but some things are more inconvenient than others. You can't just stamp on the accelerator. How naive are you?"

"But you told me you wanted to be friends... Like a little family," I teased as he scratched his head awkwardly. "Thanks to a certain someone, it's the first time since that day that I've let loose. I think you have some obligation to take responsibility here."

"You know..." He let out a sigh of resignation. "Darn it. If I pounce on you, don't go crying."

"It's okay. You don't see me as a romantic prospect anyway, right, Saku?"

I figured responding to that might be difficult for him, so I continued.

"Anyway, could you come with me to the convenience store? I need, um, stuff."

"Okay."

"And can I have a bath?"

"I'll...I'll do some practice swings outside, so you can do that while I'm gone."

"All right. I'll try not to be too long."

I knew I was being really bold.

But...just for tonight.

I just wanted to talk to him awhile longer.

I wanted to be with him awhile longer.

I mean... Yeah. I'd gotten totally carried away...

*

After shopping at the convenience store and taking a bath, Saku took another shower after getting all sweaty. By then, it was already past midnight.

Now the two of us were sitting side by side on the sofa, drinking iced lattes.

Saku told me to grab something from the closet, so now I was wearing a baggy sweatshirt that was loose and cozy.

"You won't be able to sleep if we have caffeine this late, will you?" said Saku.

"Hmm, I don't really feel like sleeping anytime soon anyway. Thanks for staying up with me, though."

"Oh, I can fall asleep after a coffee in the middle of the night."

"Oh, well, that's good to know."

Then I had a sudden thought.

"Speaking of which, Saku, you've been living alone for about half a year, right?"

"Yeah, since I entered high school."

"So you must be pretty used to it by now, right?"

"Yeah. This place has gotten pretty comfortable."

"Then what was with the sob story earlier?"

"…I make no apology."

Seeing Saku scratching his cheek as if to hide his embarrassment, I smiled wryly.

"You're a boy, so some level of messiness is expected, right? My brother's like that, too. But your food is mostly freeze-dried or frozen, or it's from the convenience store or some fast-food place, right?"

I'd found a lot of those kinds of containers and packages in the trash.

Saku shifted, embarrassed.

"Yeah, recently, I've been a little worried about that myself. Up until summer vacation, I was paying attention to my diet. It wasn't anything fancy, but I focused on cooking rice every day, grilling meat or fish, and getting vegetables in as much as possible. I was trying to build my body."

Oh, the baseball club, I thought.

But I figured I'd better not get ahead of myself and pry. I didn't want to give away how much I already knew.

Saku couldn't know that I'd been watching that scene from

the window of the music room. And I still had no idea what was really going on with him when that was occurring.

So I kept my tone light.

"Even though you look like a perfect superhuman at school, even you fall short sometimes, eh?"

"Does it awaken your maternal instincts?"

"Yeah," I answered lightly.

"Huh?"

"So from now on, I'll make the meals around here. I can't do it every day, but I can come here from time to time. I'll bring some staples, and then fresh stuff on a regular basis."

"…What, like a wife who still works?"

"Hey, watch how you phrase it! Well, when you have some free time, I'd appreciate you accompanying me to the grocery store. My brother's growing, and he consumes an unbelievable amount of food."

Saku chuckled mischievously. "You know, just a short while ago you were blubbering all like, 'Don't get involved with me!' weren't you?"

"…Was here where you squeeze?"

"Ack! Yua! Didn't I just tell you how that can kill someone?!"

Well, I'm embarrassed enough to die. Or kill the only witness.

But all I really can focus on right now is how I can do something to repay this guy for what he's done for me.

"Honestly, Saku…"

When I pouted and deliberately turned my back, he snorted with laughter behind me again.

"All right, I give." Saku held out his hand. "Then would you be so kind, Yua?"

I smiled and said, "All right. Leave it to me."

And I gripped his hand tight.

★

Before long, it started seeming like a good time to get some sleep. Saku announced that he would take the sofa so I could use the bed.

Of course, I tried to refuse, but Saku wasn't about to cave.

He's a flirt, but this was one of the ways he seemed to be oddly old-fashioned.

For my part, I could have gone on talking for hours.

I'm sure…I'm sure it would be annoying… But I wanted to keep talking right up until I fell asleep.

I wanted to listen to his voice.

That's why I suggested moving the sofa in the living room into the bedroom.

Of course, pushing the sofa right up to the bed felt weird, so I left a modest gap.

However, it was a shame that the backrest of the sofa formed a sort of wall. At least if I turned it sideways, we could see each other's faces.

Getting everything arranged kept me excited, but once it was done, and I peeled back the sheets, I felt my face burn with sudden embarrassment.

What was I doing?

Oh well. It was too late to retreat now. So I resigned myself to lying down.

When I covered myself with a blanket, the smell was very masculine, and not in the same way as my dad and my brother.

The scent of shampoo and cologne wafted from the surface, with a hint of earthiness underneath that smelled like sweat and soil, like grass on a sunny day.

After taking a few deep breaths through my nose, I seemed to view the whole setup from above, and I almost freaked.

What was I doing?

It was too late to back out now.

Has Saku noticed this tension?

Grr! No! He seems perfectly calm!

He was so casual, like he was completely oblivious to my turmoil, when he said:

"Yua, are you still awake?"

"...Yeah."

"Can we still talk?"

"...Yes, I'd like to talk a little while longer, too."

"Being stiff again."

"Er, okay. Sure. Let's talk."

"Remember when I said how it makes it feel like all the fun times were a lie?"

"Yeah..."

"Yua... Do you still hold a grudge against your mom?"

"...Yes, I do. I'm angry. I can't accept what she did."

"Oh, right."

"Why'd you ask?"

"You know, all this time, I've been thinking..."

"Yeah?"

"Just because your mom is gone, it doesn't mean all of it was a lie."

"What do you mean?"

"What I said. Your mom may have left you... But I don't think the words she left with you were lies."

"Maybe..."

"Wait, I'm not phrasing this well. Maybe your mom was secretly troubled, and part of what she said was meant to convince herself. But there was no reason to lie to you, was there? Only to herself. Does that make sense?"

"..."

"Did you hate your mom?"

"..."

"You can get mad at me if I'm misunderstanding this. To me, it seems that you wanted to take revenge on your mother who abandoned what you thought of as 'normal.' Or maybe you tried to disprove her by showing you could be 'normal' and happy, too."

"...Yeah, I think so."

"I understand it in theory, but if it were me, the first thing I'd do would be to discard the word *normal* that had been ingrained in my memories. And the music that my mom taught me, too."

"..."

"You know, Yua... Maybe you hate your mom so much you can't forgive her. But you also love her just as much, don't you? You don't want to forget the times you shared or the words she left you... Do you?"

"Agh..."

Saku's words pierced me straight through again.
What should I do?
What was the correct answer?
I...I...

"I was just starting to feel better. I was thinking I might even get some sleep. And then you go and turn everything upside down. It's irritating. Maybe you're right, Saku. I can't forgive my mom. I don't think anyone should ever do what she did. And no, I can't accept it. And yet there's a part of me..."

Tightly hugging the blanket, I continued...

"That time I spent with Mom... I was happy. I was definitely happy."

Saku laughed.

                    *   *   *

"Oh, right. So you did know. All right, then that's fine."

"Huh…?"

"If you love your mom, go ahead and keep loving her."

"But…"

"Let's talk," he said.

"I'll listen to you until you fall asleep. Tell me what you loved most about your mom."

"What I loved most…?"

"I don't know if you know this, but I quit the baseball club."

"Yeah. I heard about it from Hiiragi."

"Oh, right," Saku said, shifting on the sofa, and I could feel him turning toward me. "The balls they use in high school baseball are as hard as rocks and heavier than they look. When I hit the ball with the wrong part of the bat, my hands get numb. One day, the pitcher screwed up and hit me in the side. I seriously couldn't breathe.

"Pfft." He laughed, a happy sound.

"But if you catch it just right, with the core of the bat, it feels like it's as light as air. Even though you're hitting a rock flying at sixty-odd miles with a metal bar, it feels just the same as hitting a colored ball with a plastic kiddie bat. It's addictive."

His voice was filled with joy.

"I know it's a home run the moment I hit it. The bat, the ball, and I are one. It's like, bring it on, you know?"

He stopped, smiling with his eyes.

"I'm obsessed with that moment. The feeling of it, in my hands. I think I kept playing baseball because I wanted to go on chasing that feeling. So…"

Saku continued.

*   *   *

"I couldn't handle quitting. I was frustrated, I was lost, I was pathetic... I blamed myself over and over again. I wondered what had gone wrong, what I should have done differently. But you know, even if I never got to where I wanted... Even if my passion went unrewarded forever... Even if I could never get back to where I was... I never once wished I'd never played in the first place. The time when I loved baseball, the days I spent practicing and playing...they formed an integral part of who I am."

His gentle expression, blurred in the faint darkness, showed that this was not just him trying to comfort me, but that he was totally sincere.

From what I saw at that practice, and from how the second semester started, I could only imagine how heavy a decision it must have been for Saku to quit baseball.

But he was still able to remain...

I gripped the edge of the blanket tightly.

"...You know, she used to read picture books to me all the time."

Slowly, I began to talk, like flipping through an old photo album.

"I'd sit between Mom's legs, and she'd hug me from behind. She'd do all the different character voices. She was really good."

"Like how a certain someone uses a different voice only for me."

"Hee-hee." I giggled, continuing. "She was doing housework at home all day, but she never dressed sloppy. Her shirts were never wrinkled, and they always smelled like fabric softener and sunshine."

"I guess that's why you're so well-groomed, Yua. Your mom's example."

"She'd hum while she was cooking, and it was like a musical performance. *Dun dun dun, dat-da-da*, that kind of rhythm. When she was done cooking, there was never a single dirty dish or utensil in the sink. It was like she'd magicked them away."

"So that's why you always clean up the kitchen while you're cooking."

"And also…"

"…"

"…?"

"…!"

"…"

"…"

"…"

Like a dam that burst, I kept talking about Mom.

To be honest, this whole time, I've been conflicted.

I'd tried not to see the contradiction.

I'd made up my mind—or thought I had—that I hated my mother and I could never, ever forgive her.

When I was playing the piano, or the flute, or even when I was like, *Oh, let's just forget it all* and picked up the sax, I'd hear Mom, a smile in her voice, saying "It's enough to just enjoy music in a normal way."

When I was sad…when my heart felt like it was going to break…

I'd think of Mom. I'd see her face.

It's all right.

Yeah. Ever since that day, even now, I've kept Mom in my heart.

"I…"

I put my cheek on the pillow and looked at Saku.

"You think it's okay not to forget her? Is it okay to say that I loved her? Is it okay to pray for her to be happy somewhere?"

"Come on, that's not something I can answer." After that curt statement, he continued.

"—I will say, though, Yua…you look more at peace than you did before."

And those words were like the final fragment that was missing.
Like when I listened to the piano before going to sleep.
A gentle warmth gradually filled my body.
Mom, Mom, Mom, Mom.
I still hate you so much that I can't forgive you.

"But I loved you."

Then I buried my face in the pillow and finally cried.
For some reason, the stain that gradually spread beneath my cheeks was warm.
Saku hummed the nursery rhyme "Mother" in a soft voice, and it almost felt like a gentle stroke on my hair.
From that day on, I had never cried, even in front of my family.
No matter how discouraged I got, I tried to clench my teeth and focus on frowning.
And yet, because of this person, thanks to him….
My pillow was wet with about seven years' worth of rain.
Starting tomorrow, I…
I wouldn't have to be tied down by my nine-year-old self anymore.
I could talk with Hiiragi and ramble on.
I could ask her to teach me how to apply makeup and help me shop for clothes.
Maybe I'd try to look more like her and grow my hair out a little.
I'd have to properly introduce myself to Mizushino and Asano again.

I could clash with Dad and my brother, and allow them to clash with me.

I could embrace my memories of Mom and live my own life.

My life would be all my own.

I don't know how long I cried.

Before I knew it, Saku's lullaby was over, and I could hear his carefree breathing.

I stood up quietly so as not to make a noise and went out onto the balcony.

I listened intently to the concert the insects were putting on.

I leaned against the balcony railing and looked at the sky.

When I took a full breath, my lungs were surprised by how cold the air was.

Summer was just ending, and autumn was approaching, one slow step at a time, like walking up the stairs carrying a stack of paper.

I took stock of what I could see, the wind I could feel on my skin, the sounds, the smells, the temperature.

I didn't want to forget this night. I'd always remember it.

—I would hang this bright moon in the center of my heart, the moon I'd somehow found in a black sky.

Then I went back into the room and squatted down by the sofa.

At school, he's always smiling and joking. At times, he's embarrassingly dashing and masculine.

Right then, though, he looked like a young boy. Not so different from my brother.

Careful, so as not to wake him, I parted his bangs.

I'm not sure I'd ever looked at his face this carefully before.

I'd been looking away and turning my back all the time.

...Hmm, yes, he's very well put together, but something doesn't quite add up.

Eyebrows that look like they've been drawn with a brush, long feminine eyelashes, straight nose, sharp contours, cheeks that look softer than I thought. Thin upper lip and puffy lower lip.

Experimentally, I traced his skin with my little finger.

A little dry, but the skin was elastic, even a little plump.

Did that tickle reach him through his dreams?

His mouth moved like he was mumbling, and when I gently touched his lip, the tip of his tongue flicked out.

I hurriedly withdrew my hand from that vivid, lukewarm sensation.

When I held up my little finger in front of me, the area near my fingernails was slightly wet, reflecting the color of midnight.

Unthinking, I drew my hand toward my own mouth, then I quickly wrapped it in my other hand, as if I were hiding evidence.

I looked at the face of the sleeping boy again.

Hey, Saku.

Thank you for noticing me.

Thank you for finding me.

Thank you for lighting up the dark night.

But it's strange.

When I was younger, I thought it was okay to be normal.

At some point, I started to think that I had to be normal.

And now, for the first time, I'm making a wish.

It's okay if I'm not your favorite.

It doesn't matter if I'm not important; it doesn't matter if I'm not special.

I'm happy to be like air... Only there when you stop to think about it.

Like maybe if you're ever in trouble, you might call my name first.

*　　*　　*

—I want to be what normal means to you.

I may not have much to offer.
But maybe, someday…
If the time comes when you're alone and downcast…
When you're all alone, filled with unspoken words…
If you're lost on a moonless night…
Then out of everyone, I'll be the one to be by your side.

*

The next morning, I made us omurice using the ingredients I'd bought at the convenience store.

It was a rather simple choice for an inaugural dish when I was cooking for someone else, but I felt like it was perfect for the morning after a big cry. The morning after I'd been able to admit I still loved Mom. And to signal our new arrangement going forward.

Saku wolfed it down in no time, exclaiming how delicious it was.

I glanced at the frying pan in the kitchen to see if there was any leftover ketchup rice and made a mental note that Saku eats even more than my brother.

Then I got dressed and left the house with an unironed shirt for the first time in high school.

Saku and I walked along the riverbed while pushing our bikes. It felt so good, and the scenery looked so beautiful that I secretly decided to walk to school from tomorrow onward.

When we entered the classroom together, Hiiragi was the first to notice.

"Saku, good morning!!! Huh, Ucchi, too? Did you two run into each other?"

Apparently, Saku had texted her last night, telling her not to worry. Of course, he kept my personal stuff, and our sleepover, a secret.

As Hiiragi rushed over to him, Saku greeted her with a cool "Morning."

After clearing my throat, I summoned up a little courage and said, "Good morning, Yuuko. I'm sorry I caused all that trouble yesterday."

She tipped her head and smiled. "...Huh?"

Then she stiffened, brows rising.

She grabbed my hand, beaming now.

"Ucchi, you just called me by my first name!"

"Well, I guess it was a little sudden. But you said I could..."

"Yes! Yes!" she chirped, head bobbing. "I'm so happy! Let's talk more!"

"Yeah. Um, can you come with me when I go shopping for clothes?"

"Of course!!! And if I get called on during class, will you help me...?"

"Er... I'm not sure those two things are connected..."

As we spoke back and forth, I heard a short burst of laughter.

"Honestly, Yuuko, Yua, what a fuss to make over using first names."

I responded in my usual put-upon way without thinking. "You stay out of this, Saku."

"But I'm the class president. I have to keep track of everyone's friendships."

"You take the position way too seriously. You even manhandled me out of carrying those handouts."

"Hey, don't question my leadership skills. That's punching below the belt."

Yuuko was just watching our conversation, unusually for her, until eventually she interrupted in a voice that was 30 percent squeakier than usual.

"Okay, now I'm mad! Listen here, Ucchi!"

"M-mad? About what?"

"As soon as everyone's done with club, we're all going to Hachiban's today!"

"Um, but we only just went yesterday..."

I almost caught myself saying, "Sorry, I have to cook for my family..."

But I'd decided to stop doing that.

I've decided to eat with my friends today, so please fend for yourselves tonight.

Yeah, I could say that.

My brother, who usually eats all my home-cooked meals, might go out and buy fast food. Dad might decide to make fried rice or stir-fry veggies. Oh, in that case, I hope he leaves a little bit for me.

It would be nice to go to Hachiban's with the other two guys again, after all.

As I was thinking about it, Mizushino and Asano also gathered around.

Yuuko yelped in delight.

"Yesterday was our Let's Befriend Ucchi party. Today is Ucchi's Welcome to Our Group party!"

"Welcome...party?"

Saku grinned with one side of his mouth. "Welcome to Team Chitose."

Yuuko, Asano, and Mizushino all quickly fired back.

"Yuuko Hiiragi's Angels."

"Kaito's Dynamite Bombers."

"Kazu's Creative Agency."

All eyes were on me.

They were expecting me to come up with something.

"...Um, Yua 5?"

Chitose grinned. "All right! Disbanded due to creative differences!" He thrust out his fist.

Everyone else followed suit.

Meekly, I imitated them.

Then they all burst out laughing.

Asano shivered. "Yikes, this is so embarrassing!"

Mizushino responded coolly. "I got carried away and jumped on board, too. But yeah, that was lame."

Yuuko clutched her stomach in mirth. "Aw, it's fine! We're young!"

"Even so," Saku said mischievously, "we'll never be Yua 5 with that kind of energy."

""""No way!"""""

"Hey, guys, that's mean!"

As I jabbed back, I was thinking.

I'd been seeing the world through clear glass this whole time.

This was embarrassing, lame, a little dorky, and so dazzling bright it almost blinded me.

And just a little bit exciting.

Yeah, this is good.

This is *great*.

★

—The seasons have changed several times since then.

Wrapped up in this familiar blanket again, I gazed at the moonless night.

At some point, we stopped talking about our memories of Yuuko, and silence filled the small, square room.

I quietly slipped out of bed and squatted down by the sofa.

Gently, I combed the boy's messy bangs with my fingers.

Wow, I wasn't sure he'd ever get to sleep tonight.

Well, today *was* exhausting.

A little worried that I couldn't hear him breathing in his sleep, I brought my little finger close to his lips until I felt his warm breath.

I was about to re-create that night, but I stopped at the last minute.

Instead, I touched my own lips and gently traced them from corner to corner.

That almost indirect kiss, one year later, was somewhat sweet, like tomato ketchup.

A bitter feeling of guilt pierced my chest.

Leaving the tear-soaked, twilit classroom behind, I chased after Saku.

I have no regrets. It was something I'd made up my mind about, a long time ago.

Back then...I had a reason. I thought I had excuses.

But, I thought.

Now, here, like this, just staring at you while you sleep...being the only one by your side...

—I can't help but feel a sense of satisfaction.

I turned, spotting a crescent-shaped light on the side table beside the bed.

It appeared here after Saku's birthday party.

Yuuko brought him a *yukata*, and Haru gave him a glove for playing catch.

So maybe it was a gift from Yuzuki? Or from Nishino?

It didn't look like something he would have gotten for himself.

"Saku, you helped me discover myself. So if you went for Yuuko, or Yuzuki, or Nishino, or Haru, well...I'd have been fine with it."

I don't believe those words were false.

When I first made contact with your heart, there was already a special girl beside you.

She eventually became an irreplaceable best friend to me.

So just being with you, as a regular friend… I thought it was enough.

That's why, that day, I…

"Ugh…"

Saku grunted lightly in his sleep.

Was he having a bad dream?

Looking closely, I could see that his forehead and neck were slightly sweaty.

I gently stroked his hair, then closed the balcony window.

I switched on the air conditioner and raised the temperature a couple degrees.

I wiped off the sweat with a nearby sports towel, took out a thin blanket from the closet, and draped it over Saku's stomach.

After watching him for a while, I thought he looked calmer.

If only these days could continue…that would be enough.

That thought crossed my mind the moment I let my guard down, and I bit my lip.

I don't like myself these days.

"—*Let's talk about Yuuko*," I'd said. "*It'll be like the three of us are having a sleepover.*"

I don't believe those words were false.

My heart was forever uncertain.

I did want to talk to Yuuko right now.

I did want to hear how Yuuko was feeling.

But…even more…I just want to be by his side.

I was happy I was the one with Saku. Not Yuzuki, not Haru, not Nishino. I was glad.

I guess I can't make excuses anymore.

Still, I thought.

There's someone who can tell him what to do in a situation like this.

Someone to tell him that it's okay.

So…

Once more, I gently stroked the sleeping boy's head.

"It's all going to be okay."

Just like Saku did for me, on a moonless night.

—This time, I was going to be the one to discover his true heart.

CHAPTER 7
Fires for Returning Spirits, Fires for Departing Spirits

A few days had passed since I rejected Yuuko's declaration of love.

I spent summer vacation in a state of inertia, like tearing out sheets of a daily calendar and throwing them straight in the trash.

I'd sleep, wake up, eat breakfast, drink coffee, study, eat lunch, read a book, watch a movie, run, do some muscle training, and take a bath.

It was a slow cycle of repetition.

And when I still had too much time on my hands, I washed my futon and blankets at the laundromat, organized my bookshelves with all my miscellaneous novels, and polished my windows and mirrors instead of doing any general cleaning.

Now that I was distant from both baseball and my friends, the days without school were too long, and I wished August would end sooner rather than later. But then the second semester would start. Caught between conflicting, unpleasant thoughts, I struggled for something else with which to occupy my hands and mind.

It appeared that without Yuuko to drag me all over the place, my lifestyle had gotten a little sluggish.

I got LINE messages from Nanase and Haru.

I guess I can't keep ignoring them forever.

I took a long time deliberating over shorter responses than I usually ever sent and responded at measured intervals to avoid worrying them even more.

Nanase probed carefully, trying to cheer me back to my regular self.

"If I go over there to comfort you, is it gonna end with us both fleeing to colder climes in the north?"

"Sounds like a good place to escape the heat."

"Oh, but in the summer, we should go south."

"But you said you want to grow vegetables in your own fields."

"Shall I send you some morning glory seeds?"

"At least make it watermelons."

"Shall we all keep an observation diary?"

"Too late. For that—and the seeds."

"I see. So if we want to sow morning glory and watermelon seeds, we should do it sooner, right?"

"Yeah."

"Maybe next year, then."

"Thanks, Nanase."

"Sorry, Chitose."

Haru was brash, as if nothing had even really happened.

"Chitose! You good?"

"Getting by."

"Aw, you must be used to this by now!"

"Maybe."

"Sorry, forget I said that!"

"It's fine; I don't mind."

"I thought it'd be better to be glib!"

"Right."

"Sorry, forget I said that, too! Sorry, I didn't mean that..."

"It's okay, I get it."

"Aw, I'm not helping at all."

"It's just nice to hear from you."

"Nothing's going to change, you know!"

"It's not...?"

"Nope! You've got free time, right? Okay, So Miss Haru's gonna come play ball with you sometime soon. And you can teach me batting from scratch!"

"Thanks, Haru."

"No prob, hubby."

Everyone had their approach, but I knew they were trying to cheer me up.

I felt bad that I was making them worry like this.

Kazuki and Kenta—and Yuuko and Kaito, too.

I haven't heard from any of them since that day.

But the one who really kept me from despair all this time was...

—*Ding-dong!*

Just at that moment, the doorbell rang once.

When I opened the door...

"Evening! Chilled Chinese noodles today." Yua held up a supermarket bag in front of her.

I smiled dryly. "I didn't lock it, so you can just walk on in, you know."

"Well, I figured I'd ring anyway. For discretion's sake."

Every evening, since that day, Yua would come to cook dinner for me.

Of course, there hadn't been any more sleepovers. But even

though I tried to tell her it was totally fine, she stubbornly refused to stop coming over to cook.

Even if I asked her to at least make the meals ahead of time as usual and just bring me a portion, she would just say, "Food spoils too fast in the summer."

But thanks to her, I was able to keep one foot on solid ground.

"Saku, which do you prefer, salty or not so salty?"

"Salty."

"What kind of tomatoes do you like?"

"I prefer cherry tomatoes to sliced."

"Mayo?"

"Yes."

"Red ginger?"

"Lots."

"All righty."

Yua and I didn't even bother trying to discuss Yuuko anymore.

It may be that I'd exhausted all that I had to say that night, or it might be because no amount of discussion would lead us to a satisfactory conclusion.

However, even if I tried to return to my daily life somehow…

Every so often, I'd become acutely aware of the colossal gap in my life now.

For example, when I open my LINE messages.

The name that used to be near the top is now way down at the bottom of the scroll.

For example, whenever the skies are clear and beautiful.

When I take out my phone to take a picture of it, I just put it away because I don't have anyone to send it to anymore.

For example, whenever I have a bad dream, I don't hear that perky "Good morning!" call that always put it out of my mind.

For example, when I'm eating the food that Yua made for me.

I don't have anyone to brag about jokingly anymore.

It's like walking down an unpaved gravel road in the country-side. I try to go straight, but little detours come up and confuse me.

Something was rolling around inside me, spilling on the ground, being left behind forever. Like how a small child drags a hole in the bottom of a supermarket bag.

I wondered if it would be like this until I graduated.

The insipid redness of the setting sun came through the balcony windows, and I squinted against it.

*

After she was done cleaning up dinner, Yua immediately started getting ready to go home.

Apparently, she and her family had something to do tomorrow morning.

Maybe that was why she was late coming over to make dinner.

Only after discussing this with her did I realize it was August 12. Tomorrow was the start of the Obon period. A time for family.

As usual, I didn't notice because my own parents didn't contact me.

I called out to Yua as she was putting on her shoes at the entrance.

"Please, spend time with your family during Obon. I'm fine now."

"…Really? Are you sure you're going to eat right?"

"Don't smother me, Yua. I'm in high school. I can take care of myself, whether it's eating instant ramen or going to the convenience store."

I repeated some of the words she'd used for her younger brother, but…

"That's not acceptable." She pouted.

"I was kidding. I'll look after myself. Luckily, I have nothing but free time."

"...I see." Yua smiled, accepting what I'd said and my little joke at my own expense. "Then, see you again at the end of Obon."

"Right. See you."

With my brief answer, she opened the door, and I called after her once more.

"Thank you for everything. You really saved me."

Yua turned around, her eyes soft and smiling, and then closed the door firmly behind her.

The air was thick with silence.

I reached out and locked the door with a heavy *clack*.

After pouring some barley tea into a cup, I went to lie down on the sofa.

"Obon, huh?" I murmured, looking absently out the window.

The end of summer is almost here, I thought.

Ever since I was little, for some reason, Obon has been such a clear line in the passage of time.

When I still had most of August left, I was excited to catch beetles, swim in the pool, and ride my bike, chasing the ends of rainbows.

As soon as Obon is over, though, the sense of loneliness that comes after a festival seems to press down on me.

I'd be counting the time left, worrying about the homework left unfinished, and thinking about all the plans I had at the start of summer—and how I didn't do any of them.

No, it can't be, I'd think. *There has to be more excitement waiting... Something no one has ever seen... An adventure.* But all I feel is frustration.

And despite it all, jellyfish appear in the sea, the sun begins to set earlier, and the refreshing night sounds of insects grow louder.

To me, Obon was always about...

*   *   *

—*Ring ring ring.*

The sound of my ringtone brought to mind the autumn season that was soon to come.

I looked at my phone and saw Asuka's name.

I hadn't heard from her since I'd told her about the situation, while I was still reeling. A part of me had been worried I'd said too much.

But thinking rationally, I had to admit that she and I hadn't exactly been text buddies before, either. In fact, we'd only ever talked when we ran into each other by coincidence.

I coughed hard to clear my throat, then answered the call.

"Hello?"

"It's me, Asuka. Can you talk?"

"Sure, what's up?"

I could hear her breathing.

"Do you wanna go visit your grandmother tomorrow?"

"Huh…?"

I was taken aback.

A certain scene popped into my mind.

A hazy image, rosy with nostalgia.

Right. For me, Obon was all about…staying at my grandmother's house, every year.

That rice field–filled footpath. The girl who was my first love.

—I spent those summers with you.

"How 'bout it?"

I scratched my head. "Sorry, wait a sec."

I put my phone down on the low table and went to wash my face in the bathroom.

I got a little excited, all of a sudden. Pathetic.

I washed my face carefully, like I was removing stubborn dirt that wasn't actually there.

Then I took a long drink of barley tea, and finally, I felt calm.

Looking back, I had told Asuka that we would go see my grandma someday. There was no way she'd forget something like that.

What better occasion than Obon to visit? I hadn't seen her since I started high school.

...Great, great, a convenient excuse. I'm such a coward.

"I'm back." I brought the phone to my ear. "Maybe we can buy *habutae* walnuts at Fukui Station. Grandma always liked those."

"Great idea!"

Asuka's voice was chirpy in response.

We decided on a meeting place and time and then both hung up.

If I can't undo the decisions I've made, I have to move on.

I've made up my mind not to stagnate any longer.

I have to face it.

Past, present, and future.

*

Four PM the following day.

After riding the rattly Echizen Railway, Asuka and I stepped out onto the small platform we'd last visited two months or so ago.

Exiting the old station building, we were met with an atmosphere that can only be described as summer in the countryside.

I took a deep breath and stretched out, and Asuka did the same beside me. We both snorted with laughter at the same time.

Asuka wore a cool, sleeveless dress, which flapped in the breeze.

When I looked around, the rice fields that had been filled with water the last time we came were now bright green.

"The green wave," Asuka muttered to herself. "That's what they call it, you know, when the green rice fields sway in the breeze like this."

"Heh, that's a nice term."

Yes… The summer rice fields did remind me of the ocean.

When a strong wind blows, the rice plants tilt from the edge, and the undulation spreads out, literally like ripples. You can see the path the wind takes in the gradient shades of green.

Suddenly, an image of a boy and girl popped into my mind.

I remembered feeling nostalgic when I came here the other day, but this…this was exactly the way it had appeared in my summer memories.

"Shall we go, Saku?"

Asuka smiled at me, dropping into the cadence of our childhood way of speaking. She wasn't acting or playing it for laughs. It just seemed to flow naturally.

"Let's go, Asuka."

If I tried to do the same voice right now, it would probably sound hollow, so I refrained.

The girl walking next to me was already so much more mature, and far, far prettier than she'd ever been back then.

*

After walking a short distance from the station, we came across a detached house with a somewhat aged tile roof.

There was a small garden in front of the house, planted with fine pine trees with smooth trunks.

A long time ago, when I climbed up there and broke a branch… Man, that was terrifying.

Fortunately, Grandma forgave me quickly. "S'awright, s'awright." (*It's all right, it's all right.)

"Ah..." Asuka pointed to the front door.

Looking closer, I could see someone's small back, a person squatting down beside the sliding door.

For a moment, I worried that Grandma was sick or something, but relief flooded me as I realized she seemed to be working on something by her feet.

As we approached, I heard crackling sounds and saw white smoke rising up.

On closer inspection, I could see that she had little pieces of wood, like disposable chopsticks, piled up on top of a flat, unglazed plate, and a little fire was set there.

Oh, come to think of it.

Grandma always used to set and light tidy little welcome and send-off fires like this during Obon.

My mother is a straightforward sort of person, and my father was always a rationalist who never gave much thought to these customs, so at first I wasn't sure what Grandma was doing.

Curious, I asked what it was, and I still remember what she told me: *"I'm setting a fire to show where our home is, so that Grandpa's spirit can find his way back here easily for Obon."*

Some people might find it annoying, but I loved coming to this house and hearing superstitions and old customs from my grandma, like never stepping on the edges of tatami mats, not whistling at night, even the right way to make pickled plums.

When I looked over at her, Asuka had nostalgia in her eyes, too.

She used to get candy from Grandma every now and then. Maybe she had more memories with her than I did, since I only came to stay for a few days each year.

"Grandma."

When I called out to her as softly as possible, she showed no surprise. Instead, she slowly turned around and looked at me, as if to say, "Yes, yes, who is it?"

I don't know how it is now, but when I used to come and visit this place, the neighbors would walk in without permission and leave freshly picked vegetables in the kitchen. So Grandma was probably used to people just dropping by unannounced.

I hadn't seen her in a while; she had a few more wrinkles than I remembered, but her skin was so smooth that I could hardly believe she was in her seventies.

Her beautiful white hair, which she got regularly permed, was still the same.

Grandma stared at me, as if she was trying to recall something. "Is that you, Saku?" She sounded not quite sure.

"Long time no see, Grandma."

With that, she suddenly seemed convinced, standing up and smiling.

"Oh my! And you didn't even call to say you were coming."

She tapped and patted my cheeks, as if tracing the years of growth there, and it tickled.

"I did call. I left a message. But you didn't get back to me, so I came when I figured you'd be home."

"Ah," Grandma said, sounding convinced. "Well, haven't you shot up like a weed! You always were cute as a button, but now you've grown into a handsome young man. I made this welcome-home fire, see, and for a moment there, I thought you were your grandfather."

"Grandpa was a handsome devil, too, from what I hear," I said to Asuka, and she rolled her eyes and grinned.

Finally, Grandmother seemed to notice her.

She gazed solemnly at Asuka for a moment. "Have you brought your wife for me to meet?"

What the hell?

"Er, no, this…" Asuka was clearly panicking.

I spoke up instead. "Grandma, I'm still in high school."

"Then, your girlfriend?"

"No..."

As we spoke back and forth, Asuka seemed to recover from her shock and politely bowed.

"Um, do you remember me? I'm Nishino. When I was little..."

But before she could finish her sentence, Grandma yelped, "Oh my! Asuka Nishino? Well, haven't you grown! I was wondering who this stunning young lady could be."

"It's been a very long time." Asuka bowed again, looking embarrassed.

"I don't have much to offer you, but come in, come in."

As she spoke, Grandma entered the house.

We both smiled sheepishly at each other, then followed her.

*

When I took off my shoes in the wide entrance, I was enveloped in a nostalgic scent.

Mosquito-repellent incense that was, as always, placed on the porch.

Scratched wooden beams, tatami mat flooring, sand walls.

Shoji screens that had yellowed faintly in the sun.

Old newspapers piled up in the corners of the corridors and old, tattered paperbacks that had been read over and over again.

Grandma seemed to be in the middle of cooking something. I could smell dashi broth.

It all combined to form the distinctive scent of Grandma's countryside home.

In just a brief moment, the memories of those days returned.

—It was summer vacation of the third year of elementary school.

I was staying here alone for the first time.

My parents were both busy people, so we were only going to

eat dinner here. But as we were preparing to leave, I noticed that Grandma looked lonely, so I announced, "I think I'll stay here for a few days."

I remember being extremely excited when I was granted permission so easily.

Staying away from my parents and having freedom to play was an experience I'd never had before.

Grandma was delighted, and she put my futon in the Japanese-style room that she usually used as a guest room.

Then midnight arrived.

I was in an unfamiliar Japanese-style room, an unfamiliar private room, and an unfamiliar futon.

At first, I was excited, thinking about what I was going to do starting tomorrow, but the excitement didn't last. Then an hour passed, two hours passed, and drowsiness didn't come.

Tick, tick, tick. The sound of the clock hanging on the wall was making me anxious.

Before I knew it, the hands had gone past midnight, and I kept checking the time over and over again. I was thinking lonely, desolate thoughts like *Only ten minutes since I last checked...* and *How much longer until morning...?*

I was all alone in a large, open space.

It was a windy night.

The shadows of the pine trees were reflected on the paper screens illuminated by the moonlight, and they seemed to rage, like ferocious monsters wielding sharp claws.

I tried desperately to look away from it, but then it started to feel like someone was peeking through the back of the closet, which was slightly open. Then I convinced myself that someone other than myself was in the room, reflected on the pitch-black TV screen. I was so terrified I felt like I was about to burst into tears.

The night comes early in the countryside.

Grandma was already peacefully dreaming away.

Cars and bikes, too, sat parked and dreaming.

A silly fear took hold, like a black thundercloud... *I'm the only soul left awake in this town.*

But, I thought.

My parents had no problem staying up until two or three in the morning.

When I woke up in the middle of the night to go to the bathroom, I often found one of them still pounding away hard on the computer keyboard.

Maybe, even now...if I left this room and dialed our number on the phone in the hallway, they would come to pick me up.

I wondered if I could go home to that bright house, even in the middle of the night.

But if I did that...I would make my grandmother sad. She'd been so happy when her grandson announced he wanted to stay. She'd talked so much about the places she'd take me and the things she wanted me to eat.

I didn't want her to have to apologize to me.

So I would endure, at least until morning.

I made up my mind and closed my eyes tightly.

When tomorrow evening came, I'd ask my parents to come pick me up.

I'd sleep well in my own bed, tomorrow night.

I curled up and repeated those same thoughts over and over until I finally fell asleep.

The next day, I awoke filled with worry, but then...

"...Saku?"

I met...this girl.

It was so much fun playing with her. I felt good. Excited. All my feelings of wanting to go home seemed to have vanished.

I slept soundly that night and ended up staying here for three whole days.

When I saw her waving hard at me, from where I knelt on the back seat of the car, I felt a prickling in the back of my nose and eyes, and I couldn't face forward for a while.

Back then, I never thought that the two of us would come together again like this.

"Asuka, would you like to pray to Grandpa?"

"Yeah! I used to do that when I was little, too."

Grandma always used to invite us to do this little ritual.

First, visit Grandpa's spirit.

When we walked into the room where the Buddhist altar was located, I immediately spotted the little Obon effigy of a horse, made of cucumber and eggplant and held together with sticks.

Asuka crouched in front of it and smiled nostalgically.

"Grandma always said to arrive early and don't hurry to leave."

"I haven't seen one of those in years. This really makes it feel like Obon, huh?"

"Let's make our own next year."

"If you wanna make one, it'll take, like, five minutes. But my apartment's a rental, so it's going to be mostly symbolic."

When I said that, I heard Asuka chuckle beside me.

"Still, it's nice to see Japanese customs like this. Carp streamers, Hina dolls, pampas grass, and moon-viewing dumplings. When I have a child someday, I want to teach them all about these customs."

"Yeah, I agree."

" … "

" … "

Somehow, this conversation ended up getting kinda heavy… We quickly averted our eyes in a hurry.

Asuka backtracked. "Um, right now, I didn't mean…"

"I know. Me neither."

"I just thought that even if I got a job in Tokyo, it would be nice if you and I could still come here to visit your grandmother, and have her explain more about all this…"

"…This is awkward, but do you think you're saying too much?"

"…"

I felt uncomfortable continuing this kind of conversation in the current situation, so I let out a short laugh to put an end to it.

After praying before the Buddhist altar, we left the room and sat out on the wraparound porch.

There was an old clothesline strung in front of us, and it seemed more like a lot with overgrown weeds than a garden.

Perhaps because there's no clear boundary between the house next door and the paddy fields behind it, it seemed huge when I was little and used to play here.

"Saku, do you remember?" Asuka was looking at me. "We used to take naps out here." She lay down, her legs hanging loosely over the edge.

"Oh yeah. The wood's nice and cool." I copied Asuka.

The thin incense smoke rose from the ceramic mosquito coil.

When I closed my eyes, the cold wind gently caressed my bangs.

A refreshing, tinkling sound reached my ears.

"Just like a wind chime, tinkling on the breeze, out on the veranda on a summer's day."

Suddenly, I remembered something Asuka had said a while back.

Even now, I still don't understand the intention behind those words, but at least for a short while, I felt like I could distance myself from the sadness out here.

"Asuka," I said, with my eyes closed. "Thanks for inviting me."

"I just wanted to come."

"I'm sure Grandma will bring us watermelon and barley tea soon."

"Then we have a seed-skipping match, right?"

"Just don't slip and add even more patterns to your dress."

"Oh, why do you remember so many things?"

And so we drifted through summer in the countryside for a little while.

*

Grandma did indeed bring us watermelon, which we ate, and barley tea, which we drank. Then she called out to us.

I looked at my phone. It was only seven thirty PM, but dinner was already ready.

Asuka and I sat down at the table, and the first thing that caught my eye was the homemade pickled radish with plums and shiso, followed by potato salad with chunky vegetables and uncooked yellow pickled radish pieces in it.

My favorites.

Other dishes included boiled fish, miso soup, and boiled spinach.

Grandma was sitting in front of me. "I'm sorry for all this hay-seed (*country bumpkin) food. If I knew you were coming, I would have prepared something you young folks would enjoy."

I chuckled and shook my head.

"I like this stuff."

When I said that, Grandma clapped her hands and said "Oh my," as if she'd just remembered something. "Now that you mention it, Saku, you always did love this."

When I came to this house, even though there were dishes like meat and sashimi on offer, for some reason I preferred to eat white rice with pickled plums and stewed vegetables. "You like it simple," Grandma always joked. "You should have been born as a monk at the Eiheiji Temple."

By the way, Eiheiji Temple is known as the head temple of the Soto sect of Buddhism and is one of Fukui's famous tourist attractions. They even do a zazen experience there.

Beside me, Asuka giggled.

"I always wanted to eat something salty after getting sweets from you, Grandma, so I often asked for pickled plums and boiled pickled radish, too, didn't I?"

Come to think of it, when Asuka made us rice balls the other day, she said they tasted like something from a memory.

Together, we said a short thanks for the food, then I brought a mouthful of pickled radish to my mouth.

When you buy it at a supermarket, it's light in color and a little hard, but the one Grandma makes is soft and has a thick dark-brown color. It'll take the scales off a fish, though. (*It's really, really salty.)

I ate one piece, then shoveled a ton of white rice in my mouth. "Oh yeah, that's the stuff."

Asuka nodded with chipmunk cheeks.

"Grandma, can I have the sauce?" I asked.

"Yes, yes."

I poured Worcestershire sauce all over my potato salad.

"What?!"

I grinned at Asuka's surprise. "My mom always ate it like this. I tried it once, and it's actually really good."

By the way, if I did that in front of Yua, she'd be pissed for sure.

Grandma sighed. "That girl, she put Worcestershire sauce on everything. Even curry."

"Have you seen her lately?"

"No news is good news, and isn't it a good thing if her work is going well? When you're absorbed in something, you lose sight of what's going on around you."

"Right…"

While we were discussing my mother, Asuka was staring at my potato salad. "Can I have a little bit?"

"Sure."

When I handed her the plate, she timidly took a bite.

After chewing for a few seconds…

"It…it kinda works?"

For some reason, she sounded annoyed by this fact.

"Right?"

"Yeah. It's good. Seems like it would go well with rice."

"Why don't you try it?"

"…Mm. Delicious."

"Kinda addictive, isn't it?"

"I feel…like I just lost a fight or something."

We laughed as loudly as we ever did back then.

"Anyway," Grandma muttered. "I wish she'd come by, at least once in a while." She took a sip of barley tea, then continued. "She doesn't even seem to remember Obon."

"You know, Asu…," I started to say.

Darn. How should I address Asuka in front of Grandma?

"I mean…my friend here…"

Beside me, chair legs dragged on the floor.

Asuka seemed taken aback by the unusual way I'd referred to her. She had her hand over her mouth, and she was blushing.

But just "Asuka" sounded too informal, and calling her "Nishino" sounded too formal. Grandma knew us both when we were children. But I didn't want to give the impression I'd brought Asuka here as my girlfriend, or anything. So I had no other choice.

"Er, she was the one who suggested we visit."

Grandma's expression brightened when she heard that.

"Is that so? When you were little, Asuka, you were always such a sweet girl, always popping by and calling us Grandma and Grandpa."

"Naw, I'm just here for the sweets." Asuka was acting a little more casual; she'd dropped the formality from her speech, and she was even slipping into the Fukui accent a little.

"Wheat gluten sweets? Potato *kintsuba*? Sweet chestnuts? Them's for us old folks!"

"I know, I know, it's a little embarrassing! But I got a taste for them from you!"

"Come to think of it," Grandma said, politely placing her chopsticks down and smiling with her eyes. "Do you remember, Saku, when you broke that pine branch?"

That was exactly the memory that came back to me when I stood in front of this house earlier today.

Asuka was there, too. I sat up straighter, thinking about how she would remember as well.

I nodded, and Grandma continued.

"Grandpa took very good care of that tree. When I first heard about what happened, I thought, *What a hooligan that boy is! I oughtta give 'im a lickin' he won't forget! But you know what?"* Grandma looked back and forth between us. "Saku apologized, and sweet little Asuka just insisted that she asked him to climb it. Neither of you was willing to back down! *What good kids*, I thought, and then…I just couldn't be angry with you."

"But that was…"

Grandma cut Asuka off.

"Both of you think of others before yourselves. I'm glad to see you here again."

We looked at each other and smiled, embarrassed.

"You know, Grandma…," Asuka said, her tone serious. "Don't you miss your children and grandchildren, especially out here alone?"

My eyes flicked to her profile.

Perhaps she'd gotten too comfortable here in this nostalgia bubble.

Her beautiful eyes were colored with anxiety.

Maybe—no, I'm sure—she was thinking about her own situation, her imminent move to a solo life in Tokyo.

Away from family, away from friends, and away from...

"Not a bit!" Grandma smiled kindly. "There's nothing lonely about it. The only time we ever really say good-bye is when both sides go about cutting ties deliberately."

""Cutting ties...""

Asuka and I spoke at the same time.

"The bonds endure between grandpas and grandmas separated by death, and the children of parents who later divorce... I can see your grandpa in my memories and my dreams, and I hear that those two check in every now and again, still."

Those two—she didn't need to specify that she meant my parents.

Before they split, there was a lot of arguing... "*I don't ever want to see your face again,*" was a phrase I believe was used. Huh. The more you know.

"Saku, Asuka, you thought you'd never meet again after the big move, but you did. And now here you are, back at my house. Once you've got that bond, you can't break it so easily. When you get to my age, you stop seeing certain things as miraculous and start to see them as inevitable."

Grandma continued.

"Even if it's one-sided...holding on tightly to a connection with someone after it's been forged is a good thing. That's all you need to keep it alive."

Asuka and I were listening silently.

I couldn't help but think of Yuuko's and Kaito's faces.

Even after what happened...would I be able to hold on to my end of those relationships?

Or were those connections broken forever?

"Thank you, Grandma," Asuka said quietly.

After that, the three of us had a grand old time going over old memories.

Someone would mention something, and it would spark a whole slew of reminiscences.

It was just like how it was back then, hanging out on the veranda.

We left Grandma's house around the time the sun was turning the sky crimson and gold.

"Don't be a stranger, you hear?"

"Of course not!"

"Yeah, we'll be back."

Those words were checking the strength of the ties that bind us and designed to confirm them again.

*

"Saku, why don't we take a detour on the way home?"

After we said good-bye at the house to Grandma (who seemed about to see us all the way to the station and wave as the train pulled away if we didn't stop her...), Asuka made this suggestion.

"Well, we might as well, since we're here."

Asuka beamed.

I also wanted to breathe in this relaxing air just a little longer.

As soon as I got home alone, I'd start thinking about Yuuko again.

We started walking, chasing the trail of some old adventure.

"It hasn't changed," I muttered to myself.

When we walked around here last time, I was so preoccupied with what Asuka was saying that I didn't really pay attention to the view.

The rice fields and the river where we used to play together... were exactly the same as in my memories.

"Nope, you're wrong." Asuka pointed. "Look, over there."

"Ah…"

She was pointing to the window I once climbed to with the ladder.

The spot where Asuka's house had stood.

But now…the house there was unfamiliar.

"Right."

Beside me, Asuka's lips twisted. "It's been years since then."

My chest tightened a little.

Well, it made sense.

Someone bought that land and built a new house.

That's all.

So then…why?

I had the feeling that my memories of that time were still frozen somewhere.

So that even after ten or twenty years, we can still turn the pages of the photo album in our minds and feel nostalgic.

Suddenly, a thought came to me.

What did Asuka's old house look like, again?

The event was a pivotal one, but the more I tried to recall it, the more it faded and dissipated, as if I were trying to grope for a dream at dawn.

I still vividly remembered the feeling of hitting the window glass with my hand, your panicked face on the other side.

But I no longer remembered the shape of the front door or the color of the sandals I stole from the entryway.

"Even in a rural town like this…" Asuka, walking a few steps ahead, looked up at the sunset sky. "Things are changing little by little, even if it's hard to see. Houses are being demolished, and new ones are being built. There's even a convenience store now, within a five-minute walk. And…"

She turned back to look at me with a quick smile…

*   *   *

"My first love, Saku, suddenly appeared in the year below me in high school. And someone developed intense feelings for you while I wasn't even aware of it. And now you're suffering."

Her tone was doleful.

"Well, you see…" I found myself scrambling for words.

"It's odd… This reminds me of Hiroshi Yoshino's poem 'Sunset.'" Asuka took a bouncy step forward. "Hey, did you get to talk it through with someone?"

There was a certain sadness in her eyes as she gazed at me.

"All my friends were there. And I talked to you."

"You know that's not what I mean, don't you?"

"…"

This girl…

She can always see through me when I'm bullshitting.

"You know…" Asuka scratched her cheek near her mole. "I was hoping this jaunt could be a little distraction for you. I bet you were shut up at home agonizing over everything. So I figured we could come to Grandma's house, eat together. Then take a walk around the nostalgic old town and chat like this."

"I'm sure I already said this, but I'm glad I came. And I'm grateful that you invited me."

And I meant it.

"But I ended up getting more out of your grandma. I wanted to give you a pep talk, but it didn't turn out like that. That chat on the veranda—I feel like it actually helped *me* a lot."

"Well, me too…"

"I think we both needed some wisdom… But let's get back on topic," Asuka said. "You turned Hiiragi down."

"Yes."

"Everyone was there, and everyone saw it. And it was even obvious to me what happened."

"Yes."

"But…"

She stopped, gently putting one hand on my chest.

"…But you weren't feeling it, were you?"

Ah. Darn it, I thought.

I should have been more careful about what I told Asuka.

I should have tried not to worry her.

I wouldn't lie outright, just stick to the facts.

But now, here we are.

She could read the intentions hidden behind my every word.

She didn't seem fazed by my sudden deer-in-the-headlights look.

"Maybe I should ask you this…," Asuka said.

"Why did you turn Hiiragi down?"

"…"

She was watching me directly, and I couldn't return her gaze. I clenched my fists and my teeth, but I still didn't want to lie to her.

So I had no choice but to say nothing.

Asuka continued, as if she'd predicted this response.

"You don't have to tell me. If you won't confide in me, I won't push the issue. You can talk to Uchida, or Nanase, or Aomi, or Mizushino, or Yamazaki. Asano…might be out of the question right now. Anyway, you have a good reason for turning her down…don't you?"

Her smile was slightly lonely.

*   *   *

"Because even with what you've told me, you've never mentioned what *you're* feeling."

Once again, she put her hand on my chest.

"You told me what happened and what was said. But you haven't said why."

Asuka took one, two steps back.

"What I'm about to say might help. Or it might make everything worse. But I think I'm the only one who can tell you this... Because of our conversation, on that blue night. So I'm sorry, Saku, but..."

Her eyes were focused, both sad and determined, as she said...

"You've grown so used to being loved, but you don't know how to love, do you?"

Her words pierced my heart.

"Because sidestepping the issue felt like the obvious thing to do. You felt you had to pull back. You'd always end up losing people, at best, and at worst, they'd come to hate you. Or maybe... you only knew how to give yourself away for free."

"You know," Asuka said.

"...You were the marble, rolling around inside the bottle of Ramune soda."

* * *

Clatter.

A lonely heart, rolling around.

Without saying anything more, Asuka turned and walked away.

The clouds in the pale sky were colored with sunset.

There was a loneliness in the air. Maybe that's just part of Obon.

Crick, crick, crick.
Ree, ree, ree.

The call of the cicadas filled the red-stained country lane.

Two long shadows rippled in the green sea.

Smoke from an Obon welcoming fire rose into the sky like a thin thread.

Crick, crick, crick.
Ree, ree, ree.

Summer…was almost over.

*

This is…for the best, right?

I can't be the moon in your sky with an impure heart.

*

We acted as if nothing had happened.

The two of us walked along the nostalgic country lanes for a while, then got back on the Echizen Railway and ended up at Fukui Station.

Asuka's father was coming to pick her up at the rotary, and I accidentally made eye contact with him through the car windshield, which was awkward.

He looked like he was feeling the same way.

I went home, showered, and pulled on my sweats.

I could still smell Grandma's house on the T-shirt I stripped off.

After drinking some cold barley tea, I felt more relaxed, and I lay down on the sofa.

The day went fast. Was it because it was too uneventful? Or too eventful, after all?

Now that I was alone again, I couldn't stop thinking about what Asuka said.

"You don't know how to love, do you?"

Yuuko…

She's loved by far more people than I am.

Does she know how to love?

And where will that lead her?

Nanase, Haru, Asuka.

Kazuki, Kenta.

Kaito.

And then…

—Ping.

My phone sounded, interrupting my thoughts.

After seeing the name on the display, I answered the call.

"Hello?"

"…Hi."

"What's up, Yua?"

"I was just wondering if you ate a real dinner."

"I'm fine; you don't have to keep tabs on me."

"Okay, I lied. Actually, I kinda just wanted to hear your voice."

It wasn't the sort of thing Yua usually said.

Maybe I was imagining it, but she sounded a little less tense than she did yesterday.

Darn, I wanted her to spend today with her family and unwind a bit.

"Seriously, what's wrong? You can tell me if you want."

"Hmm. It's not like talking to you about it will help in any way, though."

She wasn't dismissing me. It was more like she was trying to convince herself.

"Yua…"

"Sorry, that came out wrong."

"It's fine; I didn't think anything of it."

"It's a personal issue."

"Oh, right."

"But hearing your voice has helped me calm down. Can we chat a little more?"

"Sure."

"Thanks. So um, what did you do today?"

"…"

"Er, Saku?"

I wasn't sure what to say.

It wasn't like I did anything particularly wrong, but I wondered if I should really tell Yua the truth when she was acting this strangely.

That said…I hate to lie.

While I was mulling it over…

A giggle came through the phone's speaker. *"It's okay; you can tell me. I'm not dumb; I know that the others will be wanting to get in touch with you sooner or later."*

"…You won't squeeze my neck once I've told you?"

"I don't recall ever doing that?"

"I need you to promise you won't!"

"*Spill ya guts, boy.*"

"Spill my guts like die?! Or like tell you the truth?!"

With a chuckle, Yua started sounding perkier.

I still didn't feel much like bantering, but I could do at least this much for her, after all she'd done for me over the previous few days.

Slowly, like I was reliving the day, I told her about going to Grandma's house.

I didn't hide the fact that Asuka had been with me.

I told her that she and I had met when we were little, along with the general events of what happened two months previously.

I'd told Yua that, someday, she and I would be great friends, like our own little family.

So I couldn't betray that sentiment now.

It might have been a bit late coming, but I figured it would be better to tell her the whole truth.

"...Oh really?" After listening to the whole story, Yua spoke in a dull, flat sort of voice.

"Listen, Yua. I never betrayed you."

"*So you mean, the very second I stopped coming over to cook you dinner, you go off with this mysterious older girl you like for a nostalgic date to a place filled with memories for you both...? Yeah, I don't remember you and I being involved enough for that to constitute a betrayal...?*"

"So you say, but your tone is scaring me..."

We did our usual bit, and then we both snorted with laughter.

"*Just kidding. It's a bit of a shock, though, you having known her when you were both little.*"

"I'm...I'm sorry. I didn't mean to, but if you look at the facts, it really does seem like I went off with someone else the minute you were otherwise engaged."

"*I told you: I was kidding,*" Yua said. "*Besides, you're not my boyfriend, Saku. And I'm the one who kept insisting, even when*" *you said it was fine. So why should you feel indebted to me? Why should that affect what you do with anyone else?"*

This felt like a reversal of another conversation with Yuuko.

Yua continued, without hesitation. *"If you're apologizing to me in this situation... I think you'd better think carefully about what that means, hmm?"*

What it means...?

Just as I was about to ask for clarification, Yua muttered something else. *"Knowing how to love, huh..."*

That comment seemed more for herself than for me.

"I'm not sure I know, either..."

"But you pour love into your family, don't you, Yua?"

"If you're going to deliberately sidestep the subject...can you please not?"

"Sorry..."

"You know, Saku, sometimes, you hurt people without meaning to."

"..."

"Sorry, that came out wrong again."

"No, I'm the one..."

"Anyway!"

Yua's voice had a "discussion over" tone to it.

"I don't want you to think about how this affects me. That's not what I want. I don't think Yuuko wants that, either."

What was she trying to tell me? Why did she sound frustrated?

To be honest...I didn't have the capacity to figure it out right now.

So I took a deep breath, and...

"Okay, I'll think about it." I just gave a brief response.

"All right. Thanks for chatting with me."

"Right, good..."

"*Um, one last thing.*" Yua raised her voice, speaking over me. "*Don't ask me what's up, but could you just...maybe...reassure me?*"

I knew she was acting odd today.

But since Yua said not to ask...

"It's all right. You're going to be just fine."

That felt like the right way to react.

"*...Thanks, Saku.*"

"Good night, Yua."

"*I...*"

Then the phone beeped in my ear as the call ended.

If I were Yuuko right now...

Would I know what to say to a friend who called, seeking reassurance?

★

"*It's all right. You're going to be just fine.*"

★

When I awoke the next day, I found myself on the sofa.

I must have been more tired than I'd thought. It was already early afternoon.

I had the feeling I'd dreamed all night, cycling through different ones.

I couldn't get rid of the feeling that my feet weren't on the ground, and I didn't feel like reading a book. So while I was washing my clothes and drying the futon, I thought about my conversations with Asuka and Yua.

But the more I thought about it, the more the answer faded and blurred, like I was wading through the haze of a summer's day.

Before I knew it, the sun had set again.

I was watching my summer vacation slip away, wasted...

      *   *   *

—*Ding-dong, ding-dong.*

An impatient ring on the doorbell.

Yuuko…?

The jaunty sound reminded me of the face of a person who would never visit this apartment again, and I scratched my head.

Couldn't be.

I couldn't be bothered to check through the fish-eye lens, so when I opened the door…

"Hi."

Nanase stood there, her expression clear.

I felt myself relax.

Oh, right.

Even Nanase has her guard down around me these days.

She tilted her head coquettishly. "Good evening; this is a beautiful girl delivery. ♡"

"Don't say that at the front door; people might get the wrong idea."

"Would you like to switch for another girl?"

"Could I switch my order to a beef bowl or ramen instead, perhaps?"

"I'll give you a *far* more delicious experience."

"You know, Nanase… I think you're probably aware of this, but I'm not in the mood…"

"I'll get you in the mood, if you know what I mean! ♡"

"All right, all right, come in already."

But even as we performed our usual banter, I kept thinking only of Yuuko and Yua.

It felt wrong to them both to invite Nanase inside at the present moment.

However…

*   *   *

"If you're apologizing to me in this situation… I think you'd better think carefully about what that means, hmm?"

I realized that last night had been a piercing blow.

At the time, I'd sensed frustration in Yua's tone.

I knew I shouldn't go getting swept away by words I hadn't even processed yet. But if I ruminated over it, it would just end in yet another deadlock.

Either way, I had to face people. I couldn't keep running away.

"Chitose…?" Nanase stepped inside and gave me a look. "Are you asking me to jump into your arms…?"

Oh, right. I was still holding the door open, my arm outstretched.

"Oh, whoops, I was spacing."

As I spoke, I lowered my arm.

Today, Nanase was wearing a boyish outfit with a tucked-in T-shirt and shorts.

She took off her sandals and grabbed some slippers with a practiced air.

Once inside, she placed the plastic bag she was holding on the kitchen counter.

"Chitose, you haven't eaten dinner yet, have you?"

"What, did you really buy me a beef bowl?"

Nanase turned around and hopped up onto the counter. For some reason, her eyes were lowered a bit shyly.

"By the way, how have you been managing so far?"

Since we were on the subject, I assumed she meant about meals.

Just as I hadn't hidden from Yua, I didn't want to hide from Nanase, either.

"After that day, Yua's been making meals here for a while."

"…Oh, I figured," Nanase muttered in a small voice. She

waggled her toes above the floor, the slippers almost falling off.
"So what, is it Ucchi's night off?"

"Yeah. I told her she should relax with her family during
Obon."

Nanase's chest heaved.

Grasping the hem of her shorts, she turned her face away.

"...Fine. I'll..."

Her voice was so faint I could scarcely hear her.

"Sorry, what?"

Nanase slowly turned her head in my direction.

I could see that her cheeks were tinged cherry blossom pink,
her lips in a tight line.

"I said..."

Grabbing her left elbow with her right hand, she looked away
again.

"...I'll make it for you."

Her words were clearly enunciated.

Then I finally understood the reason for her uncharacteristic
behavior.

For whatever reason, whenever Nanase came over, I would
either cook for us or she'd buy something at the store on the way.

The only other occasion was when she happened to run into
Yua. Come to think of it, she'd been acting weird that time, too.

Now certainly wasn't the time to make a joke or to decline her
kind offer.

"Great," I said. "I was just getting hungry. Thanks."

Nanase looked at me with some unease.

"I mean, compared to Ucchi, I..."

She shook her head, closed her eyes, took a deep breath.

＊　　＊　　＊

"Don't go blaming me if you fall in love over my cooking."

Then she gave me that coquettish, Nanase-esque smile.

＊

Nanase pulled her hair tie off her wrist and put it in her mouth, then gathered her hair into a neat ponytail like she always did before a basketball game.

Then she took out a neatly folded apron from her bag and slipped it over her head.

It had crisp blue vertical stripes, and the bottom part fluttered like a skirt.

The waist was tied with a navy-blue ribbon in front of the stomach, as a sort of color accent.

I was definitely staring when she said…

"What, does it look stupid?"

She sounded really unconfident.

I burst out laughing.

"Hey!" Nanase snapped.

"Ah, sorry, sorry."

I managed to hold back my uncontrollable laughter as I continued. "It's just an odd thing to say when you're standing there posing like a swimsuit model."

Nanase turned away. "It's not my body I'm worried about."

"Why are you more scared of how you look in an apron than in a swimsuit?"

"Because a swimsuit is basically underwear."

She paused, then continued.

"This, though… I'm not used to it."

*   *   *

She looked down, red right to her ears.

"Like, maybe I'm trying to be something I'm not..."

Even Nanase feels insecure, I realized.

Times like this, she feels confused and anxious.

Even though one glance at her tells you she has no cause for concern.

So...

—Honestly, I was a little stunned by the contrast between the usually cool Nanase and her in this homey apron.

It's cute and a little sexy. It definitely suits her.

I was about to list my honest impressions, as usual.

But I immediately swallowed back the words.

"Let go! This jerk! This freaking jerk! He knew how Yuuko felt, but he acted like it was no big deal and went off chasing whatever other random girl he could find!"

I recalled what Kaito had said.

Even though the pain had long since subsided, I felt heat begin to gather again in my face where he'd punched me.

He might be right.

Originally, I acted casual in order to draw a necessary line in the sand between myself and girls.

I'd built a wall so no one could get inside my heart.

To maintain a facade, right from the get-go.

But Nanase...

She's already become too important to me for me to treat her like that.

Maybe I should quit acting so casual.
So I smiled brightly at her and said:

"There's no clothing invented that doesn't suit Yuzuki Nanase, right?"

I chose words that were as innocuous as possible, but still reassuring.
Was this all right?
You look good in that. That sentiment got across, right?

Nanase's eyes widened in surprise, and for a moment, she bit her lip as if she were about to cry.

"—That's right! Thanks!"

The chirpiness of her voice sounded like a forced smile.

That moment…
A sadness spread from the center of my chest up to my throat and made it hard to breathe.
…Huh?
Nanase and I were both laughing.
I praised her. She said thanks. That was a textbook interaction.
I couldn't help feeling like I had made a mistake.
Nanase jumped down and stood in the kitchen. Her back was to me. I reached for her, wanting to tell her to wait…
I didn't mean it… What I actually meant was…
Stopping at the last minute, I clenched my fist tightly.
No. It's better this way.
This sadness, this pain, is the result of my own selfish thoughts.
I wish I could have praised her from the bottom of my heart.

I wish I could have laughed more heartily.

But you hurt Yuuko doing that. Over and over.

Nanase no longer seemed to be awkward or on edge. In fact, she seemed to have returned to her usual form.

She washed the rice, set the rice cooker going, boiled water in a pot, and started shredding cabbage.

I stood nearby, watching.

"Never peek when food is being prepared."

She spoke with an absurdly theatrical intonation.

What's wrong with that?

What is this, the fable of the grateful crane? I thought, forgetting about what had just happened and trying to focus.

"While you were asleep, you rode on the back of a turtle to the Palace of the Dragon King."

"I think you're getting your folklores mixed up."

"You were never allowed to leave there again and lived happily with me, the princess, until you died."

"Hey, so it just ends with me being kidnapped and dying?"

"A very happy ending…"

"No, it ain't!"

Just our usual sort of banter.

Nothing's changed, but nothing's progressed, either.

We weren't really moving forward.

Chop.
Chop.
Chop.
Chop.

A rhythm different from the one I'd been hearing for the past few days spread through the air in the room.

Careful, accurate.

Measuring, planning, evaluating.

Chop.
Chop.
Chop.
Chop.

The kitchen knife struck the cutting board methodically.

It was a very Nanase-like sound.

I wanted to listen to it better, so I turned down the Tivoli Audio.

Every now and again I peeked at her. Her side profile was serious, like when she was aiming for a three-pointer in a game.

Before long, when the pleasant smell of frying oil began to waft in the air, Nanase finally looked over her shoulder at me, smiling.

Her apron didn't have a single stain. That, too, was very Nanase-like, I thought.

When our eyes met, she scratched her cheek as if she'd finally remembered my existence.

"Oh, uh, I was concentrating way too much." She stretched a little. "Guess I can't turn into Ucchi overnight."

I cast my eye over the sink, cluttered with used bowls and cutting boards.

"I was afraid you'd cut me if I distracted you," I teased.

"I went about it like it was a game against Ashi High."

"Thanks to that, I never got bored."

"You couldn't stop staring, hmm?"

"Nanase, keep your eyes on the oil."

"Oh, whoops."

It looked like the finishing touches were coming soon, so I

wiped the dining table and prepared chopsticks, cups, and barley tea.

"Chitose, just sit down. Don't look until I bring it over."

"All righty."

Along with the fragrant aroma of fried food, a sweet-and-sour nostalgic scent tickled my nostrils.

My stomach rumbled involuntarily.

"Okay. Chitose, keep your eyes closed until I say you can open them."

"All righty." I closed my eyes, just as I was told.

This was Nanase.

No doubt I was going to be presented with a meal the likes of which I'd never even dreamed of.

Some kind of fancy, avant-garde sauce.

To be honest, I don't really like cream-based sauces, so I hoped I could stomach it.

There was a clack, a clatter, the sound of bowls lined up on the table.

Nanase pulled out the chair and sat down on the opposite side.

"Well, thank you for waiting. Let's see what's on the dinner menu at Café Nana tonight!"

Enough buildup already, I thought.

I opened my eyes slowly, half with expectation and half with anxiety...

"...This isn't a freakin' set menu restaurant, is it?!"

In front of me was a salad, tofu-and-seaweed miso soup, pickles, and then...

A bowl of rice and fried pork cutlets covered with sauce...the Fukui staple.

*   *   *

"Boys like this sort of thing, right?"

Nanase gave me a smug grin.

"N-no mistake there!"

I burst out laughing as well.
We looked at each other, grinning.
"I was expecting—"
"Something French?"
"Well, yeah, if I'm honest."
Maybe not French cuisine, but I thought it would be something fancy. Something Nanase-esque.
Some kind of dish I'd never heard of. Clever but not overly pretentious.
"Hee-hee," Nanase chuckled.

"I've stopped all that."

She paused. "...Almost.

"Any Fukui citizen worth their salt would eat katsudon at a time like this, right?"

Her expression was pure.
There was nothing more to say.
"Let's eat," Nanase said, putting her hands together in front of her chest.
I followed suit. "Wow, thanks for the food."
When I took a sip of the miso soup, it tasted completely normal, and I mean that in a good way.
It didn't need anything added to it.

I could drink this every day and call it good.

The salad with dressing had surprisingly finely shredded cabbage. You only realize how difficult that is when you try shredding cabbage yourself.

But the pickles had a slightly odd shape.

"Is this celery...?"

Nanase responded with some unease in her tone. "Yes, I pickled it at home. You don't like it?"

"No, it's good. Especially with mayonnaise like this."

"Really? Well, that's how we do it in my house."

I took a bite, and the taste of dashi stock spread over my tongue.

No vinegar used. The celery's unique aroma and faint saltiness would go well with the rice.

"This is really delicious."

"I'm glad. I had some extra, so I put it in the fridge for you." Nanase sounded happy.

I picked up my katsudon and grabbed one of the three pieces of pork with my chopsticks.

Gently, I took a bite from the edge.

Then I followed it with some rice.

With Fukui katsudon, we don't pour the sauce on top. We soak the cutlets in it instead. Nanase seemed to have also glazed the surface of the rice with sauce before placing the cutlets on top.

"How is it...?"

"..."

I ignored Nanase, who seemed to be on tenterhooks.

Before I realized it, I'd gotten so engrossed in eating my pork that a third of the rice was already gone.

"...The heck? This is really freakin' good!" I yelped with genuine enthusiasm.

"Did I grab ya by the stomach?" Nanase said, a little bolder now. She appeared much more confident.

"Oh man. I think you did."

When I said that...

"All riiight!"

Nanase pumped her fist, like she'd just pulled off an epic buzzer beater.

"I mean it; I'm not just saying that. This is as good as anything they serve at Europe Ken."

For example, in the case of curry, even if you use commercially available roux, the meat, ingredients, and secret flavors all depend on who makes it, so I think there is definitely such a thing as "homemade curry."

Similarly, in Fukui, we have homestyle katsudon.

When you make it at home, the sauce is generally a mixture of Worcestershire sauce, Chinese sauce, ketchup, mirin, soy sauce, and sugar.

First of all, it's troublesome to make, and in most cases, the sauce is too strong or too sweet, resulting in a stickier taste than you get eating at a restaurant.

Even more difficult is perfecting the texture of the cutlet.

It's a completely personal opinion, but I stubbornly believe that the thin and crispy cutlet from Europe Ken is the best, so I can't help but balk at the thickness of *tonkatsu* made at home. It feels somewhat unrefined.

In that regard, the bowl that Nanase made was, shockingly, exactly to my taste.

"What kind of meat are you using for this?" I asked.

"Normally, it's pork loin. However, meat tataki isn't common in ordinary households. So it's the stuff for frying, not for *tonkatsu*. Thinly sliced meat is the key, you see." Nanase giggled with pride.

"Hmm, that's why it looks like something from a restaurant. What about the sauce? It's just a little sweet-and-sour; it's perfect."

"I tried using apple juice as a secret ingredient."

"Oh, genius. By the way, can I have seconds?"

"Oh, I'm sorry. For the cutlet, I only fried three pieces for you and two for me; isn't that enough?"

"No, I meant seconds on the sauce."

"…Huh? I still have some, but why?"

"For the second bowl, I want to pour it over the white rice and make a soup."

"People eat it like that?"

"What, you don't know? It's a way to really appreciate the sauce."

"No, I've never heard of it."

She twisted her lips, like she was trying to hold back but couldn't.

"That is really weird."

Then she started laughing, doubling over and everything.

"You like the sauce that much?"

"When you eat at home, you gotta make the most of it."

Nanase smiled, looking reassured.

"—Then I'm glad I gave it my best effort."

All of a sudden, we stopped grinning.

I hurriedly started eating the rest of the meal.

If I kept looking at her face, I was sure I was going to blurt out unnecessary things again.

*

After washing the dishes and removing the oil, the two of us went out onto the balcony with a plastic bottle of soda each.

I wouldn't really describe the air as cool, but the nights that make you sweat just by existing seemed to have passed. The wind that blew from the river now and then had hints of the coming season.

"What about club?" I suddenly remembered.

"We have three days off during Obon."

"Still, it's only for three days. Aren't you aiming for the Inter-High competition?"

"Speaking of which..." Nanase, leaning against the balcony railings, turned toward me. "Has Haru been by yet?"

"Here, you mean?"

"Yeah."

"No, but I got messages on LINE."

"...What an idiot. She's hopeless."

The last sentence was so faint that I almost didn't catch it.

"Nanase, have you...?"

"Hmm?"

"Have you been in touch with Yuuko, since what happened?"

Nervously, I voiced something that had been bothering me for a long time.

Maybe, if it was Nanase...

But Nanase only smiled sadly.

"Of course I contacted her, but there was no response, either on the phone or LINE. She didn't even mark me as read."

"..."

I thought for a moment that I shouldn't have asked.

A part of me was hoping, I guess.

It was about time to get my thoughts together a little. In fact, I got the feeling I needed to.

Things with Yua would still be uncomfortable because of what happened, but at least I wanted Yuuko to be able to rely on her other friends.

"Wait," Nanase said quickly. "I did get a call from Kaito. It seems Yuuko has been meeting and talking with him. She's depressed, but Kaito said she seems like she's going to be okay. So we probably don't need to worry too much."

"I see. Kaito, huh?"

"Not sure how to feel about that...?"

"No," I replied. "I'm relieved. If he's by her side, she'll be fine."

And I really meant it.

My only concern was what would happen if Yuuko was left alone with her pain.

If Kaito was with her... He was an idiot, but he would watch out for Yuuko.

"...I'm glad, actually."

I murmured, looking at the sky, trying not to acknowledge the emotion I felt burning the backs of my eyes.

Gently, Nanase put her arm around my waist.

"Hey..." Before I knew it, I started talking. "Nanase, what would you do at a time like this?"

I knew it was a pointless question.

But Nanase was a lot like me.

Maybe I was curious to know how she'd answer.

"First of all, I'd keep a distance until everyone had a chance to calm down. Then when the second semester starts, I'd set up a place to talk properly again, and we'd make up. After that, we'd be friends as usual..."

Nanase laughed, a short laugh that sounded like a sigh.

"I wish I was still able to say something like that."

She continued, her voice faint.

"But right now, that's kind of impossible."

I really am an idiot.

Even Nanase must be frustrated that she can't get in touch with her friend.

I should have thought about it more, simply because we're so similar.

If I were Nanase, seeing my friends hurt in front of me, knowing I can't do anything to help them—knowing I was such a useless friend that they couldn't even come to me for help...

"Sorry, I shouldn't have asked."

I felt Nanase's fingers tighten into the back of my shirt.

"...Katsudon."

She mumbled a word that seemed a bit random.

Even I knew this wasn't the start of a joke.

It meant something.

I silently urged Nanase to continue, which she did.

"It doesn't seem very Yuzuki Nanase-like to have the first homemade dish you made for a boy be a katsudon set meal, right?"

"I guess not."

But as a result, there was no artifice...and the outcome was insanely delicious.

Still, I can't deny that I was surprised.

It certainly wasn't what I'd expect from Nanase.

"You know, we— Can I say 'we' right now?"

I nodded as she scrutinized my face.

"I think we tend to care too much about formality and good manners. Appearances and aesthetics, in other words."

She looked at me with some unease as she spoke.

Perhaps she was worried about how she was coming across.

"Nanase, I'll listen to anything you have to say. You wanna keep going?"

After taking a deep breath, she nodded.

"Of course, it's also an aesthetic we can't compromise on. It's because we've lived like that that we're the Saku Chitose and Yuzuki Nanase here today. But...who exactly would you make fancy pasta for?"

She was speaking as if she were talking to herself.

"I wanted you to say 'Boy, this is delicious,' not chuckle and say 'Well, this is exactly what I'd expect from you, Nanase.' I wanted to help you cheer up, even if only a little. And that sentiment…is part of who I am, as Yuzuki Nanase today."

She let go of my T-shirt, and I sensed her hand clenching.

"—So, Chitose, don't go dying on the wrong hills, okay?"

With a light touch, her fist knocked my cheek.

Just a short message.

In Nanase's words, which meant even more.

She seemed a lot like me on the surface, but on the inside, she was stronger and more beautiful than I was.

It touched my heart.

*

I wanted you to understand me more than anyone else.

That's all I could say…

*

After sending Nanase home, I was walking alone on the riverbed path, when the phone I'd stuck in my pocket began to vibrate.

After glancing at the name on the display, I answered the call without hesitation.

"Hello?"

"Hello?"

"I was good. I ate dinner."

"…Er… Oh, ha-ha."

It was Yua on the line.

"Sorry, I know it's getting a bit late to call…"

"It's okay, I'm just out walking anyway."

"You went for a walk?"

"No, I was sending Nanase home."

"Oh really?"

"I'll explain, so you don't have to be so tense, okay?"

I told Yua about everything that had happened.

After I finished speaking, Yua responded in a slightly sullen voice. *"Was it really that good? Yuzuki's katsudon, I mean?"*

"It was excellent."

"Hmph."

"I'm not talking about how it compares to your cooking, Yua. Anyway, you've never made me katsudon before."

"I know that. However, I will not be making katsudon at your place in the future, either."

"Why not?"

"HMPH!"

"That's mean; I tried to sugarcoat it."

"And that's beside the point."

Finally, we both chuckled at the same time.

Lately, Yua had been a little childish.

I think she and I both felt an urge to distract ourselves from worrying whenever we thought about Yuuko.

"You know, Saku…"

"Hmm?"

"Even though you barge into other people's secrets and say all these lofty things, you can't see anything about yourself clearly, can you?"

"Hey, are you really mad at me?"

"Hmm, if I had to say, I guess…I'm always mad."

"Yua…"

"However… There are two people who deserve a telling off. So…"

She paused, then said…

"Thanks. I think I'm good for tonight, too."

Her voice was calm.

"Okay, good night, then."

"Yeah, good night."

At the very least…I wanted Yua and Yuuko to make up.

I wanted to see them laughing together again.

*

The last day of Obon arrived.

Around four PM, when the heat began to ease a little, my door-bell rang again.

When I opened the door, I found Haru standing there in a sporty outfit.

After Asuka and Nanase comes Haru. I guess that was why I wasn't so surprised to see her.

"'Sup."

I raised a hand in greeting…

"…Listen!" Haru's head snapped up. She'd been looking at her feet, as if she was trying to find the right words, and I guess she'd found them. "I'm still a child, maybe, so I don't know what to do at a time like this…"

Wow, it was obvious she had a lot on her mind.

I responded with a mix of gratitude and apology. "Thank you. It's really nice that you came. Would you like some tea?"

Haru shook her head.

"Then, do you want to play catch?"

She shook her head slightly again.

"I thought about that, too. I was trying to find the best way to cheer you up. Maybe I could take you out to eat something yummy, lend a sympathetic ear. I could take you shopping. Even write you a letter. But none of that is very 'me.' Or more like I can't see myself pulling any of it off…"

Haru looked down again.

"In the end, the only thing I thought I could do was to help you get out and move your body, get some of it out of your system. But against me, it'd just be child's play for you."

"No, it wouldn't..."

"And so!"

She cut me off.

"I brought someone who can give you a real run for your money!"

She reached out her hand to the blind spot beside the door, grabbed something large, and yanked it toward me.

"   "
......
"   "
......
"   "
....
"   "
....

"What the heck are you doing here, Atomu?"

"...That's what I'd like to know! Dumbass!"

*

Haru, Atomu, and I went to Higashi Park and started stretching.

"I'm impressed you managed to get him over here."

I smiled wryly.

If she wanted a Haru-esque plan, she certainly had one, although this was pretty out-there, even for her.

Going to all this trouble, just to cheer me up...

Haru grinned back. "Really? But when I asked, he came right along. Right, Uemura?"

"Are you insane?!" Atomu snarled, then turned to me. "This

little pip-squeak. I don't know who told her, but she found out that I train alone in the park, and she cornered me. 'He'll get more into it against a real batter, won't he?' she said. 'Yeah, if it feels like a real game, he'll definitely enjoy it more!' Then she was like, 'I'll treat you to Hachiban's if you come,' she said. On and on!"

I could picture the scene, and a snort of laughter escaped me.

Haru scratched her cheek sheepishly.

"*Tsk*," Atomu groused. "Then she was like, 'You're Chitose's main opponent, aren't you?' and 'I really need you to come help cheer him up.' And well, here I am."

So he gave in.

I grinned.

"Is this because of your famous tsundere nature?"

"You're gonna pay for that, asshole!"

Atomu put on his glove and stood up, slamming the ball against it.

"Since Aomi had her fun manipulating me, I'm going to take my frustrations out on your face. Get ready for a broken nose."

Come to think of it, they even had a helmet and a ball case. No idea where those came from.

I picked up my wooden bat and got to my feet as well.

"If you feel lonely during the summer vacation, you can call me anytime."

Spinning the ball on his fingertip, Atomu grinned. "Huh, what good is a brokenhearted puppy like you gonna do me?"

"Hah, okay, now you're gonna get it, my friend!"

"How's your wrist, by the way? Is it actually functional again?"

"Would you like to try me? Playing with kiddie balls ain't exactly sports rehab, you know."

Sniping back and forth, we took our places at the mound and the batter's box.

Scrape, scrape. Atomu smoothed the dirt beneath his feet.

"Do you still have some New Year's gift money from your mama? Because those wooden bats break easily."

Scrape, scrape. I smoothed the ground beneath my feet, too.

"I'll take your pride as collateral."

"Haru!"

"Aomi!"

"All right, all right, on my way!"

Delighted, Haru dashed off to the outfield.

I did my usual routine and gripped the bat.

"…Hey, Atomu. Think Koshien is heating up right about now?"

Atomu entered a windup stance.

"Hmph. How would I know?"

—Clank.

A fastball, strong enough to blast away all other thoughts, went flying…right to the low inside corner, my sweet spot.

★

About two hours later.

Once again, we were all slumped around the mound.

It wasn't the frenzied practice we'd been doing before the tournament not so long ago, though.

Somewhere along the way, Haru entered the batter's box, and we taught her the basics, and Atomu took the bat while I stood on the mound.

Haru sighed happily. "Yep, whenever life gets tough, a good workout solves everything."

Atomu rolled his eyes and sighed, too. "Dammit, what the hell have you two dragged me into?"

"What are you talking about? Once you got into it, you really enjoyed yourself."

"Shut it, Chitose."

"Excuse me?!!!"

"Aomi, are you really going to continue playing basketball at your height?"

"Duh! Of course I am!"

"…Hmph. You're both crazy."

"Why am I crazy?"

"Because someone like you should go all the way to the top."

"Huh…?"

"Otherwise, your potential is wasted. Like little burned-out chips of cinder, lying in the dirt."

I snorted. "Behold, the bonfire of my dreams."

"You never shut up, do you?" said Atomu. "You're still practicing your swings, right? Are you thinking about starting over in college?"

"What if I said yes?"

"…Well, you can talk to me about it if that's the case."

"Are you getting mushy?"

"Are you getting ready to *die*?"

Geez, this guy.

Atomu got up, brushing off the dust. "Well, I'll leave you two to clean up."

Haru quickly sat up, too. "Why are you leaving? I said I'd buy you dinner. Let's all go to Hachiban's."

Atomu snorted. "Look, if you want the guy so bad you're willing to cry about it, then just jump him and have at it. Luckily, you seem to have plenty of stamina."

"What?!"

Leaving Haru spluttering, Atomu, having said his piece, walked off without looking back.

"…"

"…"

There was a silence in the air between the two of us who remained.

"I wasn't crying!" Haru yelled suddenly.

"R-right."

"I'm the type who sweats like a waterfall; that's all!"

"I know, I know. But I don't think that's a very delicate, maidenly way to deny something…?"

Oh, right, I thought, scratching my cheek.

That good-for-nothing jerk didn't just come along because he felt like it.

No doubt Haru begged, whined, pleaded, even cried to convince him.

"Thanks, Haru," I said.

She turned her back in embarrassment.

"I…I'm sorry. I tried, but all I could think of was something dumb."

"What are you talking about? Anyway, if anyone's dumb, it's me. And I haven't felt this refreshed all week."

I wasn't trying to flatter her. I honestly meant it.

Ever since that day, I'd been worrying about all kinds of things, repeatedly hitting dead ends and feeling depressed. Playing ball had helped me finally empty my head for the first time in a while.

"Still, that was pretty funny how you dragged Atomu along."

"Ugh…," Haru grunted, fiddling with the soil with her fingertips. "I thought it wouldn't work unless you were up against someone who really challenged you."

She looked so funny in that moment, I couldn't stop myself from snorting with laughter.

Yua, Nanase, and Haru are completely different in their approaches, I thought.

More than anything else, though, I was just glad to know that Haru cared about me.

"You know me well," I said.

She finally turned to me and grinned.

"I've been observing you closely, Hubby!"

—Drip, drip, drip.

As we chatted back and forth, I felt cold droplets on my cheek.

I thought it was sweat dripping from my hair, but...

"Oh, gah."

When I looked at the sky, black clouds had come rushing in.

"Looks like it's gonna rain. Haru, we'd better split."

"Aw, it's fine."

She lay down, totally ignoring what I'd just said. "Didn't you love the rain when you were a kid?"

She squinted up at me a little sadly.

"Hmph. If you get wet and your shirt goes see-through again, don't take it out on me."

"Unfortunately, I'm in a sports bra today."

"...Well, even a sports bra can be—"

"Listen, you!"

I quickly moved the bat and ball cases under some shelter.

In the blink of an eye, the rain was pelting down harder. Soon, it was bouncing down like hail.

Too late now, I thought, lying down beside Haru.

"Heh... Ha-ha-ha!" I laughed out loud. It was so funny.

"This hurts, doesn't it?"

Raindrops beat down on my eyelids, lips, and cheeks, *splish splash splosh.*

"Ah-ha-ha, what are we doing?"

Beside me, Haru clutched her stomach with laughter.

I propped myself up.

The air was thick with the scent of rain.

Fresh showers washed away the dust and asphalt that had been baked by the summer sun.

Many large puddles formed on the ground, and waves spread across their surfaces.

Haru propped herself up, too.

We put our backs together.

In the cold rain, the warmth of each other's bodies felt nice.

"When I was little...," Haru began. "I was able to play like this without overthinking everything."

"...Ah."

"We'll be dry once the sun comes out...right?"

"Yeah, this does bring back some memories. During baseball club practice, we'd be worn out and find our second wind when it rained. Did you know if you slide as hard as you can in a downpour like this that you can go about thirty feet?"

"Hmm?"

"No, don't actually try it. You'll get in big trouble if you go home with your training outfit dripping with mud."

Then we laughed together again.

"Hey, Chitose?"

"Yes, Haru?"

"I'm not experienced enough to give advice on love and friendship."

"Uh-huh."

"Let me just say one thing."

Haru leaned her back against me.

"You can feel free to lean on me sometimes.

"Yuuko, Yuzuki, Ucchi, Kaito, Mizushino, Yamazaki," she continued...

"—We're all important as friends, girls and guys."

*　　*　　*

She was like the sun peeking through the clouds.

"Everyone has their strengths and weaknesses. Sometimes they have darkness in their hearts, sometimes pure intentions. So you don't have to carry everything on your own shoulders."

Then she thunked her skull lightly against mine.

"That's why we play in teams, right?"

Haru was the one who carried her team on her back.
She was always striving to overcome obstacles.
She knew the value of cooperation.
Her frank words carried a certain weight.
Suddenly, the warmth disappeared, and Haru stood up.
Then, with a loud *thwack*, she slapped me hard on the back.

"So get it together, General!"

"…That hurt, you doofus."

Before I knew it, the rain had stopped, and the western sky was burning bright red.
A lakelike puddle soaked up the twilight and reflected the moon.
A bluish drizzle dripped down from the soaked leaves of the trees, and a double-blurred rainbow drew a faint arc in the sky.
I got to my feet, held up my hands, and squinted a little.
I get it, Haru.
We arrived at this new summer together—and I can't let it end like this.

★

See, I knew it.
This is the only way I can stay by your side.

★

After returning home, I briefly washed my muddy training gear by hand, put it in the laundry basket, and then slowly soaked in the bathtub.

Haru had said this was all she could do, but her idea of drawing me outside had worked wonders.

A pleasant feeling of fatigue enveloped my body, and I even felt like the heavy sediment that had been resting on my chest for so long had been washed away.

When I finished drying my hair after getting out of the bath, my phone rang.

"I had Hachiban's with Haru tonight. I chose veggie ramen for once, so that should appease your concerns, Yua."

"Well, aren't you a good boy."

"You call me every day, but how are you? Have you been having any fun, or has it been all family, all the time?"

"Yeah, cook the meals, do the laundry, clean up, and then..."

"Aren't you resting at all?"

"Keeping busy calms me down."

"Hmm, come to think of it, me too. At least these days."

"You're not going to end up like how you were last year?"

"I thought I'd grown up a little, but maybe I was wrong. Anyway, I have to take care of myself, or I'll worry everyone, won't I? Including you."

"Hee-hee, thanks."

"That's my line."

"So how was Haru?"

"Oh, right."

I told her about the day's events.

Even Yua was surprised that Haru had dragged Atomu along.

"That's our Haru."

"She has the crazy ideas."

"That's true, but she also knows you very well, Saku."

"Well, I really like baseball."

"Yeah, I know."

"Obon's about to end, huh?"

"Yeah."

"Only a little bit of summer left."

"Yeah, just a little bit more."

"Hey, what are you going to do with the last few days?"

"I'll come over and make dinner."

"I think you know this already, but you don't have to force yourself anymore."

" … "

"Yua?"

"Hmm, you don't need me anymore because you got encouragement from Nishino, Yuzuki, and Haru, huh?"

"Give me a break."

"Hee-hee, just kidding. But I'm still coming."

"…Okay. I'll be waiting."

"Okay!"

"Well, see you tomorrow."

"Yes, see you tomorrow."

"Good night, Yua."

"Saku…"

"Yeah?"

"I won't let go, so just be aware."

"Huh…?"

"Good night."

And then she hung up on me.

She won't let me go…

Those words echoed deep in my ears.

*

—*Ding-dong.*

It was the evening of Obon itself, and my doorbell was ringing again.

I, Yuuko Hiiragi, paused in the act of getting ready, checked the mirror just in case, and went down to the first floor.

Mom and Dad hadn't come home from work yet.

When I opened the front door…

"'Sup!" Kaito held up a convenience store bag. "I bought ice cream. You wanna eat it in the park?"

I chuckled. "How many ice creams have we had in the past week, Kaito?"

"What, you don't like ice cream?!"

"I like it, but I don't think it's the kind of thing you give a girl every time."

"Is that right?!"

Ever since the day Saku rejected me, Kaito had been coming around every day, except for the days when he was kept late at club games and practices and during Obon.

At first, we only exchanged a few words over the intercom.

But once I'd calmed down a little, I was able to talk to him a bit at the front door.

Even before Obon, I was finally able to go out to the park where I'd taken those detours and hung out with Saku before.

I couldn't face anyone, but Kaito would still call and message me on LINE.

Even if it was just over the intercom, he always came to see me.

When Mom was at home, she would always invite him in, and he would say, "Nah, it's cool."

Yuzuki, Haru, Kazuki, Kenta, and…

Well, I've been getting calls from everyone all this time. But I couldn't forgive myself for ruining the fun summer vacation.

And I felt so terrible for wrecking such precious friendships. And for hurting the person I love most.

Like a coward, I turned a blind eye to it all.

I don't know what to say, I don't know how to apologize, I don't even know if I can still call them friends.

That's why, even yesterday, I ran away...

I wonder why...

Kaito was the only one I could show my weaknesses and complain to.

Even if I showed him the most miserable side of myself, I felt like he would still accept me.

Even if I made excuses or lashed out at him, he would just laugh.

I felt like he would forgive me for everything.

The two of us walked into the park that was filled with so many memories and sat side by side on a bench.

When we first came here together, Kaito suggested the steps.

But that was where Saku and I always sat. So I found myself gently positing that the bench was a more normal place to sit.

Kaito was like "Oh, sure" and scratched his cheek, but he didn't seem to think anything of it.

I hated myself a little.

Somewhere in my heart, I was always chasing the traces of Saku.

Saku would say something like this.

Saku would do this.

If Saku were here, he...

Thinking back on the last year and a half...I was always around him.

When I arrived at school, I would run to him first, eat with him during lunch break, sometimes walk home with him after school, and force him out on dates during the weekends.

Those everyday moments were so precious.

I should have noticed, but I thought I knew everything.
When I lost him, the world turned black-and-white with astonishing ease.

Even when I wake up to clear summer skies...
Even when I open up the new makeup Mom bought for me...
Even when I spritz on my favorite perfume...
Even when I look at myself in the mirror...

—Nothing makes me feel much anymore.

Hey, Saku, it's nice weather, so why don't we go on a date?
Hey, Saku, how about this makeup?
Hey, Saku, don't I smell so good?
Hey, Saku, I'll do my best to be cuter.

Just imagining it was enough.
I was happy with that.

"Here, Yuuko."

I realized I'd been lost in thought as Kaito handed me my ice cream.
I tore open the package and bit into the first block of my chocolate *monaka* ice cream wafer.
"So cold..."
Lately, the meals Mom cooks don't taste good at all, but for some reason, the food that Kaito buys for me is always really sweet.
The crispy wafer, the snappy chocolate, and the nostalgic vanilla ice cream.
They're all such good friends, I thought sadly.

"You know," Kaito said quietly, "Kazuki and Kenta came to my place yesterday."

"Huh…?" I paused, looking over at him.

Kaito had already finished eating about half his ice cream.

"Then I got into a fight with Kazuki."

"Why?!" I yelped, and he laughed sheepishly.

"He asked how long I intended to act like a child… That pissed me off."

"What?"

"We were discussing Saku. He said I needed to cool off already."

"…"

I couldn't keep from reacting, and I jerked in my seat.

"In the end, I haven't been in touch with him since then. Kazuki asked how long I planned to continue sulking. He said he can't say that what Saku did was right, but he can say that what I did was definitely wrong."

Kaito scratched his cheek gloomily.

"'It's not his fault you're giving up,' he said."

Kaito let out a big sigh.

"…I know as well as anyone. I know that what I did wasn't fair to Saku…"

Why? I wanted to ask, but Kaito continued.

"What about you, Yuuko? Have you gotten in touch with everyone yet?"

"…Hmm. Mostly."

"Yuzuki, Haru, Kazuki, Kenta—they're all really worried. I've told them you're doing okay, though."

"Thank you, Kaito."

"It's fine. I can do that much, at least."

Since I didn't know what else to say, I took a bite of the ice cream.

When the two of us had finished eating, Kaito opened his mouth again.

"You know, you didn't do anything wrong, so there's no need for you to cut contact with your friends, right?"

I gripped the hem of my skirt tightly. "I did do something wrong. If I hadn't confessed my feelings in front of everyone, I would have been able to enjoy the rest of the summer vacation. I got ahead of myself and destroyed an important relationship."

"If that's the case, then I'm guilty of the same thing. Punching Saku just made the whole situation ten times worse."

"You were just angry because of me. Okay, you went a little bit too far. But I still think most of the blame lies with me."

"If that's really all there was to it, maybe I would've been able to clap back at Kazuki properly."

I didn't understand what he meant, and when I looked at him, I saw that he was smiling sadly.

He seemed to have his own complicated feelings about all this.

I can't go on letting everyone indulge me, can I?

I tried to lighten the mood.

"What a mess, and over nothing." I spoke in the most carefree voice I could summon. "I'm the only one who got my heart broken here."

I forced myself to laugh.

"Even if the second semester starts, and we can make up… It'll never be the same as it was. Everyone will know I was rejected by Saku. I can't go dashing up to him squealing his name anymore. I mean…there's another girl in his heart. And it's probably…"

"No, you're wrong." There was some anger in his voice.

"Huh…?"

"I don't think you're the only one, at least." Then he grinned. "Hey, do you remember what we talked about the other day on the way home from Lpa?"

"Er… Something about something that happened around the time of the entrance ceremony, right?"

"That's it."

I couldn't imagine what he was referring to. And he wouldn't elaborate, either.

"You know how the boys' uniform at our school has a tie?" Kaito pinched the collar of his T-shirt. "When I was in junior high school, we had that military-style uniform with the button collar. I had no idea how to tie a tie. I mean, I'm not the type to practice that stuff. I figured I could ask a parent."

He chuckled with a somewhat nostalgic look in his eyes.

"But I was so nervous that I couldn't sleep the night before, so I overslept and ran to school with my tie in my pocket."

I could imagine it, and I chuckled, too. "That's so like you, Kaito. You act all brash, but really, you're a complex guy."

"That's right! My hands are, like, shaking before every game," he said. "I didn't know anyone in the same class. I didn't even have time to get to know anyone, and it was already time for the entrance ceremony to start. I didn't have a choice, so I just knotted it around my neck and ran to the gym."

Little by little, my memory began to come back.

"Now, obviously, it looked completely skewed and terrible. Two long flapping bits. And you know, I'm a big guy, so people notice me, right? When I got in line, I could hear snickering. And some even pointed. I was like, *Wow, first day and I already made an ass of myself.*"

Oh yes, I remember that.

"And then, Yuuko, you…"

Kaito's eyes softened warmly.

*   *   *

"You were like, 'Hey! Don't laugh at him! He clearly hasn't had a chance to get used to tying a tie yet!' In front of everyone."

Finally, the memory of that day came back to me vividly.

"Then you were like, 'This is how you do it,' and you retied my tie for me."

"What? That brief moment before the entrance ceremony?! Yeah, you're so tall my arms got tired."

"After that," Kaito said, lowering his gaze shyly.

"And you told me you'd read over the rules in the student handbook because you wanted to be fashionable without breaking the dress code, and it didn't say you have to wear a tie all the time. 'You can just leave it off, you know?' you said."

"I did—I did say that! And you never wore the tie after that day."

Going through that memory had lifted my spirits a little. I was feeling some warmth and connection, too.
...After that, I started chatting with Saku—and Kazuki as well...

Back then, Kaito said so casually...

"I fell in love with you, Yuuko."

"What...?"

*　　*　　*

What did he just say?

"I'm a simple guy. You know, at first glance, you looked like an idol, like you were way out of my league. But you helped me out and covered for me the very first time we met, without worrying about what people watching would think. *This girl's amazing*— that's what I remember thinking."

Hold on a second, Kaito.

"So I thought I'd found the girl of my dreams. I started seizing any chance to talk to you. I introduced you to Saku and Kazuki, too, because I wanted to start out as friends."

What was he talking about…?

"Now that I think about it, I guess that was a mistake. See, at first, things between you and me were a bit distant—or maybe a little awkward. It was like I was trying to get you to join our group. We all got along well…but you got along well with everyone in class, Yuuko. So I figured it didn't mean much of anything to you."

All I could do now was listen.

"But then there was that day in homeroom—you know, when you and Saku butted heads? To be honest, I hadn't known Saku long, so it was like, whose side am I going to take? Well, Yuuko's. I guess our friend group's over."

Kaito gazed at the sky. "But…"

*   *   *

"After that day, you started calling him by his first name. You were so happy, laughing and everything. You never made that expression around anyone else."

But... That's...

"Ah, man. If only Saku really was an asshole. Then I could just punch him hard and feel better about things."

He was smiling, scratching his cheek...

"But he's a good guy. There was a time when I played basketball in the first year, and I was getting picked on pretty bad by a third-year team member. I was really depressed. After practice, Saku told me to make him eat his words with my abilities. And he helped me train. At some point, Kazuki came and joined in. We'd all had similar experiences to a greater or lesser extent, so they helped me out, too...

"Now that I think of it, we were just a trio of idiots," Kaito said, a faraway look in his eyes.

"There were a lot of other things, too. When Ucchi joined the group, when there was all that stuff with Kenta, Yuzuki, Haru. I thought, *As a guy, maybe I'm not good enough to go against him.* So once I realized you had feelings for him, I gave up. I accepted defeat."

"Kaito..."

"That's why, at the very least, I wanted him to be the one who made you happy. If that was how this was gonna end, I could accept it. Because there was a good, solid reason why I withdrew from the race. And then..."

He crinkled the empty ice cream wrapper.

"I didn't realize I was doing it, but I blamed what you were going through on Saku."

Kaito stood up and looked at me.
I still couldn't quite grasp what he was talking about.
I got up and faced Kaito.
His eyeline was a little higher than what I was used to with Saku.
Then Kaito smiled, as if a weight had been lifted.
As if he were saying good-bye...

"I like you, Yuuko. Would you...ever consider me?"

His face was so gentle.

"Kaito..."

Now that he'd said it outright...I finally understood.
...Kaito had feelings for me.
Why? He'd never shown any hint...
I mean, didn't he just say the other day that he was focusing on the basketball club right now?
Even when I was confiding in him, he said...

"If they were such a good friend, then I guess I'd take on the challenge, even if it meant coming between the two of them."

He said that... He encouraged me...
Maybe that was...

*   *   *

For me?

Because I said publicly that I like Saku?

Because he saw how conflicted I was?

Right...

Once I realized it, the time I spent with Kaito, the words he said to me, and the kindness he gave me all played in my head like a video on fast-forward.

It was painful, almost unbearable, and the guilt nearly crushed my chest.

How many times...?

How many times must I have talked about the boy I like in front of the one sitting here?

"What would Saku like?"

"I wonder if Saku's into this."

"Saku this, Saku that, if Saku were here..."

Each time, Kaito smiled and indulged me.

When I was conflicted, he worked through things with me.

When I was feeling down, he encouraged me wholeheartedly.

I'd been so cruel to him, all this time...

I had no idea... I had my head in the clouds...

If I put myself in his shoes for just a second, I could see how bad it must have been...

If it were me...

If Saku had talked to me endlessly about Yuzuki...

About Haru...
About Nishino...

I never could have just smiled and heard him out.
But Kaito...
Was he burying his feelings behind a smile this whole time?
Was he rooting for me?
Had he never had ulterior motives? Had he been looking out
for me after Saku rejected me?
Was he trying hard to comfort me?
This past week...Kaito never once took advantage of my
depression.
He just kept saying it would be okay, that this wasn't the end,
that there might still be a chance. He was so soothing.
What he said and what he did were totally different.
He didn't take on the challenge at all.
This guy... He was so kind and warm.
I was right about him.
If I became Kaito's girlfriend, I'd have no more worries. I'd be
able to spend every day laughing, telling him I love him from the
bottom of my heart.
What if I nodded right now?
At first, I'd be hesitant. I'd still need time to heal my broken
heart. But maybe Kaito could help me patch up my wounds,
little by little, until the pain was replaced with entirely happy
memories.
It might make me forget about Saku.
But no...in the end, no matter what...

With tears in my eyes...

"...I'm...I'm sorry, Kaito."

*   *   *

I gripped his T-shirt.

"If I can't have Saku, I don't want anyone."

Even though I knew I shouldn't, I instinctively buried my face in his broad chest.

"I'm sorry I forgot such an important moment for you. I'm sorry I didn't notice your feelings. I'm sorry I hurt you so much without knowing it."

I love you, Kaito; I really do love you.
You're always so silly, acting goofy and self-effacing... Sometimes, you're so manly, and as your name suggests, you've got a heart as big as the ocean.
I want to be in your life, always.
But...
There's a gap between my love for you and my love for Saku, and it can't be bridged.
No matter how long it takes, I'm sure my love for Kaito will never change into what I feel for Saku.
I'm so sorry.
Hands dangling by his sides, Kaito said...

"Yeah, I knew that!"

In his usual voice.

"Huh...?"

I lifted my head in confusion...

*　　*　　*

"But you know…"

He gave his usual winsome grin.

"Now we've both been rejected by someone we like. You're not the only one suffering now, Yuuko."

"Kaito… Kaito, you… Oh…!"

Then I cried hard against Kaito's chest.
It hurts. It hurts so bad!
Even though I do love him so much.
Even though he supports me so much.
Even though I want him to smile forever and ever.
Even though I just want him to be happy.
Someone, someone, please…

Oh. Oh, right.
This must be…exactly how Saku feels.

*

One evening, a few days after Obon…

—Ding-dong.

The doorbell rang briefly.
Yua said she couldn't come because she had something to do, so it had to be Nanase or Haru.
When I, Saku Chitose, opened the door…
"Hey."
"Um, evening…"

Kazuki and Kenta were standing there.

"You guys……"

For a moment, I had no idea how to react to this.

"Figured it was about time for a wellness check." Kazuki grinned. "Seems you really have been through it."

After glancing at my face, Kazuki took off his shoes with a practiced air.

"We brought McDonald's. Let's eat together."

"Oh, thanks." I called out to Kenta, who was fidgeting outside the door. "What are you doing, Kenta? Come in."

"Uh… I'm not really used to going over to guy friends' houses…"

"Please, stop being weird."

With that, he finally timidly took off his shoes.

Kazuki's been here many times, but I was just realizing this was Kenta's first visit.

He looked around the room curiously.

"I heard that you live here alone, but…I guess it's true, huh, King?"

"Yeah. So you can feel free to come around anytime you like, Kenta. Kazuki and Kai— Well, people usually swing by without even needing to call first."

I was hesitant to mention Kaito's name, but my omission was obvious—and obviously weird.

Kenta changed the subject, and I'm not sure whether he picked up on it.

"Hey, you don't have a TV or a computer, do you?"

"Oh, right. Kenta, are you a PC geek?"

"I wouldn't call myself a geek. There are geekier geeks. But I do dabble."

"I'm thinking about buying one, but when I get to the electronics store, I have no idea what to do."

"Ah, I think I can give advice at that level."

"Then maybe you'll come with me next time?"

After a bit of chitchat…

"Okay. Sit down, Saku." Kazuki, seated at the kitchen table, finished spreading out the food he'd bought.

"Oh, right." I sat down across from him.

Kenta sat down beside Kazuki.

"Okay, Saku, we got you a Big Mac set with grape soda. And I wasn't sure, so I got you a salad, too. We bought a big box of nuggets, so we can all share those."

Except for the salad, it was the exact order I always had.

Kazuki had a bacon lettuce burger set with fish on the side, and his drink was an iced coffee. The guy we weren't talking about always orders a Big Mac set with two extra cheeseburgers on the side and a Coke. And all three of us always get fries with loads of ketchup.

The three of us have been to McDonald's together so much… I have our orders memorized.

Kenta had a fried-chicken sandwich and a Coke.

We all bit into our burgers.

I glanced at Kazuki's face.

Kenta was probably along for the ride, but knowing Kazuki, he hadn't just dropped by to hang out.

"So…"

As expected, Kazuki cleared his throat.

"How have you been since that day?"

"What do you mean…?"

"You don't look like you've been in bed crying. Has Ucchi been here?"

I'd told him before that Yua usually comes to cook for me, so it's no surprise that her name came up.

"Yeah, a bit."

"Hmm. That's bold of you, after rejecting Yuuko." Kazuki's words were prickly.

Beside him, Kenta quivered.

I realized he was just sitting there holding his food. He'd only taken one bite.

Knowing Kazuki's personality, I found none of this surprising. "I have no intention of making excuses. I could have said no. But I let Yua indulge me."

"You don't have to justify it. You're not doing anything wrong."

"She said as much."

"Ucchi's the steadiest one of us all, isn't she?"

To be honest, I didn't really want to keep discussing this. But there was something else I really, *really* didn't want to discuss.

"So? Who else?" Kazuki looked me right in the eye.

Maybe he could sense it.

I didn't want to lie, but I was afraid to face up to him.

Either way, he wasn't someone I could expect to deceive with a half-assed lie.

"I went to my grandma's house with Nishino. And Haru brought Atomu over, and all three of us played baseball together."

"Who else?" Kazuki wasn't going to drop it.

"…Nanase came over and cooked dinner for me."

"…Huh?" Kenta dropped the nugget he was reaching for. "Uh, sorry."

Kazuki and I continued talking. "So what did she make you?" he asked.

"Katsudon. Not what you'd expect from her, huh?"

"Huh. I find that a little hard to imagine."

"Sorry."

"You've got no reason to apologize."

"Are you going to hit me, too?"

"I don't have the right to hit you." He gave a lonely sort of smile. "So what are you going to do?" He seemed to have regained his composure.

"You can't just keep going like this, right?"

"Well…"

I knew he was referring to my relationships with Yuuko and Kaito.

Ever since that day, I've been thinking about it, taking a step forward, coming to a dead end, and just repeating the same pattern endlessly.

Yua, Asuka, Nanase, Haru.

I feel like the clues are hidden in the words everyone has given me, but I can't seem to find them.

"What do you expect me to do?" I mumbled, and I realized I was crushing my burger in half.

"'I can't go out with you, but can I just ask you to go on being my friend as if nothing happened?' Is that what I should say to her?"

"Saku…" Kazuki paused, hand hovering over the fries.

"What should I say to Kaito? 'I'm sorry I couldn't make Yuuko happy, the way you wanted. Could you do me a favor and take care of her yourself?' Do you want me to say something like that?"

Kazuki sighed heavily. Cheek propped on his hand, he said, "Well, that won't work, will it? That kind of decision has to come from them. You can't just suggest it on your end."

"Right."

And this is where I always pause.

I have no choice in this, because I didn't accept Yuuko's feelings. Anything I did—trying to apologize or make up or act like it never happened—would just hurt the other person even more.

Dryly, Kazuki continued. "You have no choice. You have to wait for them to come to you."

"I know that."

"We went to see Kaito first, you know."

"…How is he?"

"Angry, to no one's surprise. We had a fight."

"Huh? Why?"

Kazuki shook his head slightly and said, "I dunno."

"I took out my anger and self-pity on him because I didn't make my move, either."

Kazuki narrowed his eyes sadly.

"And I'm not proud of my reaction."

"I see," I replied briefly.

At the time, he said something like, "*…I don't feel like covering for you, Saku.*"

I didn't need to ask for specifics.

If he had really drawn the line in the sand exactly as he'd claimed, he never would have spilled his true feelings in the hot spring.

Kazuki is probably still searching for a safe place for his feelings, in his own way.

When I was thinking about that…

"Excuse me!" Kenta piped up.

I smiled a little. "Sorry, Kenta, for getting you involved in all this…"

"No, I mean…"

Kenta stammered, grabbed a fry, and dipped it in ketchup. Then he stuffed it in his mouth, slurped his soda, and spoke again. "I have no idea what you two are talking about here!"

Then he looked down, as if ashamed of his outburst.

I tried to keep my voice soft. "What do you not understand?"

"…Any of it."

"Yeah, it's complicated," I said. "To put it simply, while she never asked me out in official terms, I've known Yuuko's feelings for me for a long time. In a roundabout way, I asked Kaito to take care of Yuuko on my behalf. On top of that, I got close with Yua, Nanase, Haru, and Nishino while things with Yuuko stayed ambiguous. And so now, I can't face either Yuuko or Kaito. Does that clear things up?"

Kenta kept his head down and said, "I still don't really get it." He repeated his position very clearly.

"I see. Well, anyway, it's my fault."

"No, I mean..."

Kenta clenched his fists tightly atop the table.

"...I said I don't understand!!!"

He got to his feet, knocking the chair away with a clatter.

"To me, it looks like both you and Mizushino are just giving up! You've got a couple educated guesses, and you're acting like that's an excuse! Can you please explain what I'm missing, here? You're so sure your hands are completely tied. You're sure you can't take the first step, because of how things went before. You can't do anything because of X, Y, and Z. Man! Just shut up!"

His shoulders shook with emotion.

"Or does someone like me not have the right to an opinion like that?"

""Kenta...""

Kazuki and I said at the same time.

*   *   *

"Okay, so some romance-related stuff has caused a rift in the friend group. I get that things are awkward right now. But why are you both talking like this is the end? You're acting like things are irreparably broken, as if they'll never be the same again…"

Kenta's voice was faint, strained.
I shook my head slowly as I responded.

"But they won't."

"You're *wrong*!"

BAM! Kenta hit the table.

"If that's the case, isn't it just the same as the superficial group I was in? No, you guys are different, right? You understand each other on a deeper level; you trust each other. That's why you can't act. Right?"

"…And I hurt someone who trusted me."

"So then *why*?!"

"Kenta, maybe someday you'll be able to tell someone you like how you feel. When that day comes, you'll understand."

"Bullshit! Hey, King. This is a loser-to-popular-kid story, right? And so telling you you're wrong when you're wrong just shows that I've grown, right?"

Just like when we first met, he was glaring right at me.

*　　*　　*

"It's true that you're the logical type, King. I'm the type who always gets bogged down in arguing, but you always make important decisions with your heart, don't you? That's one thing I've learned about you in our brief friendship so far. When you smashed my window, when you got mad at Starbucks, when you confronted that Yan High guy, when you played baseball again…"

Before I knew it, Kenta's eyes were filled with tears.

"King, what do you want to do? Do you really want to stay like this? Are you really happy to just let it end this way?"

I clenched my fists tightly, gritting out the words.

"If I could have my wish…then I'd want us all to be friends again…"

"In that case!"

Kenta hit the table once more.
His voice strained, throat sounding raw, as if he were attacking me with his whole soul…

"Try a little mutual understanding!!! You're the one who taught me that it's not about whether you can do it, it's about the will to try. Or are you really just that man-slut shithead?! Take a step forward; reach out to the moon!!!"

"…"

My breath caught in my throat.

He was echoing the things I'd said to him over the past few months…

Oh. Right.

The one who said those arrogant words…was me.

Kenta stared at the table.

"…I'm begging you, King. It just can't end like this."

I closed my eyes and slowly chewed on those words, then…

"Thank you, Kenta."

My earnest words for a friend who'd reminded me of something vitally important.

Our situation has been reversed, I thought.

The words struck such a chord because they were coming from a guy who had actually put them into practice.

What matters most is…what I *want* to do.

Like Kenta said.

I made eye contact with Kazuki, whose mouth was hanging open.

We stared at each other for a moment, then snorted with laughter.

"Huh? What?" Kenta looked at us with confusion.

Kazuki was still laughing as he said, "Kenta got one on us."

Shoulders shaking with mirth, I concurred. "Totally."

Kenta didn't seem to understand why we were laughing.

He stood still, as if stunned.

Well, of course he wouldn't immediately get it.

But it was seriously so funny, the two of us getting schooled by Kenta like this.

I gave Kenta a lopsided grin. "You've learned to speak your mind. Starting today, I shall call *you* King."

"P…please don't."

After that, we devoured the rest of the fast food, and then the three of us went out onto the balcony.

The sun setting behind the distant mountains felt strangely warm.

*

The next day, Yua came to cook dinner as usual.

Lately, she'd been a little unsettled, sometimes acting a little gloomy, a little childlike. But today, for the first time in a long while, she seemed somewhat refreshed.

When I told her about Kazuki and Kenta's visit…

"Hmm. Kenta, huh?" She smiled.

Come to think of it, when I went to extract Kenta from his room, I brought Yua with me before anyone else.

Maybe she was reminiscing about that time we spent talking to him through the door.

After dinner, we walked along the riverbed on the way to take Yua home.

"Saku, you wanna stop for a coffee?" Yua suggested. It sounded like this had been her plan all along.

We didn't even drink coffee after our dinner today, I realized.

At times like this, whenever one of us suggested coffee, it was customary for us to buy a takeout drink instead of going to a café.

We stopped at a nearby convenience store. Yua bought an iced *houjicha* latte, and I bought an iced latte, and then we settled down on the riverbed bank.

Together, we sipped our drinks.

"Summer vacation will be over soon," Yua said quietly.

Today was the twenty-third. There were eight days left in August.

I thought how ironic it was that after the summer study trip, the days felt so long, but looking back, it seemed to have gone in the blink of an eye.

"For me, summer vacation is already over." A self-deprecating response escaped me.

"Oh, there you go again."

"In the second half, all I did was sit around and have you take care of me, Yua."

"Oh, please. You loved it."

"And you got to indulge your maternal side, right?"

"Honestly, you're a lost cause. You don't have to force yourself like this, you know?" Yua rolled her eyes. "Hey, Saku?"

She peered into my eyes.

"What?"

"I have one request."

"That's unusual."

"Will you hear me out?"

Basically, Yua's requests are all really trivial things, like wanting me to accompany her on a grocery shopping trip or open the lid of a hard-to-open bottle.

But even then, she would politely explain the situation first.

So this was the first time she'd asked me to promise I'd do something for her without saying what it was yet.

"Okay." I shrugged.

She had to have a good reason.

We'd built a relationship of trust, enough that we didn't need to quibble over every little thing.

"Really?" Yua asked.

"If it's something I can do. If so, then I promise."

Yua gently held out her right pinkie finger. "Swear it."

"Do you want to go that far?"

"It's standard."

"I see."

I suddenly remembered the last pinkie promise I made—when Nanase was being stalked by those guys from Yan High.

Yua had gotten angry. "*You have to tell us what's going on,*" she'd said. "*Don't go acting the tough guy by yourself.*"

At that time, the three of us made a promise.

I was sure Yua hadn't forgotten it.

So this must mean she was trying to make an equally important request.

I gently looped my little finger around Yua's. "I swear: I'll do what you ask, Yua."

I had no reason not to.

Yua smiled and said:

"—Then will you go to the festival with me tomorrow?"

"…Huh?"

I wasn't expecting that at all.

"Huh? A festival?"

"Yeah."

"Why a festival again?"

"You promised you'd wear a *yukata* and go with me to a festival, right?"

"…The situation is a little different now, isn't it?"

"I'm sorry; that was a little mean."

Then Yua continued. "But when I saw that scene between you and Yuuko, and I heard you talk about Yuzuki, and Haru, and Nishino, I realized…I can't go on like this."

Her little finger tightened around mine.

"Hey, Saku."

Sweetly smiling…

"August twenty-fourth is like the Christmas Eve of summer. We might not be able to spend the real Christmas Eve together, so…"

*   *   *

She wasn't sounding like herself.

"Yua…"

"Heh…"

The knot between us slipped loose.

"I wanted to try an awkward date invitation just once, so I could be like you." Yua smiled, like she was sidestepping the issue. "Look, when we went to the fireworks with everyone, I was the only one who couldn't dress up. I was kinda sad about it. And besides, even though this was my summer vacation, too, I feel like all I did was housework and cooking for you the whole time. Before summer ends, I want to make at least one special memory."

It would be rude to mention Yuuko now.

But I couldn't forget the situation I was in, which was still unresolved.

If I brought it up here, it would be like questioning her. Like asking, "Don't you care about Yuuko?"

Are you saying that, even with everything going on, you still want to go out and have fun with me?

We never know what's going on inside another person.

But for the most part, this is all my fault to begin with, and I'm also the one who stole Yua's time.

If I couldn't indulge even one wish of hers…

And without her around, I might be doing a heck of a lot worse.

"Okay, let's go," I said.

Yua's face relaxed. "Okay!" She nodded with a big smile.

I'd talk to her again after the festival was over tomorrow.

For now, this was fine.

She should focus on herself more than on me.

On Yuuko more than on me.

I wanted her to put herself first.

And as for me...
I was going to have to get on with resolving all this.
Somewhere close by, a cicada chirped.
When I looked up, I saw a beautiful moon floating on the surface of the rippling river.
Like the night sky had been split in two.
I clasped my outstretched hands in something like a prayer.

CHAPTER 8
A Gentle Sky

I pulled on my *yukata* over my underslip.

The design was white peonies blooming on a violet background. I'd secretly bought it new, just for today.

After a little hesitation, I tied on the obi belt with flowers in the same shade of violet, in a windflower knot. I was putting my sentiments into the flower symbolism.

I, Yua Uchida, looked at myself in the mirror.

For some reason, a nostalgic image arose from my memory.

Maybe I look a little like Mom.

The thought made me smile.

I'm glad that moments like this give me more warmth than loneliness and sadness now, and in turn, it makes me think of Saku.

He seemed disappointed to see me wearing ordinary clothes last time, so he'd be sure to give me some exaggerated compliments this time around.

He would do that for anyone.

Because he was kind to everyone.

Lately, he'd been so depressed all the time. I hoped I'd be able to make him smile a little.

As the thoughts ran around and around my mind, I did my hair.

It's actually more efficient to do it before putting on the *yukata*, so I wonder why I left it for last?

I may have wanted this kind of contemplative time today.

Come to think of it, I thought, *it really is just like her...*

The hair that I'd started to grow out with such tender hopes was now quite long.

I ran my fingers through it, thinking about how this length symbolized the time we spent together and the memories I'd accumulated.

Various emotions swirled in my chest.

The night you discovered me, the days I spent with you, the feelings you taught me, the pain you made me realize.

And the feelings I've hidden from you all this time.

Picking up a *kanzashi* for my hair, I noticed a beautiful seashell on my desk. I slipped it into my purse as a good-luck charm.

Then I got dressed, went down to the first floor, and took my wooden geta out of the shoe closet.

Clonk. One of the clogs fell on its side and made a heavy, empty sort of sound.

When I reached out to right it again, my fingertips trembled slightly.

I put my hand on my chest and took a deep breath.

"It's okay."

I murmured those words again and slowly threaded my toes through the thong strap.

*

I, Saku Chitose, stood in front of the *torii* gate of the shrine that was a few minutes' walk from the Fukui prefectural office.

Yua and I planned to meet at five PM.

Even though it was late summer, the sun was still very much up.

Inside the shrine grounds, small children were running around clutching sticks of cotton candy and candy apples.

279

In the adjacent park, groups of middle and high school–aged couples were giggling together.

The festival should have happened much sooner than this, but I'd heard it was postponed this year.

It's nice, though, at the end of August, I thought.

—*Clonk, clonk, clonk.*

As I took in the sights and sounds around me, I heard the careful approach of wooden shoes.

"Thanks for waiting, Saku," Yua said shyly.

"How...how do I look?"

This was the first time I'd ever seen her wearing a *yukata*. She seemed to embody that term from another era, *yamato nade-shiko*: a traditional Japanese beauty.

Her hands, gently folded in front of her body, her graceful straight-backed posture, her toes that were pointed slightly inward. Graceful, modest, beautiful.

Like she'd been snipped out of a book of festival photographs.

But I didn't say any of that.

"I'd expect no less of you, Yua. You wear that very well."

I limited myself to a general evaluation.

Yua's eyelashes twitched, and then she grinned, as if she was covering for some other emotion.

Her little purse swayed on its cord, as if she'd gripped tighter with her hands.

Her fingertips were painted with an unusually pale violet shade of nail polish.

Her lips, brighter than usual, seemed to move cautiously.

"Thank you. I was worried because I'm not used to tying my own obi, but I'm very happy that you said that. I think I can relax and enjoy the festival now. Thank you."

*   *   *

It seemed to me that she was using a few more words than were necessary, and the double thank-yous alluded to something that Yua wasn't saying.

My chest was a little heavy, but it's fine like this.

I shook off the memory of Nanase's fake smile in the back of my mind.

"...Saku, you're wearing plain clothes...," Yua muttered quietly, as if she were talking to herself.

Looking down, I saw my own worn-out sports sandals, light denim jeans, and white T-shirt.

I chose this outfit on purpose.

I didn't want to make it a special day.

I didn't want to make an event of it.

"Then, I'll wear a yukata *next time, too, so let's go to the festival together, okay?"*

I'm sure, back then...

Yua hadn't said "both of us" when she was talking about dressing up.

Even though I understood, I pretended not to notice.

One of the *yukatas* I had was given to me by Yuuko.

After the day Nanase and I dressed up for the festival, Yuuko was salty about it.

So I fake-smiled and said:

"I never seem to be able to put it on right by myself."

It was just a line.

Yua smiled somewhat sadly.

"Well, next time I'll help you put it on again."

*　　*　　*

She spoke like I was a wayward puppy. "Let's go, Saku."

"...All right."

And so we headed out to the summer festival, just the two of us.

Clatter, clatter, clatter.
Clomp, clomp, clomp.

The narrow walkway made me feel uncomfortable.

I didn't think this through, did I? I scolded myself.

I agreed to come. I agreed to come with you. At the very least, I want you to enjoy it.

At this rate, I was going to ruin it.

"Yua, is there anything you want to eat?" I tried to force myself to be cheerful.

"Hmm, maybe something light for now."

"Yakitori or something?"

"Is that light to you, Saku?"

"Then, mini cake balls?"

"Those are for sharing. I'd rather save those for later."

"You're surprisingly detail-oriented, aren't you? Even at a festival, you've got it all preplanned, huh?"

"Hee-hee, sorry?"

"You know, Yua…"

"Ye-es, Saku?"

"If you're wearing a *yukata*, no one will notice if your belly sticks out a little."

"—That's a jugular squeeze. No backsies."

We finally found our normal rhythm.

In the end, we didn't touch the food and went for the shooting booth. I got a lot of the colorful plastic balls and bought a fox mask for Yua, who looked distinctly unimpressed.

When I put it on the side of her head, it actually looked really good on her.

We got thirsty and lined up at the stall to buy a drink, when...

"Saku, what time is it?" Yua asked, looking around.

I fished my phone out of my pocket. "It hasn't even been half an hour yet. It's almost seven thirty."

"I see; thank you."

It was still early evening, but the lights were starting to come on at the stalls.

The voices of the beer-swilling old men grew louder, and colorful *yukata* sleeves and hems fluttered in the air.

Dood dood doot.
Piyo piyo piyo.

Maybe I was imagining it, but the festival music playing throughout the shrine grounds seemed to be heating up, too.

When it was our turn, I grabbed a bottle of Ramune soda.

"What about you, Yua?"

"Hmm, I guess the same."

"Roger that."

When I picked up a second bottle, Yua pulled back her *yukata* sleeve, rummaged in the crate of ice, and pulled out one for herself.

"It's okay. Yua. Let me get you one. As a thanks for all the dinners."

"Okay, thanks."

"   "
...
"   "
...

"Um, aren't you going to put that one back?"

"It's okay; I'm still buying this one."

"Are you that thirsty?"

"Don't worry about it."

In the end, the two of us bought three bottles of Ramune between us and left the stall.

I was worried about her unexplainable behavior, so I looked over at her and cleared my throat.

But when I saw her side profile, I swallowed my words.

Why was she...?

Yua looped the elastic strap of the mask around her upper arm, gripped the Ramune bottle tightly with both hands, and stared up at the *torii* gate with a somewhat sad, prayerful gaze.

She moved toward the gate, her feet dragging in her clogs.

As if she didn't want to go that way, but she was being drawn there just the same...

I couldn't say anything.

One step, two steps, three steps.

Gradually, she closed the distance, and...

"Huh...?"

With a thud, I dropped the plastic bag I was carrying in my left hand.

Colorful plastic balls rolled across the stone pavement, and the red sunset cast soft tones all around.

One of the balls hit someone standing by the *torii* gate, and it came to a stop.

"Yuuko...?"

It felt like it had been years since I said that name aloud.

Without a doubt, it was Yuuko, hands gripping her skirt, eyes downcast, looking as if she might disappear in the blink of an eye.

Why was she here?

Just a coincidence? No. It couldn't be.
Ignoring my confusion, Yua stepped forward.

"You came, Yuuko."

Yuuko finally, slowly raised her head and looked back and forth between Yua and me.

"Saku… Ucchi…"

Her voice sounded like it was about to crack with tears.
The three of us stood in a perfect equilateral triangle.
The shadows stretching out from us made it look like we were all standing side by side.

"Saku's here. Yuuko's here. And so am I."

Yua stood tall and folded her hands in front of herself.

"Maybe there's still things we've left unsaid."

Clomp, clomp. She took Yuuko's hand.

"We've been hiding our feelings, both for ourselves and for others…"

Clomp, clomp, clomp. She took my hand, too.

"*…Holding on tightly to a connection with someone after it's been forged is a good thing.*"

"So…," Yua said, smiling softly, looking down at our connected hands.

*   *   *

"—Let's talk."

She squeezed my fingertips tight.

*

On the first day of Obon, I, Yua Uchida, lied to Saku when I said I had something to do at home.

I finished cleaning and doing the laundry while it was still light out.

Then, when the sun began to set, I headed alone to Yuuko's house.

Since that time when I chased after Saku, I hadn't contacted her even once.

It's not that Yuuko didn't respond. It was me. I avoided sending LINE messages or making any phone calls.

There were several reasons.

I was a little angry with Yuuko.

I was a little worried about what she might think of me, too.

I wouldn't have known what to say to her anyway.

…A not insignificant change had taken place in my heart, as well.

So I took some time—for Yuuko, for Saku, and for me.

I thought it would be better for everyone.

But amid all that thinking, I found myself at Yuuko's house.

I spotted Kotone, crouching on the front stoop.

It seemed like she'd been lighting a small welcoming spirit fire for the Obon festival, and soon the smoke was rising into the air.

I wouldn't have expected Kotone to follow that kind of ritual, I remember vaguely thinking.

I felt a tightening in my chest.

Yuuko and Kotone got along so well.

She'd probably told Kotone all about everything, about me.

Would Kotone be angry with me? Or sad, disappointed, or...?

Last autumn, after I became friends with Yuuko, I came to hang out here loads of times. Each time, Kotone welcomed me with exuberant warmth.

She gave me cookies and juice, cooked me meals, and drove me to the store to go shopping.

When I told her about my family situation, she cried and hugged me like a real mother. *"You did a great job after your mom left. You've been doing so well. Come visit me anytime."*

I put my hand on my chest and took a slow, deep breath.

Then I approached the front walk and hesitated, trying to decide what greeting was best for this time of day. Eventually, I said...

"Good evening."

I called out to Kotone's back, beyond the gate.

The look on her face as she slowly turned to see who was behind her... She seemed a little tired.

"Ucchi?!"

As soon as she recognized who had called out to her, her face suddenly lit up.

She hurriedly stood up and opened the gate with a clatter.

"Well, I was wondering when you'd be by!"

She hugged me tightly. Her elegant perfume tickled my nose.

"Um, well..." I wasn't sure what to say.

"I'm sorry, Ucchi. My girl caused a real mess," she murmured softly behind my ear.

"Oh, no, if anything, I'm the one who made Yuuko—"

"No, no." Cutting me off, Kotone let me go and took a step back. "I heard the whole story. Of course, Yuuko's been doing some soul-searching. But it sounds like she was the one who started it and hurt you and Chitose, too. Please, forgive her," Kotone said, bowing her head. Before I could say anything, she continued. "But you know, as Yuuko's mom, I was happy that she spoke up about her feelings. So I'm sorry, too. I'm sorry for the burdens that got placed on you both as a result."

She bowed deeply, once again.

"Wait a minute. I'll go call Yuuko."

As I watched her disappear behind the door, I smiled a little.

It was a completely different reaction than I'd expected, but one that seemed to fit Kotone perfectly.

After all, she was Yuuko's mom.

In the end, Yuuko wouldn't even talk to me through the door that day.

Kotone apologized over and over again and tried to sugarcoat things.

She doesn't want to talk to me. She doesn't even want to look at me.

…No, knowing Yuuko…she can't.

I think that's what it is.

In this past year, I've spent as much time with Yuuko as I have with Saku.

At first, I felt like she was doing me a kindness by getting to know me and being my friend. But at some point…

Yuuko became the first truly good friend I'd ever really had.

So I could kind of tell how she was feeling.

I was sure that tomorrow Yuuko would feel sorry. Then she would come around and decide to talk to me.

…Right?

I thought I was prepared for the first-ever rejection from my best friend, but it still brought a prickling pain and anxiety that I was sure would swallow me if I let my guard down.

Will I really be able to talk to you tomorrow? Will you call my name again, or am I just totally kidding myself?

I held in my weak inner whining as best I could.

It's okay.

I told Kotone that I would be back tomorrow and turned away from the front door.

Wow, I guess I didn't need to go to all the trouble of making up a cover story to explain why I would have been late.

I could have gone to make him dinner, after all.

*

The evening of the following day.

When I rang the doorbell on the front gate…

"*Ucchi…,*" Yuuko answered the intercom, just as I'd hoped.

"Evening."

I breathed a sigh of relief, and then there was a period of silence. I waited, no rush, until Yuuko finally spoke again.

"*Sorry about yesterday. But I'm still…*"

"No, it's okay. Do you want to talk over the intercom today?"

"*…Would that be…okay?*"

"If it's easier like this for you, Yuuko, I don't mind at all."

As I spoke, I felt a sense of nostalgia.

"Hee-hee. You know, Yuuko, you're a bit like Yamazaki now."

"*Hey!*" Yuuko yelped. After a moment of embarrassment, she said, "*Ucchi, you're angry, aren't you…?*"

There was a plaintive tone to her voice.

"Yeah, I am," I replied bluntly.

"…"

I could hear her holding her breath even through the intercom.

Without going into further details, I asked her a question of my own.

"What about you, Yuuko? Are you mad at me for chasing Saku?"

"*I'm not…angry. Just a little sad, I guess? No, that's not right. I guess 'I'm sorry' is the closest to how I feel.*"

"I see."

"Ucchi, I think—"

"You know, Yuuko," I interrupted. "We've talked about a lot together, haven't we?"

"Yeah."

"Fashion, beauty, club stuff, homework, the past, the future, everyone we know, and Saku."

Yuuko laughed briefly. *"The last one—I feel like I was the only one doing any talking."*

I continued with a small smile. "Do you remember how that happened?"

Yuuko thought for a moment before responding. *"I guess it started after we went to Hachiban's together for the first time?"*

"No, that may have been the catalyst for us becoming friends in the first place, but not for our current close friendship."

"Current…?"

"We're best friends. Can I say that?"

"If you still feel that way, Ucchi…then, of course you can!"

Her voice cracked a little at the end.

Her words reassured me… But at the same time, I wanted to bite my lip and apologize.

"The real catalyst," I said, suppressing the tremble in my voice…

"…was that day."

I looked away from the camera; Yuuko was probably watching me.

"…Because we shared our weaknesses with each other."

But I was still facing her head-on.

* * *

"Huh...?"

"That's right, Yuuko."

"What...?"

"Did you think you were the one holding on to a huge secret all by yourself?"

"I mean..."

"You and I are the same."

I leaned against the wall to avoid the camera's gaze.

I was glad we were doing this over the intercom. Right now, I couldn't stand to have anyone see my expression.

"I'm going home today. I'll come again tomorrow."

"Okay."

"But that will be the last time."

"Huh...?"

"See you then, Yuuko."

Without waiting for an answer, I walked away.

It was getting dark all of a sudden.

I wondered if Saku had a real dinner tonight.

*

The evening of the last day of Obon.

When I visited Yuuko's house, I found Kotone lighting a bonfire.

The crackling smell of burning wood reminded me of a distant summer day.

Noticing me, Kotone gave me a small smile and nodded, then went into the house without saying anything.

When I rang the intercom, Yuuko appeared right away, as if she'd been waiting impatiently.

"Ucchi?!"

"Evening."

"*After what you said yesterday, and then you left so suddenly, I was worried...*"

"I told you I'd come again today." I smiled a little and continued. "Hey, Yuuko, how long do you plan on keeping this up?"

"*Keeping what up...?*"

"You're just gonna run away from Saku and the rest of us?"

"*What...what gives you the right to question me? I was trying to face Saku head-on, you know? And after how that turned out, how can you blame me? I don't even know how to face him! It isn't my fault!*"

"Did you really face Saku head-on?"

I knew my best friend was hurt, but I still spoke my mind.

"*What do you mean...?*"

"At least, it didn't seem that way to me."

"*That's horrible! Why are you saying this?!*"

"Do you really have no regrets?"

"*...*"

"Is it okay with you if it just ends like this?"

"*You've been weird since yesterday, Ucchi. You're not being very nice.*"

"Yeah, I'm aware of that."

"*I'm sorry, I want you to go home today.*"

"You still won't let me see you?"

"*I'm sorry, I'm sorry...*"

"Then... Koff...sniff..."

Drip, drip, drip.
Patter, patter, patter.

"Wait, Ucchi, what was that?"

Oh right. Yuuko wasn't watching the monitor.

Well, I was also standing off camera so she couldn't see me.

I parted my soaked bangs as I responded. "Um, it's been raining a little for a while now."

With that one word, the conversation suddenly stopped, and the front door was flung open.

"Ucchi?!" And Yuuko finally showed me her face.

"Long time no see."

She smiled. "It's a little embarrassing for you to see me dressed like this."

The rain that suddenly started to fall intensified in an instant, and before I knew it, I was completely soaked.

Yuuko's face twisted up, as if she was about to cry.

"You dummy! Why didn't you tell me sooner?! You're gonna get sick!"

She'd rushed out in her pajamas.

"I'm sorry; I was in the middle of an important conversation."

"Don't give me that!" She grabbed my hand and yanked me inside the front hall.

"Hey, Mom! Bring me some bath towels!" she called.

Kotone popped up from farther back in the hall.

"Oh, that was all your fault, Yuuko! Sorry, Ucchi!"

"Not the time, Mom!"

"All right, I'll bring you a towel, so wrap her up and take her straight to the bathroom. The bath is already filled."

I panicked and waved my hand in front of my face.

"Y-you don't have to go that far…"

Kotone laughed and sighed at me. "A towel's not going to do much good when you're soaked through. Yuuko, hop to it."

"All righty! I'll prepare a change of clothes and new underwear for you."

"Wait a minute… Whoa!"

In the end, the two of them dragged me into the bathroom.

★

After I took a quick shower, Yuuko called out to me from the dressing room.

"Ucchi, I'll put a change of clothes here."

"Okay, thank you. I'm sorry for all the trouble."

"No... I'm the one who's sorry." Through the frosted glass, I saw Yuuko plop onto a chair, then she timidly continued. "We were in the middle of a conversation, weren't we?"

I put my arms on the edge of the bathtub and rested my chin on them. "Hee-hee. I got into the house, and yet we're still talking through a door."

"Ah-ha-ha, that's true." After laughing awkwardly, Yuuko muttered. "What did you mean by '*the end*'? You said that yesterday."

I could hear her anxiety without even seeing her.

"I mean cutting off the relationship entirely."

"...No, I don't want that!"

Despite how bad I felt, Yuuko's fervor made me burst out laughing.

She must have been thinking about the significance of what I said for a while.

That was by design, but maybe I had been a little too mean.

"Wait a minute, Yuuko. Will you hear me out?"

"Ucchi, you were talking about cutting off the relationship..."

"No, let me finish. I meant to say, 'but not like how it sounds.'"

"I don't get it."

"You jumped the gun."

"I never know how to respond when people say that..."

"Well, it's mostly been you who's been hiding, Yuuko."

"You're saying mean things again."

I submerged myself up to my shoulders in the bathtub again.

The hot water was slightly pink with the bath salts that Kotone put in.

The scent was sweet and floral and sort of calming.

I made a water gun with my hands and tried to shoot a little arc, but the hot water just splashed in my face.

"Yuuko..." I rested my head on the side of the bath and gazed at the ceiling. "Today will be the last time I come to talk to you like this."

"Huh...?"

"That's what I mean by cutting off this current relationship."

"So you don't want to be around me anymore?"

"Hmm, it's not like that."

I scooped up hot water in my palm and let it splash away.

After doing that several times, I got out of the bathtub and stood in front of the door.

"That was my plan if you kept this up, Yuuko—if you isolated yourself and decided never to talk."

Yuuko also stood up on the other side of the frosted glass, as if she'd sensed my presence.

I put my hand on the door softly.

"—I'm going to be with Saku after this."

I spoke clearly.

"U...Ucchi?"

Yuuko put her hand against mine on the other side of the door.

"Everyone says you're the endgame girl—but if you stepped aside, it would be fine if I moved up, right?"

"Wait a minute, you mean...?"

"At the festival. On August twenty-fourth. At five thirty PM."

I gave her the name of the shrine where we would meet.

*   *   *

"Will you come, if you feel like having a conversation between the three of us? If you don't show…that's fine. I'll be there on a date with Saku instead."

"…"

I heard the door bang shut as Yuuko left the dressing room.

I took a deep breath and opened the bathroom door.

I dried myself with the bath towel and put on the clean underwear and dress that Yuuko had laid out for me.

Oh, I remember this dress.

"It's not really me, so how about I give it to you, Ucchi?" That's what Yuuko said. And she sent me a pic of it.

I placed my hand on my chest for a moment.

After that, I quickly dried my hair and thanked Kotone before leaving the house.

Apparently, Yuuko was up in her room again.

"I'll be waiting for you, Yuuko," I muttered, looking up at the window from the front step. Then I left.

I won't be long…Saku.

*

—Back to today.

Yuuko came to the festival.

I believed it would all be just fine.

But a part of me was worried.

If we missed this twilight chance, we'd never be able to return to our original relationships.

I just knew it somehow.

When I saw Yuuko standing behind the *torii* gate, I had a sudden urge to hug her and start crying, but I managed to hold back.

*　　*　　*

"So let's talk."

Right. That's what I said.

The hands through which we connected were warm, and my heart swelled a little.

In a row together, we started walking. Saku, Yuuko, and me.

The two of them seemed a little confused, but they came along without saying anything.

The festival venue was a little too lively for us to talk about something this important there.

We went to the Yokokan Garden, which was about five minutes on foot from the shrine.

We paid the entrance fee and went inside.

This place used to be the seat of the Matsudaira clan, the feudal lords of Fukui.

I don't know much about it, but the facade of the mansion is in the style of a traditional Japanese teahouse. The architecture of that era is very beautiful, and it looks stunning when it's lit up at night.

On a non-festival day, it's usually pretty quiet.

I was thinking of moving to the nearby park if there were too many other people there, but when I looked around, it seemed like we were the only ones.

There was still plenty of time until it closed, so we'd have a good chance to have a calm discussion.

It's been a long time since I've been here, and I wished I could take my time and look around, but instead we went around the promenade and sat on the mansion's long veranda.

It was Saku, me, and then Yuuko.

The setting sun spilled across the glossy green garden in front of us and the surface of the pond beyond it.

The cool breeze that came through the mansion brought the calming scent of wood and tatami mats.

"Well, where shall we begin?" I asked, and I felt the shoulders on both sides of me twitch.

Sitting so close together, I could sense how they were feeling. After a short silence, Saku spoke first.

"Well, to start off… What exactly should we talk about?"

I smiled a little and then answered.

"I think there's several things. Saku, don't you have anything you want to ask Yuuko?"

"…"

There was no response, so I continued.

"Well, I do."

I looked at each of them.

"—For example, why did you confess your feelings to Saku, Yuuko?"

I'd been waiting to ask that one.

"…"

Both of them inhaled sharply.

"I mean…" Saku's voice was strained. "Isn't it obvious?"

"So then, Yuuko wanted to be your girlfriend… That's why?"

"Right."

"Is that really true, though?" I asked.

"…What do you mean?" He looked slightly angry, as if he thought I was making light of Yuuko's feelings.

No, no, that's not it.

I shook my head mentally, then continued. "Saku, didn't you have any doubts when she confessed?"

After thinking a little about my question, Saku spoke.

"…Honestly, I wondered, *Why now?* It was right after the summer study trip was over. I may just be unobservant, but I felt like it wasn't really the right situation for a big confession…"

"For sure," I said. "I don't have any experience with that kind of thing myself, but normally when a close friend confesses their feelings to you, it's a gradual process, isn't it? But I guess Yuuko's made no secret of the fact that she likes you. So maybe this could have been an exception."

Saku looked down sadly, no doubt reliving the past.

Yuuko tugged the sleeve of my *yukata*.

I put my hand gently over hers and kept talking.

"That's all that stood out to you?"

"…Yeah, I guess."

"I think there was more about the situation that seemed unnatural."

"Unnatural how?"

Yuuko's fingers closed over my wrist. Like she was begging me not to say anything.

I'm sorry, but…if I don't do this, we'll stay stuck where we are.

I looked straight ahead.

"—I wonder why Yuuko chose that occasion to confess at all."

Saku seemed surprised.

"I mean, we'd just made some long-lasting memories together."

As I spoke, I narrowed my eyes, fumbling through my memory. I think Saku had noticed this odd discrepancy, too.

I held Yuuko's hand tightly.

"No, what I mean is: Why'd she specifically do it in front of everyone?"

*   *   *

"…"

I didn't wait for a reply.

"I mean, it goes without saying, if you're going to confess, it's usually when you're alone, right? It can be in the form of a phone call or a LINE chat. I mean, if you're both friends, you both want something more, and you both know it, one person has to break the stalemate and confess. But that's not what this was. If Yuuko did get turned down, it would put everyone's friendships at risk, including her friendship with Saku. I think Yuuko knew that it would have a big impact, right? But suppose her dream came true instead. What if Yuzuki, Haru, and I also like you, Saku? Wouldn't it be a bit cruel to do it in front of us? We all know Yuuko causes people to run around after her without meaning to, but I can't see any way that she wouldn't have been aware of that possibility… We're friends, so I'd know."

Yuuko had my hand pressed against her forehead, and I ran my free hand over her hair.

"And more than all that…"

I continued, enunciating my words.

"…Yuuko, did you ever have even the slightest hope that your confession might go well?"

Saku looked confused by that.

"Ucchi…"

*   *   *

Yuuko had tears in her eyes.

I took out a handkerchief from my purse and mopped her eyes.

"Maybe it has something to do with that day?"

Yuuko looked down and tightly gripped her skirt across her knees.

"Can you tell us?"

"I can't…I can't tell you that…"

"It's okay. I'm here with you, okay?"

I patted my best friend on the back as she trembled slightly.

*

I, Yuuko Hiiragi…am a sneaky bitch.

What sparked my interest in Ucchi was that day, in homeroom.

My actions put her on the spot, so I went to apologize again to her the next day.

At first, that was all I was going to do, but it was kind of funny how the calm and quiet Ucchi was so combative with Saku.

I wondered if maybe she hid part of herself, the way I had. I wanted to know more, so I found extra opportunities to talk to her.

Ucchi was always so polite.

She chose her words carefully, trying to make sure she didn't offend anyone.

She was like that during the homeroom incident, too. I tend to speak without thinking, so this was fresh and intriguing. As we talked, she had a calming effect on me. And I even started to feel a little lonely.

I'd always felt like there was a transparent wall around me that led to me getting special treatment from the other kids at school. But Ucchi seemed to have surrounded herself with a transparent wall of her own making, one designed to keep people out.

It seemed to me that she was holding back something, and that her airtight room was suffocating her.

But for some reason, she was never that way with Saku, right from the beginning.

She showed irritation. And her words seemed designed to sting.

When they talked, Ucchi seemed to breathe a little easier.

I guess, in a way, she reminded me a little of how I'd been until I met Saku.

I kept trying to get to know her better. Then the second semester came.

I decided to invite Ucchi to grab ramen.

I wanted to get to know her better, of course, but also…I thought Saku could be the one to break down Ucchi's glass walls.

So…

When Ucchi panicked and ran out of the ramen restaurant…

"Saku, go after Ucchi! We'll take care of the tab!"

I completely meant it, too.

…And then the next day came.

Ucchi called me Yuuko for the first time.

She was different. Her entire aspect had softened and grown warm. And instead of the awkward smile she'd always worn, this new smile of hers bloomed bright as a dandelion.

Wow. Even Ucchi can smile like that, I thought.

I was glad I left it to Saku after all.
She needed him… Just like I'd needed him, that one time.

"Honestly, Yuuko, Yua, what a fuss to make over using first names."

"You stay out of this, Saku."

Huh? Saku…?
It was just a minor change.
She'd changed how she referred to *us*. Both of us.
Ucchi's tone was friendly toward those she'd opened her heart to; the distance between us was so much closer than it had been only a day ago.
Nothing strange really.
Saku had recently started calling me by my first name, too.
I invited her to grab ramen, thinking it would be nice if this happened someday.
I sent Saku after her, thinking he would be able to help her.
So this is fine. It's what I wanted to happen, right?
So then, why?
Even as we all welcomed Ucchi together, it felt like something was stuck in my throat, making it hard to breathe.

After a week of quiet inner confusion, lunch break came around.
Our group, which now included Ucchi, got our desks together and opened up our lunches.
"Hey! Saku! Where'd you get that homemade bento?!" Kaito yelped.
"Keep your voice down." Saku laughed and rolled his eyes.
"It's the same as Ucchi's!"

"Well, you know how it is."

"No? How *is* it?!"

Ucchi and Saku have the same bento...?

Wait a minute.

What does that mean?

Saku frowned and looked at Ucchi next to him.

Ucchi shrugged very slightly, as if saying "It's okay."

Like a secret form of telepathy that only the two of them could understand.

"You know," Ucchi said, "My parents got divorced when I was in elementary school, and my mom left. So I basically do all the housework, including the cooking. And Saku lives alone, right? So I just gave him some of our leftovers 'cause I made too much."

"What? Wow, Saku! Nice! What about me, Ucchi?" Asano asked her.

"You always bring a big lunch, don't you? You don't need more."

"Nooooo!!!"

I didn't know what to do as the exchange unfolded in front of me.

I just didn't get it.

Was Saku eating a homemade bento from Ucchi?

No, more importantly...

Just like Saku, Ucchi's family is also divorced. And her mom's gone. They understood each other's pain and sorrow more than anyone else ever could.

They had a special connection I could never understand.

My heart was prickling.

This was unfair.

That horrible word suddenly sprang into my mind, and I was horrified.

…What…am I doing?

That's the first thing that comes to my mind when I hear about the awful stuff that happened with Ucchi's family?

I'm such a bitch.

Even if it was only for a moment, I couldn't help but think of my new friend's extremely painful past as convenient, a tool to shorten the distance between the boy I like and me.

Even just imagining my own mother away…was an unbearable thought.

Trying to distract myself, I shoved a mouthful of food into my mouth. It was a hamburg steak, with half ketchup and half Worcestershire sauce.

Mom's not really good at cooking, but she always wakes up early every day and makes me a bento. Usually from leftovers or the frozen section.

But today…the food tasted like cardboard, and I couldn't swallow it.

Even though I knew I shouldn't, I couldn't stop these terrible thoughts.

What happened after Saku chased after Ucchi?

What does Saku think of Ucchi, and what does Ucchi think of Saku?

Why were they getting along so well when they just became friends?

Why did they walk into school together that day?

And it was the first time I'd ever seen Ucchi wearing a wrinkled shirt…

What should I do?

—Ucchi's going to steal the lead out from under me.

Even though I fell in love with him first.

Even though I'd been by his side longer.
Even though I invited Ucchi to Hachiban's.
Even though I was the one who asked Saku to go after Ucchi.

It was the first time in my life that I'd felt like this.
I've always gotten along well with both boys and girls.
When someone fell in love, I cheered them on, and when couples got together, I congratulated them from the bottom of my heart.
But now I...

—I'm not the only girl who likes Saku—or who Saku might like back.

I came to realize that really obvious fact.
Plenty of girls had liked him since school started.
He never told me about it, but I know from the rumor mill that several girls had confessed to him.
Fundamentally, though, Saku tried to keep his distance from them, and the only ones he's on really good terms with are Yuzuki and Haru on the basketball team.
But even with them, it's just casual chitchat in the halls.
I'm the only girl who was always by Saku's side. Was I wrong in thinking I was special?
I assumed I was the only one who was really in love with Saku.
At the very least, I was the only girl who watches over and understands Saku the most.
I was naive.
And that was a big mistake.
Right under my nose, the distance between Saku and Ucchi was closing.
Maybe they'd already become closer than he and I were.
Maybe I can be Saku's girlfriend someday..., I'd thought. God, I was delusional.

That hope of mine could end anytime... If not today, maybe tomorrow.

After all, Saku had rescued Ucchi the way he'd saved me—there was no guarantee she wouldn't fall in love with Saku the same way, too.

There was no guarantee Ucchi wouldn't confess her feelings right away.

When lunch break was over...

"Ucchi, do you have some time after school?" I asked, and I wasn't totally sure why.

"Yeah! We don't have club today, so it's okay."

My heart ached hearing how light and happy Ucchi's voice was.

I didn't know love until I met Saku.

Jealousy and envy were growing in my heart—I couldn't resist it, but I couldn't acknowledge it, either.

After school, I borrowed the key from Saku and Ucchi, and I headed up to the roof.

I lied to the person I liked, saying I just wanted to show it to Ucchi once.

"I didn't know we could get up here." Ucchi looked around by the railing, breathing in the fresh air.

I stood beside her. "Actually, we need to get permission to come up here. Although Saku got a key from Kura, so he comes and goes whenever he wants."

"Ah-ha-ha. Yeah, sounds about right," Ucchi said. "Come to think of it, Mr. Iwanami told me once that Saku and I are similar."

"D-did he, now?"

"Although, I'm not sure he knows what he's talking about. We're not similar at all."

Gazing at the distant sky, her hair fluttering, her eyes narrowed with love.

Oh, I knew it.

Just by looking at her profile, I could tell.

When Ucchi said Saku's name…she felt the same way I did.

But maybe now…

"Listen!" I said, surprising myself.

Ucchi's eyebrows rose.

"It may be rude to ask this so suddenly, but…can I ask you something important?"

"What?"

I nodded once. "I want to get along better with you, so I want to make this clear first."

"Yeah, I understand."

Ucchi turned to me and stood up straight. She held her folded hands in front of her elegantly, and I was a little distracted by the sight of them for a second.

"Well, um…"

I took a deep breath.

"Ucchi, do you have a crush on anyone right now? Because I have a crush on Saku!"

Before I knew it, I'd said something I shouldn't have.

Actually, I was just going to ask if there was someone she liked.

I was going to hold back.

But I exposed my own feelings…

"Huh…?" Ucchi's eyes widened in surprise, and… "Um, uh…"

She looked around, then squeezed her eyes shut.

A small crease formed between her brows, and she pressed her lips together.

Her fingers were now splayed, tightly grasping the folds of her skirt.

She opened her mouth briefly to speak, then closed it again.

After repeating that several times, she put her right hand on her chest, closed her eyes, and took several deep breaths.

The next time Ucchi looked at me, she smiled just like when we first met.

"I don't have a crush on anyone."

She was very clear and direct.
Her eyes were colored with gentleness.
"Ah...," I mumbled.
This isn't right. I shouldn't do this.
I should take it all back and apologize...

...Crick.

Just then, the roof door opened, and...

"Hey, I was thinking of going home soon, just so you know."

With his hands in his pockets, Saku came ambling over.
It's okay. I still have time.
I'm sorry, Ucchi. Forget what I said. Let's discuss this again tomorrow.
I tightened my fists and looked at the blue sky...

"You know, Saku..."

I said.

"Hmm?"

He yawned and looked at me, and I said...

*   *   *

"...I like you."

Before I knew it, my lips formed the shape of a faint smile.
At the edge of my vision, Ucchi's shoulders twitched.

"Oh, right. You're my one true love, et cetera."

He'd taken it as a joke.

"No!"

I took one step, two steps closer.

"In a romantic way! Like, a boy-girl way! I want to be your girl-friend! I like you *that* much!"

I made sure he could see the sincerity in my eyes, so he couldn't dismiss it.
But...

"...What's this all about?"

The moment I saw the sadness on his face, I knew.
I could see right through to that beating heart.
Oh, that's right.

"Yuuko, I'm..."

So I...

"Wait a minute! You don't have to answer now!"

*   *   *

I forced my words and my feelings into a different shape.

"Huh…?"

I forged ahead, before he could say anything one way or another.

"I just wanted you to know that I think about you that way, Saku. But I don't need an answer until I confess properly someday. I want to stay friends, like we were before. Is that okay…?"

For a moment, Saku just looked dumbfounded, like Ucchi did a moment ago.
Then slowly…

"…I understand. If this isn't a real confession, then there's no way I can turn you down, either way. For now, I'll just accept your feelings."

"Okay! Then the three of us should walk home together!!!"

I'm a sneaky bitch.
Even though I tried to be friends with Ucchi myself, even though I convinced Saku to go after Ucchi and help her, even though I'm happy that we finally became friends, even though I'm convinced that Ucchi likes Saku…
I'm still doing this.
And I was still basking in that sweet afterglow.
Saku didn't reject me.
He said he would accept my feelings.
Sneaky, cunning, horrible, selfish.

And yet…
There was a smile on my face.
And yet…
My heart was crying.

*

—About a year had gone by since then.
Yua and I just silently listened to Yuuko talk.
It was so painful.
It was obvious how bad she felt as she spoke. It sounded like she was about to cry.
I kept trying to make her stop, over and over. I told her it's okay, you don't have to do this.
Of course I remembered the incident on the roof, but it was the first time I'd heard about the exchange between the two of them, or about the secret feelings behind her open declaration of love.
Oh, right.
Yuuko and me, Yuuko and Yua, and the trio of all of us… Our friendship had lasted until this summer vacation, and I feel like it had really begun on that day.

"Guh… Ngh…"

Yuuko let out a sob, but she never stopped talking.
She seemed to deeply regret what she'd done.

"I'm sorry, I'm sorry, I'm sorry; I'm so, so sorry, Saku."

As she listened, Yua continued to rub her best friend's back, occasionally wiping her tears away with a handkerchief.
But those acts of kindness seemed to hurt Yuuko even more.

*　　*　　*

"I'm sorry, I'm sorry, I'm sorry..."

Yuuko just kept apologizing over and over, like a scolded child.

"I don't deserve to say that you betrayed me as a friend... Or that I'm his endgame girl... I don't have the right to try keeping others away... And yet..."

I wanted to tell her that she was wrong. *It doesn't matter how it started*, I could say. *The time we spent together was real.*
But I couldn't say such shallow words of comfort.
Yuuko continued, her expression pained.

"Honestly...I should have expressed it earlier; I should have apologized... That's what I kept thinking. But I was scared."

Yuuko grasped Yua's *yukata*.

"Because if I talked about it, it would all be over. I'm in the wrong, I know. I've been deceiving you both this whole time, and I knew I shouldn't, but I still..."

She sucked in a breath, her voice cracking as she spoke...

"I didn't want either of you to hate me!"

Her shout was like a strangled prayer.
"Gack, ack," she coughed.
Her shoulders heaved as she fought for air.
Watching her cling to Yua was breaking my heart.

*   *   *

"I thought I was prepared, but...I didn't want that. It doesn't matter if we're not friends anymore. It doesn't matter if I can't be your girlfriend. All I care about is just being around you. So please...don't hate me..."

What should I say?
What could I say to make her feel better?
What could I do...?
As I stood there, at a total loss...

"It's okay."

Yua spoke, stroking Yuuko's hair.

"I told you, right? We both shared our weaknesses that day."

"Ucchiii..."

"So let me ask again," she continued.

"Yuuko, did you ever have even the slightest hope that your confession might go well?"

Why? I wondered.
Why was Yua...?
Why was she still hung up on that?
Ever so gently, she was driving Yuuko into a corner.

"I knew..."

I realized Yuuko's hands were shaking.
She was fighting for breath and wiping away her tears.

*   *   *

—*Thump.*

She got to her feet, as if squaring up against Yua.

She glared back and forth between us, her eyes filled with a mix of sadness and anger…

"I knew it wouldn't!!!"

Yuuko yelled at the top of her lungs.

"I've been watching Saku this whole time, ever since the day I fell in love with him! Every day I fell asleep thinking about Saku, and when I woke up, I'd be thinking about him, too! I know better than anyone that I could never be special to Saku that way—not yet!!!"

"Huh…?"

That was something I never expected to hear, and I asked exactly what I was thinking.

"Then why…?"

Yuuko gripped her skirt tightly and looked down.

"You might not believe me, but…"

Slowly, she began to speak.

"It's true that I kept thinking that, one day, I'd have to correct the mistake I made. But the relationship between the three of us, the time we spend together, made me so happy. I wasn't paying attention. I started to think…it would be fine to stay like this forever."

She narrowed her eyes, as if reminiscing. "But…," she continued.

"In the second year, we all became friends with Yuzuki and Haru. Yuzuki had that stalker… And then there was the stuff with Haru and baseball and basketball… And they got closer to you, Saku, just like Ucchi did… By the time I realized it, we weren't that well-balanced triangle anymore."

She twisted her fingers in front of her, like she was making excuses.

"To tell the truth…it made me nervous when I saw the announcement of the class change in second year. And when Yuzuki and Haru immediately started talking to us in the classroom. Our group was Saku, Ucchi, Kaito, Kazuki, and me. I didn't think we needed anyone else. I knew that both Yuzuki and Haru got along with Saku. That's why I joked around that Saku and I were endgame, and Ucchi was the sidepiece—so I could keep them in their place. I really am a bitch."

The tears that had started to dry were flowing down her cheeks again.

"Ugh, those two… It would have been so much better if they were as bad as me."

Yuuko smiled forlornly.

Her glistening eyes were red with the cast of the setting sun, a light that seemed both ephemeral and fleeting.

Before I could reach out my hand, Yua stood up and gently put her arm around Yuuko.

Yuuko continued with tears in her eyes.

"At first, I thought Yuzuki might become my archnemesis. She made a move on Saku right away, almost like she was try-ing to provoke me. It was only temporary—and necessary—but still. She was playing the role I'd dreamed about—being Saku's girlfriend. So she and I butted heads a bit. But I've never met another girl who can talk so much about fashion and beauty stuff. We promised to go shopping together in Kanazawa. She's cool but occasionally stubborn, and it's hard not to love how she tries her best for the people she cares about. I really, really like Yuzuki."

She chuckled, tears slipping into her open mouth, and I heard her swallow hard.

"And Haru—you know, I thought she was really cool from the beginning. She has something she's thrown her whole life into, and she fights toward that goal. It's like how Saku was when he was still playing baseball, I thought. So it made sense that Haru was the one who made you deal with the baseball stuff. Okay, so she sucks at fashion, makeup, and girly things. But she tries her best at those, too, for the person she cares about. And how could I refuse to help her with that stuff when she came to me so ear-nestly? I really, really like Haru, too."

Her voice was trembling.

Hiccupping, she sniffed hard.

The expression on her face was one she would normally never show anyone.

*   *   *

"You know, Saku...I was watching."

Yuuko looked down, a little apologetically.

"On the day of the fireworks festival, when I went looking for you. I saw Yuzuki holding the sleeve of your *yukata* while you watched the fireworks together."

"—Listen, that was..."

But Yuuko cut me off.

"I asked everyone, at night, during the summer study trip... 'Does anyone have a crush on someone now? Because I have a crush on Saku!' I used the exact same words I said to Ucchi that day."

Her expression twisted, as if she'd lost all control of it.

"But no one... No one was ready to be honest. Not Yuzuki, not Haru, and not Ucchi, either. Of course, I don't know for sure if everyone likes you, too, Saku. Maybe they just didn't feel like telling *me*. But...but you know...!"

She clenched her fists atop her knees, as if she was trying to hold herself together.

"Yuzuki was so happy watching the fireworks with you... there's no way she doesn't have deep feelings! And Haru—there's no way a girl would cheer that passionately at your baseball game and not secretly wish for something!

* * *

"And again," Yuuko muttered.

"Again, I got in the way of people I thought were precious friends. It's my fault. I act all ditzy and stick to you like glue and talk about how I like you—I wasn't your girlfriend, but I sure acted like it. Some girls are nice and keep their feelings to themselves for the sake of other people. And some girls can't really face their own feelings for people. Ever since I was little, all I wanted was to have friends who were dear to my heart and a person I loved."

Wait a minute, so that means...

"So I thought I had to bring this situation to some kind of conclusion. That day on the roof, I was the first to do something unfair. I really didn't want to confess like that! But—but—but..."

She pressed her lips together, then forced them apart.

"I knew that if nothing changed...Ucchi and Yuzuki and Haru..."

She clutched her chest, as if she were in physical pain.

"And Saku, who I loved the most... I knew that as long as I was in the way, that you were too nice to let me get hurt. You'd try not to see sadness on my face. I hesitated to take the first step because I was lying to myself. Because I'd lose the chance to tell the people I love how much they meant to me. That's why!!!"

With both eyes brimming full of tears, she looked right at me.

*　　*　　*

"I wanted the guy who was special to me…to find the one who was special to him!!!"

She shouted the words with all her heart and fell to her knees, like a puppet whose strings had been cut.

"Yuuko!"
"Yuuko!"
Yua crouched next to her, and I quickly followed suit.
Yuuko was breathing heavily from all the crying and talking.
Yua slowly rubbed her back.

"I'm sorry, Yuuko. That was painful, wasn't it? It must have hurt so much. Thank you for talking to us about it."

I bit my lip as I listened.
I was sick and tired of my own stupidity.
I didn't pick up on any of this, even though Yuuko was always right by my side.
I should have known what kind of girl she is.
I couldn't believe it. This whole time…

—Her love confession wasn't about starting something new. It was about bringing something to an end.

Only now did I understand what Yua was trying to get at.
I found my mouth moving before I could put my thoughts in order.
"So the reason you deliberately chose to do it in front of everyone…"
Yuuko, who had calmed down a little, giggled a bit.

"Like I said, Saku, you're kind. If I confessed to you when we were alone, I was sure you'd just pretend it didn't happen. You'd

keep it a secret from the others, and we'd go on as before. That wouldn't have worked. I had to end it for real, in front of everyone. I had to make sure everyone knew it was over."

"…You're silly, Yuuko."

Her trembling hand reached out and touched my cheek.

"I caused trouble for you, Saku. But you're my hero. I knew this wouldn't be enough to break you."

Tears like glass beads spilled down her cheeks; her eyes were scrunched up, like a letter that would never be sent.
I held her hand tightly.
Leaning on my shoulder, Yuuko slowly stood up.
She was carrying such a weight with that delicate frame.
Yua and Yuuko sat back down on the porch.
Yuuko looked embarrassed as she spoke. "So that's my story."
Yua nodded softly. "Yeah." Still next to Yuuko, she looked at me. "And now it's Saku's turn."
She met my eyes.
I wasn't surprised by what she said.
Yuuko had laid her heart bare.
I wasn't just here to watch and listen.
So then, what?
When I said nothing, Yua spoke for me.
"Do you want me to give you a prompt?"
Her face didn't change at all when she said…

"—Saku, why did you choose those specific words when you rejected Yuuko?"

I never imagined she'd hit on that, too.

* * *

"…Yua…"

Beside her, Yuuko tilted her head.
"What do you mean, Ucchi?"
Glancing at me, Yua responded.

"He said, 'There's another girl in my heart.'"

Yuuko lowered her head and winced, no doubt reliving it.
"I think it's obvious… Saku likes someone else."
"Nope." Yua shook her head emphatically. "If that's true, I think he would have clearly said, 'There's another girl I like.' Knowing Saku put it that way at a time like that… It's uncharacteristically vague."
Yuuko's eyes widened. "Yes, but in that case…"
"Right, so now…" Yua looked at me again. "I'm asking Saku."
I stood in front of them, bowed my head, and clenched my fists tightly.

"…Sorry. I can't talk about that."

It was a secret I planned to keep for the rest of my life.
Because it's too pathetic.
Because it's too selfish.
Because I'm too arrogant.
Because it's unbeautiful.
Because it's not Saku Chitose.
And…because I can't do that to Yuuko.

"I can't tell you."

I'm sorry, Yuko.

I'm sorry, Yua.
I'm sorry to all of you.

—That was when something started shouting at me from the depths of my memory.

The words Kenta said…

"Try a little mutual understanding!!!"

The words Nanase said…

"—So, Chitose, don't go dying on the wrong hills, okay?"

The words Haru said…

"—We're all important as friends, girls and guys."

—Oh, I see.
I fumbled for the house key I'd stuck in my pocket.
I traced my fingers over the leather key chain Yuuko and I bought, the ones that match.
Like puzzle pieces coming together, everyone's faces came to mind. Click. Click. Click.
My amazing friends had already taught me something important.
Kaito got all hotheaded for the sake of the girl he likes.
Even cool-guy Kazuki struggles with the part of himself that isn't so cool.
Even innocent-princess Yuuko faced her own weaknesses and shook us out of a tough stalemate.

"So let's talk."

*　　*　　*

I wondered how much Yua knew.

After looking at their faces, I closed my eyes briefly, and…

"…That day, one year ago…"

Nervously, I began to speak.

"Yuuko, when you confessed to me on the rooftop, the first thing that came to my mind was *Again?* and *Please, give me a break.*"

Yuuko flinched.

"I'm sorry. Up until high school, so many girls I thought were my friends confessed to me, and when I said no, they weren't my friends anymore. I got sick of it. I started to get annoyed by stuff like that."

And in my first year, I was still trying to measure my distance with others much more carefully than I do now. I wasn't even completely open with my friends.

"But at the same time, I loved hanging out with everyone… Yuuko, Kazuki, Kaito, and then Yua, too. I really mean it—you were all so special to me. It wasn't love, but I definitely wanted to be with you, Yuuko, always."

If it's someone you don't care about, you can just say sorry and that's that.

Which was why I was so lost at the time.

"So when you told me that you didn't need a response, I really held on to that. Of course, I enjoyed having a pretty girl like you be into me, Yuuko. So I thought if I maintained the status quo, we could all go on being friends the same way, for a little longer."

I bit my lip, then continued.

"If I really thought about your feelings, Yuuko, then I should have given you a clear no. I knew this ambiguous relationship couldn't go on forever, but the more time we spent together, the more comfortable I became with it. I was dragging my heels. That's why…"

I laughed, as though I was ridiculing myself.

"If you call yourself sneaky, Yuuko, well, that makes two of us."

While I was talking, Yuuko took a step forward.

"Honestly, I know how stupid and lame this sounds." I lifted my head and looked at their faces again. "But will you...let me say one thing?"

Yuuko and Yua nodded without saying anything.

Embarrassed, I forced myself not to shake.

"—You *are* there, Yuuko. In my heart."

I had never said that to anyone before.

"Huh...?"

Yuuko opened her eyes wide in surprise.

I slowly shook my head and continued.

"When you confessed to me on the roof... To me, you were a close friend, nothing more and nothing less. But it's been about a year since then, and...well, really it's been ever since I started school here. You were always by my side, Yuuko. I figured you'd get bored eventually and leave me. But you didn't. You didn't get anywhere close to that. The more time passed, the more you believed in me, relied on me, and treated me like a hero. Well, to be honest, I might have felt a little pressured at the same time."

"Saku, I..."

I held up a hand, smiling wryly as Yuuko was about to get up.

"I didn't know what you liked about me. The Saku you seemed to be seeing was far better than the reality. You had to be dreaming up tons of illusions about me. When you confessed to me in the classroom, those feelings became even stronger. I had no idea it was triggered by something I forgot I'd even said. I thought, *Isn't that just love at first sight?* ...But that wasn't it at all. You were always close by, watching me, so you had high expectations of me. 'Saku can do anything,' you said. I had to be a stubborn show-off so I wouldn't disappoint you. I'm sure that's what I was thinking. That's how...you always showed me a brand-new perspective, Yuuko."

Since Yuuko and I had been separated, I'd become aware of my own feelings for the first time.
I had to tell her, from the heart.

"I didn't recognize it at first, but you've become someone incredibly important to me, Yuuko."

Then, before my spilled emotions caused a misunderstanding...

"However!"

I heard the tension in my voice.
I had to keep myself from running away.
I had to stop myself from doing my usual thing and making a joke of it.
After biting the inside of my trembling lip until it bled...

"...But there is another girl in my heart."

I said the worst thing I could say all in a rush.
My vision went blurry; my knees went weak.
Ha-ha. I'm so lame.
Who knew talking to a girl could be this scary?

*   *   *

"Hey, Saku, that's…"

Yuuko seemed to be groping for words.

"I hope I'm not being an idiot and misunderstanding, but…"

But I didn't think we should continue this line of thought.
With a thud, I slammed my clenched fist into my thigh.
Yuuko had laid everything bare.
She confronted me with the things I didn't want to see and taught me things that I didn't want to know.
So I had to do the same.

"I think very highly of you as a girl, Yuuko. But there's another girl I think of just as highly. And there's more than two…"

I had to dredge the utmost sincerity out of my dishonest heart.

"Each one has given me things I could never replace."

Someone who was like family. Someone who was my mirror. Someone who challenged me. Someone I looked up to.

"You've grown so used to being loved, but you don't know how to love, do you?"

It's just like Asuka said.

I only learned how to dodge.
Love from others always came with an expiration date. And when it arrived, those feelings would get crumpled up and thrown into the trash like junk mail. If the sender wasn't home,

you could easily deliver it to some other address. Like ticking off names on a list.

When I turned them down, they'd move on immediately to the next person.

But now, for the first time…

—I was thinking about love.

Among the colorful lines of locked mailboxes, only one letter can be mailed.

Once the sender's been decided, that letter can't be withdrawn.

Before I knew it, tears were dripping from the corners of my eyes.

My lips were trembling.

I sniffed briefly.

That's why I—I…

"I don't know which feeling goes with romantic love."

Choosing just one was too terrifying for words.

There was a loud silence.

I'd exposed myself and laid bare the shameful things in my heart, in front of people who mattered so much to me.

I was an indecisive and pathetic guy, who never wanted to be truly known by anyone.

Yuuko slowly got to her feet in confusion.

"If that's true… If you're being honest… If this is how you really feel… Then I'll wait for your answer forever if that's what it takes."

*   *   *

"But I *can't*!"

My voice rose with frustration, and Yuuko flinched again.
But I couldn't stop. It was like a dam burst.

"What the hell do you want me to say? 'I like you, Yuuko,
but there are other girls I'm interested in, so please wait until I
decide'? 'I'm in the middle of choosing right now, so please stand
in line and wait your turn'?"

I clenched my teeth, summoning what shreds of dignity I had left.

"I never want to be the kind of guy who forces others to bear
the burden of these feelings, even if they are awful."

Because that's not the Saku Chitose Yuuko fell for. That's not
her hero.

"But at least, we could put this aside until later, and…"

I shook my head slightly.

"I think that's what got us here, wouldn't you say?"

"…"

That was everything I had to say.
Right now, I couldn't give Yuuko an answer.
On the other hand, this kind of distorted relationship could
only go on so long.
That's why this twilit moment was the end of it.

* * *

As we both stared at the ground…

"—That sounds fine to me, though?"

Yua suddenly stood up.

""Huh…?""

Yuuko and I were both confused.
Yua brushed her bangs aside with her little finger before continuing.

"Yuuko is still in love with Saku. Saku is still searching for what love means to him. What's wrong with that?"

"But… It's not honest…"
"—Saku."

Yua interrupted me briskly.

"Why are you the only one who gets to choose?"

"I don't…"

What?

"Just like you have the right to choose, Yuuko, Yuzuki, Haru, and of course I have the right, too. We have the right to choose our own love."

She took a step closer.

*   *   *

"You're free to think the same, too, Saku. But you have no right to judge the sincerity or dishonesty of our loves based on your own values."

There was a snippiness to her speech that reminded me of when we first met.

"We can postpone the response, or keep being vague—but as long as there's a possibility, I think a love like that still has merit."

Her tone softened a little, but she was no less passionate.

"I don't think there's anything wrong in asking you to wait until you've worked through your feelings properly."

I ruminated on those words: the right to choose our love.

"You see, Saku, you don't need to bear the responsibility for someone's else's love. And neither does Yuuko."

Yua continued admonishingly.

"Remember when I said, 'If you're apologizing to me in this situation... I think you'd better think carefully about what that means'?"

"...Of course."

It stuck like a thorn in my mind, and I hadn't been able to remove it.

"Then can I ask you now? Why would you need to apologize to me for hanging out with Nishino?"

"I mean, the moment you stopped coming to my house, I went out with someone else..."

"Hmm," she said. There was a lot going on behind her eyes. "You thought I would feel bad when I heard that, right?"

"Huh…?"

"In other words, you were subconsciously thinking I might be jealous?"

I inhaled. "I don't…"

"Isn't that a bit arrogant, Saku?" Yua seemed to be rebuking me.

Of course I didn't mean it like that.

…Or at least, I didn't think about it that way.

It wasn't about hanging out with a girl or a guy. But the moment Yua stopped coming to support me, I immediately went out with someone else. I just meant that…I felt wrong about it.

But now that I think about it, what if it had been Kazuki or Kenta? I wouldn't have bothered to apologize to Yua.

I hadn't realized it before. Is that the implication of my apology?

No, maybe I myself was unconsciously saying it in that sense.

What an arrogant thing to say. No wonder Yua was annoyed.

Softening a little, Yua sighed. "Well, I was joking around and then got angry, so I think we can kinda blame it on the mood of the conversation. Either way," she continued. "Suppose you do something that makes some girl jealous or sad… So what? Is there any reason why you should have to walk on eggshells?"

Earnestly, she approached her conclusion.

"I said it before, but if you're boyfriend and girlfriend, I think it's a different story. You don't have to feel responsible for the feelings of some girl you're not even dating. It's on the person who caught feelings to bear that burden."

"Yua…"

She closed her eyes for a second, then…

"No matter who the other person might be, you always have the freedom not to choose that love."

*   *   *

She lowered her voice.

"...If they don't want to be hurt, they can just go ahead and choose another love."

I suddenly remembered the last day of the summer study trip.

Even though I'm not even in love yet, I was miserably jealous in the middle of that barbecue.

Was Nanase in the wrong, for spending time with Kazuki and not considering my feelings?

Was it Nanase's fault for happily talking about Kazuki in front of me?

Should Nanase be responsible for my jealousy?

—Of course not.

"Let me rephrase," Yua continued. "Yuuko was miserable after you rejected her. At the same time, I came to your place, Saku. Yuzuki came, too, and so did Haru. Was that underhanded of us?"

"No! You were all just trying to cheer me up."

Yua didn't respond to that and changed the subject of the conversation. "Yuuko, you didn't meet with anyone until I came to your house, right?"

Yuuko shook her head, looking down. "...Kaito came to my house every day after that to comfort me."

Yua looked at me again. "Hey, Saku. Was Yuuko being underhanded? She was getting comforted by another boy right after the big rejection, right?"

"No way, not at all. It's normal to rely on friends when you need them."

Actually, I'd felt hugely relieved when I heard Kaito was look-ing after Yuuko.

"For the most part, I was the one who declined Yuuko's feel-ings. After that, no matter what Yuuko did or who with, I have no reason to blame her— Wait."

Suddenly, I feel a sense of déjà vu about my own words.

Yua tilted her head slightly and smiled gently.

"Yeah, I think so, too. And I feel exactly the same toward you, Saku."

That sounded familiar, of course.

"But you turned Yuuko down quite clearly, in front of me and everyone else. So there's no need for you to feel any type of way about what you do with anyone going forward, right?"

Yua had said that right at the beginning.

Why? I wondered.

Why did I feel like it was my fault?

I could have shouldered my pain alone, obsessed over it, refused to spend time with any other girl after turning Yuuko down. I could have rejected the kindness from Yua, by all the others, then cursed and blamed myself forever.

Would I have wanted the same for Yuuko? No.

I would have wanted someone to be by her side. I would have wanted someone to hear her out and comfort her, if she could be comforted after all that. *Forget about me, just please...please feel better. As soon as possible.*

...Yes, that's what I wanted for her.

Is the only difference that one confessed feelings and the other rejected them?

But even if the roles were reversed...

I think... No, I know I'd still blame myself and not want Yuuko to feel hurt.

As if she'd been waiting for the right moment, Yua continued.

"So it's the same this time around, right? You chose that answer based your guilt toward Yuuko, right?"

"In a nutshell, I think so..."

"In the end, it seems to me that you're trying to take responsibility for other people's loves. If Yuuko is also in your heart, you shouldn't really want to give her a definitive answer right here and now, don't you think? You should consider it a little more and really work through your feelings. And if so, then isn't it fine to carry on like this?"

"But..."

"Yuuko's the one in love, so she should get to decide for herself whether that's right."

Yua stepped closer.

Then she gently put her hand on my chest.

"I think both of us, Yuuko and I...we don't want you to be the only one grinning and bearing the hard stuff or making sacrifices on our account."

Tightly grasping my T-shirt...

"Saku, you're the one who said we should become friends who can fill in each other's missing puzzle pieces, like a real family, right? You were the one who made me realize how frustrating it is not being able to speak your mind, and how disappointing it is to feel like others can't rely on you. Right?"

She looked up sadly.

"If you truly do care about us, let us carry our own burdens."

She gently took my hand and held it in front of her chest.

"You too, Yuuko."

She held out her free hand to Yuuko, then placed it on top of mine.
Our three hands overlapped—Yua on the bottom, then me, then Yuuko.
Yua gently closed her eyes and spoke.

"You don't have to end your love for the sake of someone else. Don't worry about the girls around you. If you love someone, just say so. That's not weakness; it's strength."

"But, Ucchi…"

"It takes a lot of courage to tell someone you love them. Especially if they're a good friend. Keeping it secret is safer; you can stay friends as normal."

I could feel Yuuko's hand twitch on top of mine.
Yua slowly opened her eyes and continued.

"—But we're the ones choosing not to speak up, in that case. So there's no need for Yuuko to shoulder any of that burden."

                    *   *   *

In some way, it sounded like she was speaking to herself.

"Ever since that day, I've been watching you both. Saku is willing to sacrifice himself for someone else. And, Yuuko, you only think about people you find more important than yourself."

The hand beneath mine was warm.

"It's not good for two people like that to misunderstand each other this way, especially not when they're both trying so hard to be considerate."

"Yua…"
"Ucchi…"

"We grew up in different environments, and our values and personalities are completely different. We know that, and we still came together anyway. I think everyone should be able to find love the way they want, even if it means inconveniencing others or being sneaky for their own benefit."

That's…

"You know you taught me that, right, Saku?"

She wore a slightly mischievous expression.
"So," Yua continued.

"There may be times in the future where someone gets hurt, or someone else hurts you. But if you still want to be together, then what I think is…"

*   *   *

She put her other hand on top and gently pressed our hands between hers.

It was like she was testing the strength of where we were joined.

"—Let's hold hands and go forward together."

She was, like her name suggests, a gentle, enveloping sky.

"And then, one day, we'll all decide to face up to our own feelings of love."

Yeah… I see it now, how closely Yua watched us all.

The back of my nose suddenly stung, and I felt myself squeezing our layered hands.

Can I lean on this kindness and warmth?

Is it okay if I go looking for it?

I wondered if I'd missed something else.

Had I been wrong this whole time?

Then…

"—Wait just a second!!!"

Yuuko yelped, as if this ending wasn't good enough for her. Dropping our layered hands, Yua jumped in surprise.

"What about *you*, Ucchi?! What about *your* feelings?!"

"Huh…?"

—Drip.

*   *   *

A single teardrop ran down Yua's cheek.

*

Why was I crying?

I, Yua Uchida, gently touched my cheek. My fingertips came away cool and wet, and when I held them up in front of me, the setting sun made them sparkle.

I never used to wear nail polish because it made me too self-conscious.

I chose violet to match my *yukata*.

I had to practice applying it over several days because I was so afraid of screwing it up.

It came out really well. Good.

"Um, uh... Ha-ha."

My lips made an artificial smile.

You once scolded me for that, saying it's become a habit.

But I guess it might be a little useful at times like this.

It's funny; I thought I'd decided not to cry until the end.

The other two were looking at me in concern.

...*Oh, Saku. Why'd you have to wear plain clothes?*

Not really the right moment for that thought, but never mind.

I set our meeting for half an hour earlier than the time I told Yuuko.

I did it by instinct.

Back at the fireworks display, he'd looked sort of disappointed when he realized I wasn't wearing a *yukata*.

When we promised to go to the festival together...he looked so happy.

So there was a part of me that hoped...

*   *   *

"Ah…"

Even though I still hadn't heard their responses yet.
Even though I knew I needed to make this stop.
My tears just kept on flowing.

"Ucchi!"

Yuuko jumped up and hugged me tightly.
I've missed this scent, this warmth.
It's been a long time.

"It's okay to take it slow. But I want you to talk, okay? This time, for sure!"

She patted me softly on the back, just like I'd been doing to her minutes before.

"We haven't heard how you feel yet, Ucchi."

Right. Yuuko noticed.
I've been vague about some of these things this whole time and avoiding them…and I'd kept the other two as the focus of the conversation.
Yuuko always notices…

"…That day… I mean…on the roof."

I slowly started to speak, encouraged by the warmth of my best friend.

"I lied, too."

*   *   *

I could sense Yuuko's surprise in her body language, but she didn't stop rubbing my back.

"The day before I started calling you by your first name, the day you invited me to dinner—Saku saved me. He broke down the glass walls I'd used to keep people out for years. He freed me."

Her arm tightened around me.

"He brought color back to my memories of my mother and helped me look forward again, instead of down. And I made a decision then—he would be as important to me as a member of my own family. If I ever have to make a choice one day…Saku will be the one I think of first."

I tasted salty tears on my lips.

"But on the rooftop, Yuuko, you asked me if there was anyone I liked… I didn't understand. Whatever was growing in my heart was so new. Was it first love, or was it gratitude for a friend? I'd never been in love. I didn't have any close friends. That's why I…I used you and Saku as an excuse."

I hiccupped, and my breath caught.

"I'm sure Saku would be a great match for someone like you, Yuuko. I have nothing going for me; I don't stand a chance. Even if I told you my honest feelings, it would only cause trouble. I told myself not to make waves—to stand back and watch you two get together. It's the happiest ending I can hope for. It's enough, for me to step back and support him when he needs it. I'm happy just to be by his side…"

*   *   *

To be honest, at the time, I was so happy.

I took the hand of the boy I was supposed to hate.

His hand was strong, kind, warm.

I had a feeling it would take me to places I'd never seen before.

That night, I ended up sleeping over.

He said I was the first.

Even though he's so popular with girls.

Even though he's always joking around.

—I became the first girl.

I think, ever since I changed my glasses to contacts, I was always conscious of what Saku saw when he looked at me.

Which do you like?

What do you think?

What would you say?

You. Saku.

How crazy, that I gradually became attracted to a boy I used to hate.

It felt like I had become some shoujo manga cliché, and it kinda made me laugh.

So that day.

I still remember how I felt when Yuuko told me that she liked Saku.

It was like being plunged into a bucket of cold water.

It was like the whole past week was a lie.

I woke up from my dream.

I felt like I was separating from my body.

—I was embarrassed.

I was mortified.

*   *   *

I'd gotten the wrong idea.

Who did I think I was, working myself up when I was just one of his classmates? Saku's a nice guy, so he spread that kindness to everyone.

It was crazy for me to go thinking I was special.

But I should have known that from the beginning.

Yuuko was always around Saku.

I didn't even have a seat at that table.

I just happened to sit there for a moment on a whim.

But it couldn't be helped.

Until now, I've wanted to keep those feelings away.

And Yuuko...ever since the entrance ceremony, she kept trying to talk to me, when all I could do was fake a smile.

She was the one who created the opportunity for me to open up to Saku.

She found the real him much earlier than I did. And she spent much more time with him.

There was no room for me to intrude.

So for Yuuko's sake...I decided to accept my fate as just another one of Saku's friends.

And for Saku's sake...I wanted to avoid causing any more trouble.

It's better like this. This is fine.

"I pushed my weaknesses off on you two..."

Yuuko's shoulder, where my chin rested, was stained with tears.

*   *   *

"I'm sneaky and terrible, too."

I sighed, about to lean back, when...

"You're wrong!"

The hands that had been holding me suddenly pushed me away.
I staggered and almost lost my balance.
I managed to stay on my feet and look at Yuuko.
Her eyes flashed as her fists shook.

"You made a choice, Ucchi!"

I'd never been on the receiving end of her anger before...

"Yuuko...?"

Come to think of it, we never had a fight.
We were always just smiling and talking nonsense together, never getting in too deep with each other.

"In that moment, Ucchi, you ignored me and chased after Saku."

Yuuko was practically shouting.

"You ditched me for him! A boy who clearly meant more to you than your best friend! You *did* pick who mattered most! And yet here you are talking as if you showed such amazing restraint!!!"

* * *

"No…"

I grasped the hand that held on to my sleeve, wiped away my tears, and opened my mouth.

"Because I had to go after him then."

I bit my trembling lip for a second.

"I thought everything was about to be destroyed! Everything was about to come crashing down!!!"

I yelled, too.

"When my mother left, I couldn't do anything. Before I knew it, everything was over, and my family was one person smaller. So this time, I had to chase after him! I was the only one who could look at both of you and know you were hiding your true feelings. I was the only one who could hold both of your hands and tell you to get a grip. I was the only one. I agonized over it. It was so painful that I couldn't see it all the way through. Everyone was with Yuuko. So I…I went with Saku. If you're really such a close friend, you should know that much!!!"

My tone became harsh, as I finally let all my feelings out.
Yuuko lowered her eyes sadly for a moment, then glared at me again.

"That's a lie!!!"

"What? What's that supposed to mean?!"

*   *   *

"You didn't look like you had a hard time deciding at all! You didn't even look at me. You ran right after Saku. You didn't even turn around. You're saying all this after the fact! I know that much *because* we're close friends!!!"

"..."

Instead of swallowing my words, I quickly hit back.

"Well, what about *you*, Yuuko? You never even told me you were going to confess to Saku. You say you wanted to put an end to it for everyone's sake. But you avoided some things, didn't you? What would have happened if Saku said yes? What would you have done if he'd said he liked you back? Wouldn't you have just gone ahead and started dating him?!!!"

I was aware that I was saying something cruel, but the dam had fully burst now.

"Oh, well, what about you, Ucchi? You're the one who said 'Maybe I'll move on up.' If I didn't show up, then maybe you'll just go on a festival date together. Wasn't that how you really felt? What if I hadn't come today? You were happy to be by Saku's side in his hour of need!!!"

"You're the one going on about what a terrible person you are, Yuuko! But when you were with me, all you wanted to talk about was Saku! You wouldn't shut up about where you went with him and what you did and who said what! You'd just parade it in front of me with a big grin! Do you even feel bad about what happened that day?!"

*　　*　　*

"Argh, this is infuriating! Like, Ucchi, you never open up about anything! I asked so many times! But every time, you dodged it and just smiled at me. You're the one who didn't even try to talk to me about it!!!"

"That's because—!"

When I ran out of the classroom that evening, I decided I wasn't going to cry.
I won't let anyone see that, not until everything is resolved.

"You're strong, Yuuko…"

My best friend's face swam before my eyes.

"You're always so straightforward…"

I felt like my legs were about to give way.

"No, you're wrong."

But Yuuko's voice had suddenly grown soft as she spoke.

"I'm sorry. I'm so sorry, Ucchi."

Then she hugged me hard again, like she was helping me stay upright.

"I'm sorry for saying something mean on purpose. But I had to say it…or you'd just shoulder all the burden alone again. If I didn't say the truth…you'd just hold back again… That's what I thought…"

I realized Yuuko was crying, too.

As our wet cheeks rubbed together, our tears mingled, then dripped down our necks.

My *yukata* was getting damp.

"Thank you, Ucchi. Thank you for following Saku. Thank you for coming to visit me. Thank you for holding our hands. Thank you for finding me and pulling out the feelings I was trying to hide."

"Ah… Ngh."

The back of my nose stung, and I couldn't form words.

"I did my best, you know, Yuuko…"

"Mm-hmm, you did."

"When I ran out of that classroom, I thought everything was going to break apart if things stayed like this. You, and Saku, and me—we really would all go our separate ways…"

"Yeah, I know exactly what you mean. You have a good heart, Ucchi."

"When I was leaving, I met your eyes while you were crying… But I pretended not to have seen."

"Yeah. It was tough on you, too, Ucchi."

Still clinging to Yuuko, I continued.

"You know, what you said earlier was also true, Yuuko. At that time, I chose Saku over you without hesitation."

"I know, Ucchi. You're amazing, and strong, and cool. I'm so sorry for making you keep everything inside after that day. It wasn't fair. I'm sorry."

"I've always thought that being by his side as a normal friend would be enough. That I was the only one who could support Saku in his hour of need. Once I started to realize that Saku was relying on me…"

"Mm-hmm."

"There were moments when I forgot about you, Yuuko… I wondered if it really would be so bad if this continued forever… It was a horrible thing to think."

"Mm-hmm."

"While I was trying to talk you around… Nishino, Yuzuki, and Haru were all trying to cheer up Saku, too… And that got on my nerves."

"Well, of course it did."

"I was really scared the whole time! *What should I do if Yuuko hates me now that I abandoned her? What if we can't ever be friends again?* There were still so many places I wanted to go together and things I wanted to talk about."

"Mm-hmm, me too, Ucchi."

*　　*　　*

"But…but… I'm sorry; I'm so sorry. You're not my number one, Yuuko."

"My…my number one…isn't you, either, Ucchi."

"Oh, Yuuko…there's so many things I want to tell you."

"I have a lot of things I want to tell you, too."

"I told myself I wasn't going to cry until now. I was going to support you both…and join your hands together…because I was really terrified that everything was going to end!"

"Thank you, Ucchi, thank you."

"It's okay to cry it all out now, though, isn't? Can I just break down? Saku, Yuuko, you'll stay with me, right?"

"It's okay. We'll be here until all your tears have dried."

"Will you still be my best friend?"

"Of course, Ucchi, you idiot!"

"I don't mind being hurt by you, Yuuko."

"I'm okay with being hurt, too, as long as it's you, Ucchi."

"Yuuko… Yuuko…"

"Ucchi, Ucchi, Ucchi…"

* * *

The two of us held each other's hands for a long, long time…
We held on to each other until all the tears dried.

*

After Yuuko and Yua stopped crying, the three of us sat side by side again on the veranda.

My heart felt like it was going to burst as I'd listened to them both.

I felt terrible. And pathetic. And embarrassed.

I'd sensed what Yua was feeling, at least faintly.

There's no way she didn't care about Yuuko. She must have been desperate to be with her.

And yet it was me who she chased after.

I think I needed to take out the hidden meaning I'd locked up in that box made of night and face up to it.

But it was hard to believe…

I can't believe she went into it with that kind of determination on day one.

I'd known these two girls for a while now, and I didn't understand a single thing about the true depth of their strength, kindness, or weaknesses…

In this kind of situation, I thought…there was never any way I could choose someone and call it love.

"Ah…" Yuuko stretched, like she was feeling somehow refreshed. "I feel so much better."

"Hee-hee," Yua responded. "I haven't cried this much since the day my mom left."

"Hey, don't say sad things all of a sudden."

"It's okay. I'm not sad anymore, thanks to Saku."

"I see."

"Actually, come to think of it, I was bawling in front of him right around this time last year."

"Aww, that's not fair, Ucchi."

"Er, what's not fair?"

"Hee-hee, hey, you know what?" Yuuko grinned. "I always dreamed of fighting with my best friend."

Yua laughed and rolled her eyes. "What? That's so weird."

"Let's fight a lot from now on!"

"Well, maybe just a little, now and then."

The two of them looked at each other and cracked up.

"So what now?" Yuuko murmured after a little bit. "We had a good cry, but we didn't really come to any kind of resolution…"

Yua scratched her cheek. "Well, Yuuko, before you derailed the conversation, I was about to bring it full circle."

"That's because you're too stubborn, Ucchi."

"Well, Yuuko, don't you have anything else you want to talk about?"

Yuuko thought about those words for a while. "Yes, yes, yes! I do!"

She raised her hand, standing up.

I realized it was twilight.

"Hee-hee. Saaaku…" Yuuko took my hand and indicated for me to stand up. She gazed up at me, her face tearstained. "You said earlier that you don't know why I fell in love with you, right? You said it was just love at first sight."

"…Right."

"Well, you're totally wrong!"

She poked my chest with her index finger.

Then she gently spread her fingers and placed her hand over my heart.

Badump, badump. My heart had sped up, which was a little unsettling.

"True, it may have been something like that. You were the first person to be normal with me after everyone else in my life gave me special treatment. I'd found a boy I liked. I got overexcited. I got carried away. Yes, it might have been childish.

"But," Yuuko continued.

"No girl is romantic enough to hold on to unrequited love at first sight for a whole year and a half!"

"Huh...?"

Yuuko puffed up her cheeks, like she was trying to look angry.

"I can't believe you thought my feelings were that shallow, Saku! Boy, that made me so mad! Seriously!"

Yuuko lowered her gaze.
Her long, bright eyelashes cast faint shadows in the setting sun.

"Ever since the day I fell in love...I've been paying attention to you, Saku. You've got good and bad things about you. You're cool, and you're also lame. I like things about you, and there's some things I don't like."

She took several steps back, putting her hands behind her.

"Hey, did you know?"

She looked back at me with a slightly sweet smile.
Her long hair fanned out like wings in the evening breeze.

"Whenever you're about to put on your cool-guy act, you narrow your eyes a little like this. I like that habit of yours. It's super cute. When you lie, or try to deceive someone, you lift the corner of your mouth just a tiny bit on the left, and you get this itty-bitty dimple. So when you told me you weren't going to go with Kenta when he went off to see his old friends…I knew. You're surprisingly easy to read. I like that. Oh, and when I call you late at night on the phone. You sound annoyed, but really, you always get a little lonely. I like to chat with you for hours and hours on nights like that."

"Yuuko…"

Yuuko was describing parts of myself I'd never known about.

"I like how you want to live your life in a cool way, but I don't like how easily you disregard your own pain. I like your boyish grin. But I don't like your sneer or the way your lip curls. I like that you're kind to everyone, and I also *hate* it. I'm a little worried about the way you always try to force yourself to be the hero. But along the way, you did in fact become a hero. And I love you."

The setting sun that seemed to shine into my heart was dazzling, and I unintentionally narrowed my eyes.

"Even if it started with love at first sight, spending every day together, by your side, finding more and more things I like about you, collecting beautiful memories—it was like I was making a bouquet so big that I couldn't hold it with both hands. I'm not living in an illusion of you. In my eyes…you've always only been who you are."

With a drip, a single tear surprised me by sliding down my cheek.
Oh man…
I'm really a hopeless case.

Her feelings were so earnest and straightforward.
I was skeptical, because of my silly preconceptions.
I was so trapped in the past that I couldn't see anything clearly.

Yuuko's words, her feelings, and the time we spent together gradually seemed to seep into my heart.
My cheeks were dripping wet, as if she'd given me so much, it was spilling over.

I didn't want them to see me like this, so I turned away.
The surface of the pond reflected the bright-red sky like a mirror.
Right. It's always been within reach, like this.
You were watching me.
I should have noticed sooner.
I'd even thought it, myself.
Leaving too soon will just pave the way to disillusionment. It always does.
But that's not what happened this time.
I tried to laugh it off, but I ended up letting them see me pathetic and hurt. I let them see all my embarrassing emotions.
But nothing's changed, at least on your end.
Because the first girl I befriended in high school...had taken her time, longer than anyone else ever cared to.
Was she slowly and carefully nurturing her feelings this whole time?

Yuuko stared at me with her transparent, clear eyes, and she grinned.

Just like...

"See, that's what I'm saying, here. I love the boy who was always by my side—Saku Chitose."

*　　*　　*

Just like a lake at twilight reflecting the moon.

"…Thank you, Yuuko."

Anything else I said would sound paper-thin, so I just muttered those words.
Yuuko nodded with satisfaction.

"Yes, yes, yes, all right; now it's Ucchi's turn!"

She yanked on Yua's hand, forcing her to stand up.

"Isn't there something you want to talk about?"

"Um, yeah…"

Yua looked back and forth between us, then slowly opened her mouth with a certain resolve.

"That day, the day you saved me, Saku… It may be a bit of an exaggeration, but I planned to always think of you first for the rest of my life. I wished for your happiness more than my own. It wouldn't matter if I wasn't the one to make you smile. Just being by your side was enough."

She tugged on the collar of her *yukata*.

"But I think I was wrong. Because what you taught me, Saku… was that I was Yua Uchida. I was willing to rethink the way I was living—trying never to cause trouble for my family like my mom did—because of you. I was going to repeat the cycle and give up on so many things. So…"

*　*　*

Yua held out her hands. "Yuuko, Saku."
The three of us looked at one another.
Then Yuuko and I took her hands.
Yua tilted her head playfully.

"—From now on, can I be a little more selfish?"

She grinned, even though her grin was a little embarrassed.

"You just gave me a lecture about that yourself, didn't you?"
I replied. I was still trying to act cool, even as my face was all
screwed up from crying.
"Of course you can!" Yuuko yelled. "All right, it's your turn,
Saku!" She took my hand and raised it high.
"If we keep talking this way, I'm gonna look more and more
pathetic."
"Eh, just think of it as like a sports speech."
"Please realize that it's even more embarrassing when you
make that analogy."
Yuuko had recovered completely now, and she grinned and let
go of my hand for a second.
But the bonds between the three of us seemed to remain intact,
reflected on the surface of the water.
I knew what I wanted to say.
And yes, I was embarrassed to say it out loud, but they'd shown
me that was fine.
Yua, standing in the middle, squeezed my hand tightly twice.
As if she was telling me it was okay.
So I…

"Ultimately, I don't think I can ignore the fact that I refused
Yuuko's confession."

* * *

I spoke with clarity.

"""Huh?"""

Yua and Yuuko responded at the same time.
I could feel the two of them turning toward me.
I continued, staring straight up at the twilight sky.

"Don't get me wrong. What you had to say really resonated with me, Yua. It stung. It's not like I'm trying to be cool or stubborn or anything."

I wiped away my tears with the sleeve of my T-shirt.

"This isn't for anyone else but me. This is so I can tackle love with the honesty it deserves... So I can properly face you, Yuuko, and you, Yua. And...everyone else, too."

My words grew fainter as I spoke.

"I don't want to just pretend it didn't happen—that Yuuko never told me how she felt, and I never turned her down, and we never had this conversation today. I want to remember this summer just as it was."

I took a deep breath and spoke clearly again.

"So I'm sorry. I can't go out with you right now, Yuuko."

"...Right, okay."

Yuuko's voice trembled, just a little.

*   *   *

"However..."

I continued quietly.

"I can't make any promises. The answer may not change even if I keep you waiting. And maybe a day will come when I go out with another girl."

"..."

"But even in that case, someday..."

Yuuko gave me the impetus.
Yua gave me the lecture.
They both drew me out.
So from now on, this time—

—as Saku Chitose—as a man, not as a hero—

"What if, someday in the future, my feelings for Yuuko could be labeled as love? Could I tell you so then?"

—I won't avert my eyes from anyone else's feelings or from my own. I'll face them head-on.

—I'll hold the end of a blue thread that hasn't yet been dyed red.

Yuuko paused for a moment to think, then...

"All righty!"

* * *

She said.

"But if you keep me waiting too long, I might end up confessing to you one more time. Because my feelings for you are mine, right?"

"Right!"

The surface of the pond undulated, like our hearts. It was uncertain, delicate, transparent. Illuminated by the moon and the sun, and easily blown by the wind.

The sunset is gone, but this lake will eventually reflect the morning sun again.

When we look up, it's always there…like a gentle sky embracing us.

*

After the three of us left the *yokokan*, Yua spoke.

"Since we're here, why don't we all go to the festival?"

"Yeah, I wanna go!" Yuuko chirped immediately.

I smiled and watched the two walking hand in hand ahead of me.

"Oh yeah, Saku…" Yua looked back at me. "I didn't think much of what you said earlier!"

But her tone was soft.

"Earlier…?" I said.

It wasn't that I didn't have any idea what she was referring to. But since we talked about so many things, I wasn't sure exactly which part she meant.

"…When I asked about your impression of my *yukata*."

Beside her, Yuuko tilted her head in curiosity. "What did he say?"

"'I'd expect no less of you, Yua. You wear that very well.'"

"He said *what?*" Her shout was loud and accusatory.

Yuuko dropped Yua's hand and advanced on me. "What the heck? That was all you had to say about a girl's *yukata*? That's way too dry and technical! After Ucchi put in all that effort to dress up! Unbelievable!" She jabbed a finger into my chest.

"I mean, I didn't want to sound too frivolous after I'd turned down your love confession, Yuuko; that's all."

"That's a totally different issue! This is a special occasion! You have to praise the girl and tell her she looks fantastic!!!"

"But we just talked about this; a guy who hasn't made up his mind can't go saying things like that to girls..."

"What? I don't get it. You're so annoying, Saku."

Yua had been watching this. "Listen, Yuuko," she said. "I think Saku really believes that. If he casually compliments a girl, she might get the wrong idea and fall in love with him."

"Hold on, Yua!" I yelped indignantly.

When she put it into words that way, there was a ring of truth. But I *shouldn't* go casually complimenting a girl when I can't say for sure that I like her. I definitely got the feeling that would be the wrong thing to do.

Yuuko stared at me, unimpressed. "Ew."

"C'mon, you don't have to be so mean about it!"

The two of them exchanged looks and giggled.

Then Yuuko rolled her eyes. "You think a girl's going to get the wrong idea over a simple compliment? You underestimate us."

"You're so old-fashioned, Saku," said Yua. "And extra."

"You keep doing stuff like that, and you're never going to find out which girl you really like. Please, make up with everyone so you can get on with deciding."

"Usually, Saku's lightheartedness is one of his better features."

"Hey!"

I'm really getting kicked around, here.

But maybe they're right.

I scratched my cheek and mumbled, "Yua, um, the *yukata* looks great on you. Like, I-want-limited-edition-stamps-of-you great."

Yua looked taken aback for a second, then said, "Er, that's a weird compliment, but I'll take it." She smiled.

The three of us kept walking.

Before long, we entered the hustle and bustle of the festival.

It was early evening, with the sun completely set by now.

I could see the *torii* gate of the shrine illuminated by the lights of the stalls.

""Huh...?""

Yuuko and I both spoke at the same time.

Standing there very still, watching us, was...

"You guys..."

"Guys..."

Nanase, Haru, Kazuki, Kenta, and for some reason, Asuka.

And...Kaito.

I saw Yuuko's eyes sparkle with familiarity and love, and she dashed forward at top speed.

"Yuzuki, Haru!"

She hugged the two girls, who were standing side by side.

"I'm sorry, I'm sorry, I'm sorry!"

She said it over and over again.

Nanase gently stroked Yuuko's head, and Haru patted her back awkwardly.

"Yua, did you…?"

Yua stuck out her tongue mischievously. "Yeah, I called everyone here."

"Even Asu—er, Nishino?"

"I thought it'd be nice to have her come tonight. Actually, I figured if she was here, you'd wag your tail and be happy. I asked an older girl in the music club to get me her contact details."

"You didn't have to put it that way."

"That's because I'm still a little annoyed!"

Come to think of it, when we were looking around the food stalls earlier, Yua avoided anything heavy or meant for sharing.

She knew this would happen… No, she believed it would.

As we approached the group, Yuuko turned to us with shining eyes. "Ucchi! You and Saku didn't have any intention of going on a date together!"

Yua smiled a little. "I don't know; maybe not."

"What were you going to do if I hadn't come?"

"Well then, you'd have been left out."

"Hey, that's awful! But you don't get to have your date, Ucchi…"

"Unfortunately, that's already over."

"What do you mean?"

Yua took out her mask from the sleeve of her *yukata* and put it on the side of her head. "I mean this!" She made a beckoning, paw-like motion.

"How cute!"

"Hee-hee, Saku bought it for me."

"Aw, no fair! Saku, buy me one, too!"

A burst of laughter erupted.

Haru raised her hand toward us. "Hubby, hurry up and let's eat something. I'm tired of waiting, and I'm super hungry."

"Sorry, my bad. I'll treat you to some *marumaru yaki*, then."

Asuka spoke up, blushing and looking down. "Um, sorry to intrude…"

"Ah no, thanks for coming, actually."

It was a super awkward exchange.

Then I made eye contact with Nanase.

I scratched my head and cleared my throat. "The other day, when you asked me what I thought of you in your apron… I'm sorry for being so curt. You looked great in it."

For a moment, Nanase raised her eyebrows in surprise, then…

"Really?! Honestly, I was bummed, but I didn't want to react in front of you, and then I was all worried about it…"

Her face crumpled, and I briefly thought she might cry.

I smiled with one side of my mouth.

"But you looked more like a pinup than a housewife."

Nanase rolled her eyes at me.

"…What? You're so dumb!"

She stuck out her tongue and shook her shoulders.

Then…

"Saku…"

Kaito was hanging his head.

"Kaito."

"Hey… Back then, I…I lost my temper. I'm sorry."

"Heh."

*   *   *

I smiled a little and held out my right hand.
Kaito snorted and gripped it tight.

"All right. We'll call it even, then."

He smiled, showing his teeth.

"Right."

I pulled Kaito in, like for a hug, and then...

"Graaagh!"

Just like that, I punched him in the side.

"Guh!!! Gack! Whyyy?"

I grinned down at him as he stood there bent over.

"*Now* we're even."

"Hey, man, that's evil!"

"I only hit you with my left hand. It's not my fault I'm super strong."

Then we shook hands for real.
Kazuki rolled his eyes, but he was smiling, too.
"Damn, if that's all you needed, then you should have done that from the beginning."
"I'm sorry. It looks like I made you guys worry a lot."
Kenta, who was next to me, opened his mouth timidly.

"King…"
"Right. Don't worry. We tried a little mutual understanding."

—And so as a group, we wandered around the late August night festival.

We picked up cotton candy, candy apples, fried noodles, crepes, cake balls, and bottles of Ramune.

We bought enough for the whole group to share.

It almost felt like we were midway through a perfectly normal summer vacation.

But then, from the way we exchanged glances, the distance when we walked side by side, the warmth of our voices, and the slightly awkward exchanges, it was clear that our relationships had all taken a step forward.

Still, there was no sadness to be seen in our illuminated faces, and there was no hesitation in the sound of our footsteps on the stone paving.

Finally, the festival came to its end.

The busy stalls were now beginning to pack up their water balloons and plastic balls and goldfish and *yukatas*.

Everyday life rushed back in to pack away the remains of the special occasion, piece by piece.

This was the final ritual of the summer festival.

We moved to the nearby park, holding the sparkler fireworks Kaito had picked up from somewhere.

In the sparse, scattered shadows, we lit our sparklers, filled a bucket with water, and made kaleidoscope patterns in the night.

Yuuko drew the word *love* in the air toward me. Nanase and Haru ran around clutching fistfuls of sparklers. Yua and Asuka politely crouched and watched the sparks fly.

At some point, I paused and looked up to see a white moon that looked like a large teardrop against the night sky.

Creak, creak. See you next summer, the cicadas called.

Ree ree ree. See you soon, fall beckoned.

Before long, the family pack of fireworks was all used up.

Everyone formed a circle, and we opened our bottles of Ramune with a loud *pop*.

The sunken marbles rolled, reflecting the festival decorations.

Right… Just like this.

One person is in another's heart. And someone else is watching.

Swaying amid the churning bubbles.

The profile of the person we care about, trapped inside the sparkle of our eyes.

Finally, we each picked up a final sparkler and lit them like a farewell fire.

Our summer was coming to an end.

"See you next year…"

Someone softly muttered.

—One by one the sparkler tips dropped to the ground, like a series of silent nods.

EPILOGUE
Your Normal

I wanted to be special.

But I knew I couldn't be.

The answer to the sense of inconsistency that was stuck in my chest was so simple it was anticlimactic.

Even though I hated being treated so special.

Even though I was so happy to be normal for once.

Before I even realized it, I wanted to be special to you, and for you to be special to me.

But you wouldn't let me get close to your heart for the longest time.

Hey, honestly…

I wish I could see you each and every day.

I wish I could have a special seat saved for me next to you.

That's all I wished for.

After losing my love and feeling so empty, it finally rolled around and came right back to me.

But I don't have to be precious about it and keep it locked up safe.

If we could just walk side by side on the way home, if we could just chat together the whole time.

If I could just say your name, and have you say mine...that would be more than enough for me.

Everything I ever wanted was already in the palm of my hand.

Because the form of "special" I wanted to be to you...wasn't what's actually special, after all.

A certain special girl made me realize that, and it's just as she said.

The one I love...will be my number one.

I'll gently support him whenever he feels down, and I'll console him whenever he feels defeated.

I'll listen carefully when his cheeks are wet with tears and tell him off when it looks like he's going down the wrong path.

And on those dark nights when he's hunched up, hugging his knees...I'll keep a tight hold of his hand.

I'll be by his side, gazing at him, letting him know that the moon is right here.

—Because all I ever really wanted was to be your normal.

I took a step back.
But I also tried to move close.

I don't think I was being dishonest that night when I wished to be by your side just as a regular friend.

When I realized I was the only one you had in that moment...
When I first saw your tears.
When I had your sleeping face all to myself.
When I realized I couldn't keep you all to myself forever.

—I wanted to be the one beside you.

How desperately I wished for that.
I remember when I passed through that door of the twilit classroom.
From the moment I chose you and chased after you, I was sure.
You can't put the lid back on love once it's already started to roll forward.

Hey, Mom.

I won't forgive you, and I won't I say I understood what you did. I'm not like you at all.

But I did come to understand that sense of unfulfillment a little. Of hating normalcy, of wanting to strive and reach for something more.

So just like the girl who pushed me to act once said...

Someday, I want to face you with all the feelings I've locked up in my heart.

So that you might always look at me and me alone.

So that I might always be in your heart.

So that we never have to let go of each other's hands.

On nights when you can't see the moon, I want to be your gentle embrace.

—If I could, someday, be special to you...I could ask for nothing more.

AFTERWORD

Hiromu here, and it hasn't been so long this time, has it? Applause, please.

After the release of Volume 5 in April, we managed to release Volume 6 within four months. I'm not a fast writer. I agonize over each sentence, sometimes for days at a time. So I haven't finished a *Chitose* book this fast since Volume 2. What's more, the main story in Volume 2 was 359 pages long, and this time it's almost 250 more pages! Go, me! But as a result, the two months it took to get the first draft written...I have almost no memory of that time. (Teardrop.)

—I really wanted to publish this book in August.

One of the reasons is, as I mentioned in the afterword of Volume 5, that I felt I couldn't make you wait another six months.

Another reason is that I wanted people to read this end-of-summer story at the end of summer.

When writing a series, sometimes the season in the book doesn't correspond with the publishing season.

For some time now, I've been thinking it would be better if I could put the summer story in the summer and the winter story in the winter. So this time, I tried my best to make the most of the opportunity.

I hope that those who pick it up around the release date will feel the air outside the window, look at the sunset sky, listen to the calls of the summer insects, and enjoy the festival music. I hope that you'll experience summer with Saku and the gang, while immersing yourself in the glow of fireworks.

By the way, with these six volumes, we will conclude the first half of Chiramune.

Two years and two months after the release of the first volume. It feels solid, and it feels like it's been forever, but at the same time, it feels like it's passed in the blink of an eye. And when you don't even know how many volumes a series will be, it feels odd to look back on what's already gone.

In any case, I've been pursuing this with all I have, using up my life force (and maybe my life span, too). Maybe going forward I'll take my time a little more and write five or six volumes without so much frantic energy. However, don't worry. I'll make sure every word is meaningful. While taking breaks to improve my energy and stamina, I'll plan out the concept for the second half of the series carefully, so that it will be more satisfying than the first half of the series. So please look forward to that.

So let's move on to the acknowledgments. Raemz, I think there were more requests than usual from me and the editor in charge of this cover illustration, but the result was a degree of perfection that far exceeded my expectations. Thank you very much; I love you! Even after two years, the excitement of receiving the illustration has never faded for me. Editor Iwaasa, there are still as many things I want to accomplish as there are stars. Don't settle for the status quo, let's reach for the moon (wait a minute, is it stars, or is it the moon?).

In addition, I would like to express my heartfelt gratitude to all those who have been involved in Chiramune, such as those in charge of advertising and proofreading, and above all, to all the readers who have stuck with me so far. Let's continue hand in hand, shall we...?

HIROMU